CHARIOTS OF FIRE

Michel Parry
and
Garry Rusoff

Chariots of Fire

Futura Publications Limited
An Orbit Book

An Orbit Book

First published in Great Britain in 1974
by Futura Publications Limited

ISBN 0 8600 78132
Printed in Great Britain by
Hazell Watson & Viney Ltd
Aylesbury, Bucks

Futura Publications Limited
49 Poland Street,
London W1A 2LG

INTRODUCTION

Over the past half-century scientists have grudgingly come to admit that the creature called man has existed on this planet for over three million years. Yet in our schools and universities events of only two thousand years ago are studied as *Ancient* History. Whatever happened to the 2,996,999 or so years that passed before? Nobody really seems to know. Or very much to care. For the vast majority of people in the western hemisphere, the history of the human race begins with year one of the christian calendar – as if a ready-made instant civilization had then suddenly sprung into being. Beyond that there is only a vague, gaudy impression derived from Hollywood epics, of people rather fond of beards and sandals charging about in belligerent hordes.

And what of the professional investigators, the palaeontologists and archaeologists whose self-appointed task it is to delve into our mysterious past? Until recently, belief in Biblical infallibility shaped and prejudiced their judgements. Today, caution is the new tyrant. Scientists appear to formulate their conclusions with the same hesitant reticence with which they handle newly-excavated bones. Afraid to tread on the toes of orthodoxy, they shrink from theories which, however justifiable from available evidence, might shake the narrow blinkered view of human history and potential which has so long prevailed. In this way they resemble those astronomers who open our eyes to the wondrous immensity of the universe – yet hesitate to admit the possibility that life may exist on any planet but our own.

It is hardly surprising that the theories advocated by our timid professors trail behind them a litter of unexplained facts, facts that can no longer be ignored. One thinks of the Siberian mammoth-fossils displaying bullet holes, the baffling Babylonion artifacts discovered to be electric batteries, or the perfect steel cube found in a chunk of coal millions of years old.

The forgotten history of the world is chronicled by

forgotten men. Men who desired truth more than respectability and were prepared to suffer the consequences of persecution or anonymity. Some have been partly vindicated by time – Immanuel Velikovsky, Wilhelm Reich and Charles Fort spring to mind. These are the fortunate few amongst trespassers into forbidden regions of science. The majority of their fellows have not been so fortunate. They have been erased from memory, swept under the carpet of complacent ignorance by the academic giants – along with prehistoric steel cubes, mammoths with bullet holes in their skulls and anything else inconsiderate enough to refuse to comply with the established 'rules' of science.

Such a thorn in the side of the establishment was Felix Giradoux (1858–1901). A French antiquarian bookseller, Giradoux became fascinated by what he had read of the monolithic ruins at Tiahuanuco near Lake Titicaca in Peru. Discounting the 'official' explanation that these huge and awesome edifices had been constructed by the Incas (which is rather like attributing the Stonehenge monument to the present-day British troops who take part in military exercises on nearby Salisbury Plain) Giradoux developed the theory that Tiahuanuco was a remnant of a civilization that fled to Peru when the legendary continent of Atlantis disappeared beneath the waves. He also believed that another off-shoot of the Atlantean civilization settled in the area we know as Egypt, thereby accounting for some of the startling similarities between the culture of the Ancient Egyptians and that of certain areas of South America. In 1893 he made a decision that was to change his whole life. He sold his shop and used the proceeds to travel to Peru in search of concrete evidence to support his theory.

We know little of what happened during his expedition to South America but three years later he resurfaced in Paris, claiming to be in possession of a manuscript of unique importance. He told those that cared to listen how he had discovered, close to the Inca fortress at Cuzco, north-west of the mighty ruins of Tiahuanaco, a system of underground caves and passage-ways. In one cave, which he described as being filled to the very ceiling with solid-gold ornaments, – recalling the tantalising legends of *El Dorado* for which the conquering Spaniards searched in vain – he came across a book of incalculable antiquity, lying upon a dome-shaped altar. The book's pages, which Giradoux describes as being

6

very thin and metallic in appearance, were covered with ancient writing of a kind wholly unfamiliar to him. Not surprisingly, Giradoux was anxious to take possession of the book but this the Guardian of the Cave (regrettably, Giradoux does not elaborate) would not permit. Suspecting that the book might provide the confirmation of his theory for which he was seeking, Giradoux spent months painstakingly copying down the symbols from every page – of which there were over a thousand.

Returning to Paris with his prize, Giradoux was soon alerted to the similarity between the script he had faithfully copied and examples of Sumerian writing. He endeavoured to enlist the interest of experts in this field but found his enquiries rebuffed with varying degrees of politeness. After all, who could believe a man who claimed he had turned down an opportunity to stuff his pockets with gold just so as to copy strange writing from an old book. Undeterred, and despite the poor health in which he had returned from Peru, Giradoux immersed himself in the study of ancient writings and himself undertook the enormous task of translation.

Despite many rebuffs, Giradoux never relaxed his attempts to interest the academic world in his manuscript and its implications. As the translation progressed, he submitted extracts to scholarly journals. We can, without stretching the imagination, visualise the reaction of the high-principled editors on receiving these unsolicited submissions. None of them saw print. In fact, the only mention Giradoux ever received in a recognised academic publication was in a letter to the *Journal of Sumerian Studies* (London, September, 1899) where Marcel Bertrand cites him as an example, along with the Pyramidologists, of the sort of people who brought archaeology into disrepute and scared away backers and their sorely-needed funds.

In fairness, it must be admitted that Giradoux's personality at this time was not one to inspire confidence amongst conservative-minded scholars. Whilst living amongst the Indians of the Andes he had become addicted to cocaine. Although he himself appears to have been fairly level-headed, his few friends formed part of a circle of mystically-minded individuals whose beliefs vied with each other in fancifulness and credulity. The most prominent member of this circle appears to have been a self-advertised

7

Kabbalistic magician by the name of Sar Merodack J. Peladan. Peladan, a worshipper of hermaphrodites, was as striking in appearance as in name. He wore only a blanket, long hair and a beard. Such a costume might pass unnoticed today in London or San Francisco but it certainly turned heads in Paris even during the Naughty Nineties. Significantly, Anatole France is said to have once remarked that Peladan was more an enemy than a friend to those close to him since he brought them into disrepute as well as himself.

Eventually, two segments of Giradoux' introduction, along with introductory notes, did appear in *Le Sphinx*, an undated small-circulation magazine published in Paris. The title page of *Le Sphinx* informs the reader that the magazine is dedicated to 'piercing the deepest mysteries of the Orient . . .' Despite this grandiose claim, the pages of *Le Sphinx* are largely filled with the florid excesses of lesser poets and artists of the Symbolist movement and, other than Giradoux' contribution, there is little of lasting interest. Yet it is to this obscure magazine that we owe most of our knowledge of the background to the Giradoux Manuscript, as it has come to be called.

Giradoux does not appear to have published anything further about his discovery and soon after, in 1901, at the age of forty-three, he died. His work was nowhere near completion.

After his death, the Manuscript disappeared from sight and was assumed lost. Within a few years at least one article on archaeological hoaxes went so far as to deny it had ever existed!

That slickly dismissive mention might easily have been the final epitaph to one of the world's most fantastic discoveries. One cannot help but wonder how many other potentially world-shaking revelations and ideas have met with such an ignominious fate. The answer, if we but knew it, would undoubtedly make us bow our heads in shame. Man, it seems, finds it easier to deride anything which might alter his established beliefs, however false, than to gracefully accept the truth of significant discoveries. Consider for example, the outraged furore which greeted Darwin's Theory of Evolution. Even today, in certain parts of the United States, supposedly the most 'advanced' nation on Earth, there remain places of learning where Darwin's

Theory is dismissed as heretical blasphemy because it contradicts the story of Adam and Eve!

It is our suggestion that within a few years, belief in the probability of visits to Earth by extraterrestrial beings in Ancient Times will be as widespread throughout the civilised world as the acceptance of the Theory of Evolution is today. And it may even come to pass that the name of Felix Giradoux will be as familiar and respected as that of Darwin.

Because, fortunately, the Giradoux Manuscript was not lost. It turned up in Austria in 1947 together with Giradoux' incomplete translation. Manuscript and translation subsequently passed through several hands and in 1966 were acquired by their present owner, a private collector from Philadelphia. We are indebted to the collector's son, Roger, for alerting us to the significance of the Manuscript. His father (who, sadly but understandably, has expressed a desire to remain anonymous and undisturbed) considered the Manuscript to be little more than a bizarre literary curiosity, a very minor addition to his impressive library of European literature. After all, Giradoux was no celebrity even during his own life-time, and there was no proof of the authenticity of the material he claimed to have copied down so faithfully from the original. It was left to Roger, a keen student of Parapsychology, to realise the value of the manuscript as evidence of visits to the Earth by spacemen from other worlds, visits recorded and celebrated in the mythologies of the world as the exploits of the Gods.

Through Roger we were able to get a first-hand look at the elusive manuscript. Although it is, of course, only a copy of the original somewhere in Peru and is itself less than a century old, the manuscript does seem to convey a feeling of ages long past, the sort of feeling one gets strolling through the British Museum or any other great national museum. When holding the brittle yellowing pages with their neat rows of bewildering inscriptions, some people claim to receive a sudden illuminating impression of some underlying purpose to humanity, a fleeting glimpse of some Great Cosmic Plan in operation. This is how one person described the feeling: 'Most of the time human beings seem to be wearing blinkers. Not the kind we used to see on the horses that pulled the old ice-wagons but more like a pair of super-powered binoculars. We look at everything,

9

including the relics of our own past, with our binoculars at full magnification, seeing only one small piece of the puzzle at a time. When I was looking over the Manuscript it was as if I was looking down the wrong end of the binoculars. For the first time in my life I could see the whole picture. Suddenly everything fitted into place.'

Such experiences are undoubtedly highly subjective and may well be influenced by the mysterious reputation of the Manuscript. Nevertheless, it is an experience many people have shared.

After such a build-up, Giradoux' attempt to translate the Manuscript was admittedly a disappointment. Confused, fragmentary and not always decipherable, the text came out so strongly in favour of Giradoux' Atlantean theory that our suspicions were immediately aroused. Yet the apparent descriptions of extra-terrestrial spacecraft and their occupants immediately excited our hopes. If only we could be sure that these parts of the translation were valid and authentic! Giradoux himself interpreted such descriptions as having some sort of secret symbolic meaning related to the level of spirituality attained by his Atlanteans. But then he did not have the advantage of living in the days of Cape Kennedy and televised moon-walks!

No time was lost by Roger in commissioning a new translation. The man given charge of this formidable undertaking was John Capstan, an American cryptographer. He brought to the job the same meticulous military precision that helped him crack enemy codes during the Korean conflict. The study of ancient writings had been a seriously-pursued hobby of his for many years so he was doubly-suited to the task at hand. He worked in close collaboration with several eminent palaelogists (fortunately more open-minded than their predecessors of the last century) and was further aided by William McGough Associates, a specialised computer organisation who generously placed their resources at the disposal of the project.

Eighteen months later and the first section of the Manuscript had been successfully re-translated. And the implications of what Capstan and his colleagues came up with was shattering. The Manuscript completely overturned the apple-cart of pre-conceptions upon which our view of the Earth's past is based. It throws the world's oldest mythological stories into an entirely new perspective. It demands a radical reappraisal of human history. *It proves, as never before, that beings from other planets have walked upon this, the third planet from the sun in our commonplace little solar system.*

At this point it becomes necessary to deal briefly with the three major objections which people have levelled at the Manuscript and what it contains. They are as follows:

(a) That the whole thing is a hoax master-minded by either the present owner or someone else in recent years. There never was any Felix Giradoux.

(b) There was a Felix Giradoux and there was a manuscript but it was lost soon after his death. The present Manuscript is a fake put together by persons unknown.

(c) The Manuscript is a fake concocted by Giradoux himself.

Let's take each of these arguments in turn. Firstly we know there certainly was a real person called Felix Giradoux because of records of his existence and references to him and his Manuscript in various magazines, some of which have already been mentioned. The second objection is more plausible. However, the existing manuscript does correspond in every way to what we know of the original and in particular to the extracts published in *Le Sphinx*. It may be argued in reply that the forgers simply did their homework thoroughly and took all existing knowledge of the Manuscript into consideration when planning their deceit. The final word on this point lies with the experts: specialists in the field of antique bibliography have examined manuscript and translation and pronounced them genuine; an independent laboratory conducted tests on samples of the paper taken from the Manuscript and original translation and identified them as being of the correct period; a graphologist whose opinion is valued in courtroom testimony compared the handwriting in the translation with examples of Giradoux' writing and swore an affidavit that in his opinion both were written by the same man.

Lastly we come to the suggestion that the whole affair is a magnificently conceived fraud perpetrated by Felix Giradoux himself. The idea that the shy, moustachioed French bookseller could have devised such a complex coup, the effects of which would still be reverberating almost a century later, is quite an appealing one. Compared to such an

11

enterprise, the bogus skull of the Piltdown man is a practical joke on the level of itching powder. The notion is, however, quite implausible.

Giradoux' knowledge of ancient languages was entirely self-taught. It is inconceivable that a man with such a rough grasp of the subject could singlehandedly devise a text of over a thousand pages, written in an unknown language of his own invention, with such miraculous accuracy that it can fool expert philologists and computers alike. The idea does not hold water for an instant. Even if we were to consider it possible why should the brains behind such an extraordinary deception then proceed to spend the rest of his life trying to make sense of his own fraud, an endeavour which never brought him anything but hardship and derision and wasted away his own health? There is no better refutation of such an unlikely theory as this than Giradoux' own painfully inadequate attempts to translate the very manuscript which some would have us believe was his own creation.

We are convinced of the authenticity of the Manuscript. The facts all point that way. And if we accept the Manuscript as genuine, we must also accept its evidence as conclusive: *Men from the stars walked the Earth in Ancient times and gave primitive man a helping hand along the road to civilisation.*

Idealists might think that such startling evidence could change the political face of the Earth. That governments would topple, well-established religions crumble. That the whole of Mankind would put aside its petty squabbles and prejudices and join together in gazing up at the stars in wonder . . .

Not so.

Tons of evidence exist to prove that Unidentified Flying Objects, those mysterious objects that the press has labelled 'Flying Saucers', are real and have landed on Earth many times. The evidence includes photographs, films and hundreds of eyewitness accounts from reliable people such as civil and military pilots, astronomers, airport personnel, NASA technicians and policemen.

None of this overwhelming evidence that we are not alone in the universe has made the slightest bit of difference to our daily lives or to the insular thinking of the men in power.

A society where TV newsreels of a bloody war are interrupted by commercials for soap-powder is blasé. It demands excitement, sensation, controversy – but it also wants to sleep soundly at night. It doesn't want to be shaken to the roots of its being. It doesn't want the carpet to be whipped out from under its feet. It wants everything to carry on, exactly as before. In such a society a man possessing knowledge of the kind revealed in the Giradoux manuscript is placed in the same position as the millionaire who stood on a street corner and tried to give away his money. People are interested, they're very tempted. They want to believe that the money is real. But they're also afraid of being tricked, of being made a fool, of getting laughed at. So in the end they pass by with knowing expressions on their faces, hurrying away to business as usual.

This was the position Roger found himself in. He knew he was holding a cultural time-bomb. He wanted to share his knowledge with the rest of humanity – but how do you get people to accept a time-bomb? If he published the new translation in a scholarly annotated edition acceptable to philologists the book would quickly be consigned to the dustiest and least-browsed shelves of the libraries, unread by any but the elite few. On the other hand, if he produced a popular work sensationalising the UFO aspects of the manuscript the book would be dismissed as the ravings of a crank and lumped together with the kind of books full of Important Messages for Humanity their authors claim to have received from flying saucers or cities beneath the sea or monks in Tibet or their dead aunts.

After a lot of thought and discussion it was decided to release the Giradoux Manuscript to the public in the same spirit the original had been set down countless years ago – as a tale of adventure full of wonder and thrills. For however astounding the revelations of the Manuscript, it is still basically an entertaining piece of story-telling. Once, the tale of Boaz, the man who became a friend of the Gods, was whispered around native fires in the depths of the Amazon jungle and in the high peaks of the Andes. It probably still is. Now, for the first time, his adventures, with all their heroics, battles and bawdiness can be shared by the modern reader.

This book is an adaptation of the first section of the Giradoux Manuscript as translated by John Capstan and his colleagues. It follows the Manuscript up to the point where the revised translation ends. As work on the translation proceeds we hope there will be further volumes until the entire text is available to the reader.

In its original form, the tale of Boaz is an exciting one. Hopefully the reader will find this re-telling to be equally so. The language we have used is modern but we have also tried to keep as close as possible to the original. Out of necessity some of the dialogue is conjecture and so too are some passages of description. These have been included to make the story more understandable and also to bridge certain gaps existing in the Manuscript. It must be emphasised, however, that all the characters and incidents are exactly as described in the original Manuscript. Nothing has been added or altered in order to make the text fit in with our own theories. Naturally we hope that the reader will find the same stupendous significance in the story of Boaz as we do. But it is up to each person to make up his own mind and to draw his own conclusions.

It is time this tale were told. It is the story behind the best kept secret in the world: *the true history of mankind.*

M.P.
G.R.

Part 1

THE COMING OF THE GODS

ONE

Silence stalked the forest. A familiar silence that made my movements slow and stealthful. It was the silence of fear. Fear strong enough to freeze the chattering tongues in the trees. A warning silence too. Ahead, perhaps, a fire-eyed puma was prowling for meat like me. Or a raiding party of Jaguar People were hunting new heads to dangle from their belts. I sniffed but caught not the scent of man nor cat.

I had never believed the tales told round the night-fires by the old men of my tribe . . . tales of angry spirits of slain beasts waiting in darkness to chew the fresh torn parts of hunters.

But, tonight, I remembered them well.

I hugged my llama skin tight around me against a chilling wind shivering the trees, gripped tighter the bone-tipped spear clutched in one hand. About me the forest seemed to tense like a puma crouched to spring. I felt the hundreds of eyes I could not see, waiting with me . . . waiting for movements that would end in screams and the torn flesh of hunger . . .

Fire lashed the night sky. Shadows fled the sudden bursts of light leaping through the trees . . . I recognised the anger of the Gods. Once before I had seen such a thing. I was a boy then. Roars of anger filled the night. Flames crackled across the sky. Viracocha's tears of forgiveness battered our huts and swelled the great Lake of the Moon. I lay in Snake-Killer's arms and trembled.

But this time there were no comforting arms. No roars of anger. No battering rain. Only fire and a dazzling light that pained my eyes.

There were two moons in the sky!

I, Boaz the Hunter, threw myself shaking to the ground. I, Boaz the Warrior, felt my blood-pump pounding like that of a virgin bride . . .

One moon fell from the sky weeping tears of flame . . .

It dropped towards me as the eagle swoops on its prey, filling the forest with light and terror. The forest cried out with one voice of Fear, echoing my scream. I leapt to my feet. I smashed through the undergrowth, running as I had never run before. The forest was alive with noise and shapes. I glimpsed pigs, jaguars and bears running with the same wild fear that threw me forward. I, the Hunter, ran with the hunted.

The falling Moon scraped the tree-tops with the sound of many windstorms . . .

A stag brushed against me in its fear. My stomach twisted with hunger. I could have reached out and gripped his antlers. I could have pulled him to the ground, struggled him until his neck snapped. He would have filled my belly for days. But fear shoved hunger aside as I shoved aside the clutching branches. I wanted only to escape from that burning eye in night's black face. The stag swerved from me, springing high, and was gone.

A mighty wind screamed in my ears, blasted me to the ground. The earth trembled. Trees higher than twenty men bent like wind-swept blades of grass . . .

The Moon had fallen!

I raised myself. The air was filled with the frightened screeching of birds and monkeys but my ears caught the roar of the maddened puma running at me. Maybe it thought I was the one that shook the world and made night into day.

I still carried my spear. Dropping to one knee, I jerked it upwards as the big cat sprang. The puma howled. Sharpened bone bit deep into its golden breast. The shaft snapped, leaving me with half a spear. Claws slashed at my face. I

16

leapt aside. The puma's spring carried it past me. It fell heavily, legs collapsing. The splintered spear hung from its breast. Blood gushed from the wound in a thick stream. The puma twisted towards me. It crouched ready to spring, hate-filled eyes eating into mine. Like a powerful wave it leapt forward. Without hope, I threw my broken shaft in its face of teeth.

'Choke on my bones!' I cried, falling beneath its hungry breath.

I woke with the stink of rotting flesh in my face. The stink came from the puma's gaping mouth. Its head lay on my chest, like a babe sucking milk. Already the crawling things swarmed across its dead eyes and into its nostrils. I pushed the heavy carcass from me and sat up. My body ached. A hunter's body always aches. I looked at the puma. My spear jutted from his back. He had landed on it when he sprang. And rammed it through his body. Now his spirit hunted the darkness.

I climbed to my feet. I searched the sky. I saw only one moon, the true Moon that always rides the night. The sounds of the forest had settled into familiar restlessness. I shivered with the cold of night. I scorned myself for losing my warm llama skin when I ran squawking through the forest like a frightened parrot. Had there really been a falling Moon? I began to wonder. Perhaps only in my head. Perhaps it had been a fever-dream, a vision like those the Vision-Catcher snatched from the Spirit World. Sometimes I too could see things hidden from the eyes of others. Things for which there are no words. But I could not look at a man and say, like the Vision-Catcher, this man will die and this is how, and this is when. There were times it happened as the Vision-Catcher said and then he would be honoured with a feast and gifts and Nima would offer him one of his wives. Other times it did not happen as Vision-Catcher had seen. Then nothing would be said.

Far off, through the trees, a faint light captured my eyes. Then I knew it was no fever-dream I had seen. The dying Moon *had* fallen. Its glow was like that of a fire after the flames have sunk low. But more white than red. It lay on the cliffs above the Great Lake beyond the forest. And I, Boaz, would stand over its carcass as I now stood over the puma.

My stomach spoke to my head. I remembered my hunger. I tugged on the broken end of my spear. Grunting, I tore it from the puma's body. The victor would feast on the loser. With the spear's point of sharpened bone I cut myself a thick chunk of flesh. I bit into the dripping meat. It tasted good and strong. I felt my blood fill with the courage of the puma and the warriors it had eaten. I ate hungrily and wondered if the Moon's flesh would taste as good.

I hurried through the forest, my half-spear in my hand. Soon I had left the cover of the trees and started up the rocky slope. I was drawn by the light as a flying ant to fire. I felt Tall-Feather and Swollen-Breasts gazing down on me. I looked for them but the darkness hid the high peaks from my sight. Their cold breath swept over me. I moved fast so I did not feel its chill.

Half the night was gone when I reached the place of the fallen Moon. Light was the blood of the moon and the moon was bleeding to death. Its warm blood streamed over the cliffs washing away the darkness. The darkness crawled behind broken rocks and hid in deepest shadows.

I crept towards the bleeding Moon, my face low, my hands grasping at rocks. Before me my hand looked white as day. There was a smell of burning in the night.

I circled the Moon like a wolf sniffing round a camp-fire. When I looked at its brightness I had to look quickly away. It hurt to see into the heart of the Moon.

Above, the true Moon still flew in the sky. It was admiring itself in the waters of the Great Lake beyond the cliff. I touched the stone hanging from my neck. It was smoothed flat and round by the waters of the lake. The shape of the fallen Moon was like that of the stone.

The Moon above was small, no bigger than the joint of one finger. The proper size for a Moon. The Moon which had fallen from the sky was huge. It was bigger than all a mighty chief's huts put together. And the huts of his father. And the huts of his grandfather. And it was taller than the tallest tree.

Its skin was silver, yet many other colours, too. Like sunlight on a fresh-caught fish.

The Moon was not dead. It still breathed. It made a sound like a swarm of angry bees. Its life force touched me and I knew its blood-pump still beat strong.

I smelt men. For a moment I thought the warriors of my

18

tribe had come to capture the Moon. Like me, they would have seen it fall. But mixed with the scent of men were the smells of fur and blood. Smells that told me of men with sharp teeth and sharper claws – *Jaguar Men*.

A short throw away, black shadows became three cat-eared shapes sneaking forward. I sank to rock level, my spear-arm tensed. But the three Jaguar Men had not seen me. They were too interested in the Moon. They moved warily towards it, their shadows creeping after. One held a spear raised to throw. The other two had arrows notched to their bows. The one with the spear ran forward until he was within throwing distance of the Moon. I saw he had many heads hanging from his waist. I wondered if he was Aroona, he who had sworn to kill me. But I could not see the face beneath the hooded Jaguar skin.

He shook his spear at the Moon. He screamed a challenge. Then he ran back to the other two. Their weapons raised, the three of them looked up at the Moon. Its light shone full upon the cat-faced men.

The Moon did not answer. The Jaguar Man who shouted the challenge ran forward and threw his spear. The spear struck the Moon's skin. It made a noise like rocks smacked together and fell to the ground. The two other Jaguar Men loosed their arrows. The Moon's skin was tough. Their arrows dropped beside the spear.

For a moment none of the Jaguar Men moved. Then the one with many heads around his waist walked over to his spear. He bent down to pick it up. The Moon hissed with the voice of an angry snake. I did not see its mouth open, but its thin red tongue flicked out and licked the Jaguar Man. He screamed. His Jaguar skin started to burn. It made a good fire. Then the Moon's tongue licked his face. He screamed more. Flames leapt out of his head and he lay down.

The other two Jaguar Men turned and ran, shrieking their Fear. The red tongue darted after them and licked them too. Their skins also made good fires. Their bodies blackened. They lay down like the first man.

There was a lot of smoke. Some of it drifted towards me. It smelled good. The Jaguar Men were well cooked. I began to get hungry again. I wanted to see if they tasted as good as they smelled. But I did not want to be Moon-food.

I crept away more silently than I had come.

19

Behind me lay the fallen Moon. Ahead were the yellow flames of the tribal fires. Between the two ran the pads of my feet, racing over the shore of the bottomless lake. I glanced over my shoulder to make sure the Moon was still there. Its glow pursued me like a dawning sun.

The flames of my tribe grew closer. I could see the warriors were already in their War-Glory. Breathless, I slowed to a walk. I moved through the warriors. They were stuffing coca leaves into faces red with bear-blood. Their eyes were bright. They raised their spears to me as I passed. Soon I saw Tamba the Vision-Catcher, writhing like a wasp on the sand. He screamed that he had caught the spirit of the condor. His flapping arms beat against the sand and I knew he was riding on the back of the great bird.

Nima the chief was shouting encouragement to the warriors, his great weight supported by the shoulders of two bearers. He watched as I slowly stepped forward and picked a haunch of meat from the pile of offerings before him. I chewed casually on the meat. My blood-pump wanted to shout what I had seen. But Snake-Killer's spirit held back my tongue.

Nima screamed for me to step forward.

'Where have you come from?' he demanded, pulling at the hair of his bearers. 'And where is the meat you promised?'

'I have come from the shore where fell the Moon, Great Chief,' I said, pointing to the far-dimmed glow. Nima liked to be called Great Chief. To my eyes his only greatness lay in his fat.

He laughed scornfully.

'So the bravest of hunters has brought back a lie for us to eat!'

'I killed a puma, Great Chief. The beast lies where I left it when I went to battle the Moon.'

By now the warriors had gathered around listening.

'And did you leave the Moon as dead as the puma?' Nima asked, anger growing in his face.

'Great Chief, I watched as the Moon made the warriors of the Jaguar People burn like reeds thrown into a fire. I did not think myself worthy of so mighty an enemy . . . '

As I spoke, Tamba groaned in the Otherworld, releasing the spirit of the condor. He opened his eyes.

'Fight the Moon,' he croaked. 'Kill the Son of the

Moon. . . . the condor cries for the blood of the Moon-Child!'

The Vision-Catcher rose swaying to his feet. He thumped his spirit stick into the fire, sending splashes of sparks into the wind. All eyes were on Tamba as he urgently put words to the vision he had caught:

'I rode the wind on the back of the mighty condor . . . I saw the Sun burning in lust for the Moon. Day after day he chased her to satisfy his lust . . . but each time he came close, she hid in the kingdom of darkness where the Sun cannot enter. So always the Moon escaped the Sun and the Sun became angry, and his anger dried the waters and burnt the earth so there was hunger and thirst among men. Then Tumtoshec the Sky grew jealous of the Moon's beauty and she held open the door into Night . . . and so the Sun was able to enter the kingdom of darkness where the Moon was hiding. For three days and nights the Sun and Moon fought against each other and great was the fear amongst men who saw the battle. Then the Sun rushed at the Moon and thrust his Man-Spear deep into her and filled her with his golden seed . . . and so a child grew in the belly of the Moon. When it was time, the Moon-Child dropped from the Moon's belly but it could not fly, and so it fell to earth, flames pouring from its eyes . . . The condor swooped down after it and I saw the Moon-Child where it lay, glowing like a great fire. I saw the Jaguar Men burning in its fire, screaming like women as they died . . . I saw the coward Boaz turn blue with fright like a newly born and run to great Nima to save him . . . . I saw the brave warriors of the Huanac striking the Moon-Child with spears and sling stones. I heard the Sun speaking to me with the beak of the condor. He said, "he who slays the Moon-Child will become Chief of the Moon . . . . From the Blood of the Moon-Child rises the Chief of the Moon."'

'From the blood of the Moon-Child rises the Chief of the Moon!' Nima repeated, his eyes gleaming. His fist slashed the air.

'Nima shall be Chief of the Moon,' he decided. The Warriors roared.

'Blood of the Moon-Child!' screamed the Vision-Catcher, his eight-fingered wand striking at the Moon and the Sky. The warriors took up the chant—

'Blood of the Moon-Child, Blood of the Moon-Child!'

'The Moon-Child is mighty!' I yelled above the chanting. 'Spears and arrows cannot pierce his skin, which is tougher than the shell of a crab . . . .'

'Enough!' Nima's fat finger pointed at me.

'I will let live the hunter who hunts lies – let him live to eat the faeces of the Chief of the Moon . . . .'

The monkey-laughter of the warriors stung me like arrows. I held my anger. I did not want to substitute for the puma as food. The warriors would listen more closely to my warnings when they came as near to the Moon-Child as I had been.

I quickly smeared my body with bear-blood and the mud of the Sacred Waters. I chewed coca leaves and joined the circle of stamping warriors. I chanted, 'Blood of the Moon-Child . . . .' The spirit of the coca leaves roared mightily through me. I became One with the leaping warriors. They were a part of me and I was a part of them. Together, we were the Huanacs . . . .

In the dark beyond the dancing flames the women cowered together, holding warm heads to their milk-sacs. They wailed and cried as they always did before the War-Glory. The fathers of their babies, the strokers of their wombs, were warmer in flesh than in spirit.

Nima rode his bearers into the flailing circle, holding high his hands. The circle poised like a snake about to strike.

'I will take as many warriors with me as there are fingers on two men,' Nima announced. 'Brave Boaz will come with us to watch our Glory . . . the rest of the warriors will stay behind with Olmec to defend our children.'

He waved his war-club forward.

'We go now. Before the Sun rises I shall be his brother . . .'

We raced along wind-battered cliffs, one warrior with many arms, many legs. The coca spirit moved with us, singing a wild song of strength. Below, the Waters of the Great Lake murmured of our courage. Alongside ran Vision-Catcher, hopping and leaping, howling his words of power that called demons from the ground . . . a sea of snakes would die beneath our heels, pumas flee in packs before us . . . he shook his rattle in the face of the wind. He struck the rocks and angry sparks chased his spirit-stick. Behind rode Nima, digging his heels into the flanks of panting bearers. His voice whipped us on towards the Child of the Moon.

'It is a great egg,' said the Vision-Catcher, his face white before the fallen Moon. 'The Moon-Child has yet to be born . . . .'

We huddled amongst the broken rocks where I had crouched earlier. The glow-beast dwarfed us and the victory cries of the warriors fled their throats. Its brightness was less than before. It was like a dying fire dimmed by ashes. I wondered if it slept.

'Let the woman-hearted Boaz approach,' Nima called.

I joined him, my eyes defying his as he glared down at me from his throne of living bodies.

'You say this egg killed the Jaguar Men – where are their bodies?'

I looked. It was true. The blackened shapes were gone.

'The Moon-Child burned them with its tongue of flame,' I replied. 'Perhaps it has swallowed them whole, as the lizard swallows the fly, and chewed their bones to mush . . . And it will do the same to us if we attack it.'

'You lie!' spat Nima, shaking with a rage that trembled the bodies of the bearers beneath him. His foot swung out and struck my face. I fell to the ground.

'There were no Jaguar-Men and no tongue of flame – nothing but *your* lying tongue, Faint Heart, over which my dogs will fight when we return . . . .'

He looked up at the fallen Moon as a man looks upon a woman for whom his lust is great.

'We shall smash the egg and pull the Moon-Child from its shell,' he promised. 'I shall kill it and dance in its blood . . . and the Moon will bow low to its Chief, the Brother of the Sun!' Yelling of War-Glory, the warriors raised their spears.

The Vision-Catcher flopped on the ground like a fish on land, foam spewing from his mouth.

'The Huanacs will dance in the blood of the Moon!' he screamed. 'Nima will drink the blood of the Moon!'

'Blood of the Moon! Blood of the Moon!' chanted the warriors as one. Their feet pounded the ground.

Shaking his rattle, the Vision-Catcher sprang up and scrambled over the rocks towards the Moon-Child. In a flurry of thumps and feathers he swam through the moon-glow. Its brightness closed about him.

Nima pointed his war-club. The warriors poured over the rocks after Vision-Catcher, raising their voices in Battle-Joy. I rose into Nima's path as he urged his bearers forward.

'Stop them!' I shouted, my hands circling his wrist. 'The Moon-Child is mighty. The warriors will all—'

'Die!' Nima yelled, his war-club hacking at me. Its sharpened edge sliced through my shoulder. I saw an arm lying on the ground – my arm. The voice of pain bellowed at the Moon. I fell beside my arm, pumping splashes of blood across grey rock. The feet of Nima's bearers trampled my body, then were gone.

A strange calm settled over me. I knew I was dying yet there was no fear. I would not die alone I knew. I raised my head . . . through eyes growing dark I watched Nima's bearers hurrying after the others, sagging beneath their fat load. The spears and arrows of the warriors rained down upon the Moon-Child. They dropped like sticks from the Moon-Child's skin. . . .

The Vision-Catcher was the first to fall. The Moon-Child's tongue flicked out in hissing rage, sweeping over him. He leapt in the air as if to fly away – a bright plumed bird with feathers of red flame. But the condor spirit did not hear his cries and he fell smoking to earth, a ragged wingless crow . . . . The red tongue of the Moon-Child danced among the warriors. They became its partners, leaping torches dancing higher than they had ever done before.

Nima's two bearers fell from beneath him like snapped twigs. He pitched wailing into a stream of boiling blood. The tongue of fire swept past him towards me. I waited to taste its touch of death. It ate a path along the ground and licked at the rocks near my feet. The rocks spat and sizzled, melting like chunks of pig fat in a pot. The tongue darted forward. My head fell back to the ground. It would never rise again. I watched the tongue snake over me. I heard the crash of trees falling in the forest behind . . . then the red tongue fell away. . . . It disappeared back into the mouth of the Moon-Child where no mouth could be seen.

Smoke drifted before me. Smoke of flesh and smoke of spirit. The warriors of the Huanacs were no more. They were meat to fill the teeth of the Moon Child at his Victory

Feast. Only Nima was still alive, for I was surely dead with only my eyes remembering what I had seen. My body was dead yet a laugh struggled up my throat . . . a laugh from a dead man for a frightened Chief crawling like a sow from the slaughter.

More laughter – then empty fell my eyes.

TWO

They were eating me. The tiny creatures of the night were feeding on my flesh. I felt them crawl across my dead face. They wiggled into my eyes, humming their wings loud in my ears, louder than a nest of bees. Fat worms filled my nose, pushed into my mouth. Spiders crept through my brain on delicate legs. They spun their silver threads across my skull.

I wanted to scream . . . but found no tongue.

My spirit struggled to rise. It wanted to soar higher than the condor and spread its wings in the world of spirits: the dark sky-big world where only Vision-Catcher had been and returned. From which he would return no more. Like a live bird cupped between two hands my spirit beat against my bones. But found no escape from the trap of rotting man-skin I had become.

Fireflies danced before my shuttered eyes. Then flames spun and whirled and became the Moon battling against the Sun. As they fought, they called to each other. Their tongue was not that of the Huanacs nor of any tribe I had ever heard. Great was the battle between Sun and Moon. They circled one another like two men fighting for their lives . . . yet so fast they became as one great light which poured into my eyes, filling my head. As the light touched my brain, many last thoughts and happenings all at once returned. Too many thoughts to hold on to. They thrashed around inside my head. Then all that I knew was one throb of pain.

A sudden movement behind the great light – Man movements in a silver cave. Through eyes closed by death I looked out and saw men who were not men. Their faces were pale as the bright Moon. My spirit reached for theirs in friendship. And drew back as if from freezing cold. They looked like men yet their spirits had not the soft blood-warm touch of men. They were cold as rock, hard as the Moon-Child's skin. I looked at them and they looked at me. They looked right through me into my head. They ran their cold hands through my thoughts. They played silver music on the cob-webs in my skull . . . .

I wondered who they were, these pale lords of Death. If this was the Spirit world, where was Vision Catcher to guide me? Where was Mala, my mother, and my father, the great Snake-Killer?

A fang pierced my arm – Snakes had found my rotting man-skin! I laughed. My lips were cold and stiff but I laughed. For how can the poison kiss of a snake injure the dead? I laughed too, because the fang had sunk into my spear-arm, the same arm which Nima had hacked from my shoulder.

My laughter shook the spiders from their webs. They scrambled across my brain and out of my ears. The faces of the spirits were as round, as cold, as pale as the face of the Moon. They talked quickly to each other – in man-like voices but with words that held no meaning.

I watched the men-but-not-men walk across the shiny cave and disappear through a hole in the cave-wall. Then the hole disappeared. I moaned inside my head. The next moment the great light was gone. There was no smoke as from a fire killed by water. There was no Sun, no Moon. Nothing but darkness, a darkness blacker than the waters of the Great Lake on a moonless night. More terrible still was the silence. Total empty silence. Not a bird called to its mate, not a monkey laughed. The wind-spirit was dead, the cicadas had lost their cry. My voice poised, a spear raised to thrust at the skin of silence. But a scream could not pass through lips tight-sewn as heads drying on a shrinker's pole.

I hung in dark silence, body and spirit bound by death. I thought of my enemies in the world of spirits: The Jaguar ghosts I had mocked, the pumas and warriors I had slain. If they caught my spirit they would slash it to screaming threads – and my Spirit lay trapped in its shell of bone. Already I had heard the scratch of their claws as they padded towards me across the Spirit blackness. I knew not if I heard the sound with my ears or from inside my head. Fright-water poured from my skin. My spirit crouched in fear. Only once before had I ever felt such shaking terror.

26

Fear remembered fear. Again I saw – as in many fever dreams before – myself wandering into the forest, further from our hut than my father allowed. I smelled the forest smells as if they were new. I saw colours fresh to young eyes. I heard my sudden scream when the snake dropped from the tree. Its grip wrapped me in man-thick coils. My arms could not move. My heart shook my bones. The green body tightened. Breath shrieked from my dying body. The quick-tongued head turned to watch me die. The mouth which would swallow me grinned a hideous grin.

Then my father came running, his anger trembling the trees. He seized the flicking green head and ripped its jaws apart. His teeth cut through snake-flesh. His mouth spat out snake-eyes. I was wrapped in twisting death and lived. I crawled from under the writhing, blood-spewing serpent and crumpled into my father's arms. His giant arms had cradled me as if I was a newly-born, and I held on tightly until we were back on the shores of the Huanacs.

After that they called him Snake-Killer, for he had killed the largest snake ever killed by a hunter of any of the lake tribes. From that day I feared neither man nor forest beast. But the touch of a serpent had chilled my skin ever since.

And then the first of many miracles happened. As if in answer to my feverish memories there appeared suddenly before me the image of Snake-Killer, his face smeared with sacred mud. His smile gave forth his joy in seeing me. He was in full battle dress, just as he had died in the fight with the Falcon Tribe. His severed head grew again on his shoulders. His loin bark swelled with the vigour that made his wives fight for his man-spear, like birds over a grub.

I wanted to kneel before him but my body couldn't move. The image of my father trembled, as if seen in clear waters. He spoke:

'You have been brave. You have shown wisdom, my son. Your body has been saved from death by the Moon-Gods, so that you might lead our tribe in the battle to save the world.'

My lips could not yet speak, yet my very thoughts became words: 'But Nima is still alive, O father. And I cannot fight with my spear arm rotting on the ground.'

'The Moon-Gods in their All-Power have restored your arm, brave son. Nima shall live no longer to infect the tribe with his cowardice.'

'But I lay captured, great Spirit. What will they do to me?

27

What must I do for them?'

'Behold the truth of my words,' said the shimmering spirit. 'The Moon-Gods have been sent for by the very tears of Viracocha. They have come to save the world and teach the Sacred Duties to the men of this world. Behold their faces and listen to their words. They are those of great masters with many gifts to give those who do the Sacred Duties.'

'But I can serve no greater master than you, Snake-Killer.'

The image wavered once more as though the Wind-Spirit had blown on the face of the waters. My father appeared again. This time his smile was gone.

'You will be Chief of all the Lake tribes,' he said. 'You will be the Chief of chiefs, and you will lead the tribes into battle against the fearful enemies of this world. We in the Otherworld have pledged our power to the Moon-Gods. May you serve them with all our blessings . . . .' The vision slowly faded into blackness.

I was filled with boundless joy at seeing my father and listening to his guidance. All at once I felt the truth of his words. My body, though aching with pain, was alive and my shoulder had once again grown the arm that Nima had severed.

Light sprang back into the cave. I was now ready to follow the gods that the tears of Viracocha had summoned. When they came through a hole in the cave wall I looked at them boldly, forgetting my fear.

They had no feet to kiss, these gods. The bottoms of their legs grew hard hooves. These stuck out from the shiny loose outer skin that covered them to their necks. The white moon-skin covered only their faces and hands. They wore no feathers, no bones in their ears, and carried no weapons.

Even the words of my father could not stop the first question that came to my lips:

'Why? . . .'

'Why did we kill the brothers of your noble tribe?' continued a being with white hair, who fixed me with a wise look.

The god turned aside. When he looked back at me there were tears coming from his pale grey eyes. The tears of Viracocha! I bowed my head without words, for I knew now the gods too had feelings.

'We lament the slaughter,' said his voice without emotion. 'We come from beyond the man-world, where gods do not kill other gods. There we do battle with the demons who would destroy the sky itself, with all its stars and planets. We bring gifts of wisdom and peace to all peoples of the starry sky. And those who revere our guidance will share in our glory. Those who attack must themselves be attacked.'

My mind found truth in these words. Truth that chased away anger. The god continued:

'You, who told your Chief to stop the attack, have been brought back from the dead. The arm which Nima cut off will deliver his own death.'

'Great Fathers, I worship you. But will my arm come fully alive?'

'It will, Boaz,' said the god, 'and where your blood spilled to the ground a stone will rise for the Huanacs to worship.'

'What shall the Huanacs call the gods?' I asked.

'By our names, so we may understand each other better,' the god smiled. 'I am Oraan, whose duty is to be friend and father to man. Ravaan is the healer of your arm, helped by young Askar, who will heal the sick in the days to come. Looth will come amongst you with knowledge of taming plants and animals so that you may never starve over the long winter again. Chiruwi is our Vision-Catcher and will lead you in the building of temples. Mahala will direct the digging of the Sacred Rock and see to it there are no halts in the Sacred Duties.'

'And do you have a chief?' I asked.

'Sett is the Great Master whom we all obey. It was he who brought power to this great craft and guided us towards your Sacred Lake. There are others but these are the names of the gods who will walk amongst you. We are the gods whom you will worship alongside the spirits of your ancestors. We will reward you with new pleasures for carrying out the Sacred Duties.'

I looked at those surrounding me carefully. I would serve them as the Huanacs would serve me. But I knew I would continue to serve myself and the great spirit of Snake-Killer above all.

Oraan turned his back to me and vanished through the hole. The god Ravaan ran his cold fingers over the seam

29

where my arm joined my shoulder and applied a magic grease over the join.

'Within two crossings of the Sun you will fight,' said the god of Healing.

'And you will win!' said Askar with great excitement.

'And the Sacred Duties, O gods, when will I learn more of them?'

'You need only relax now, brave Earth-man. All will be made known,' said Ravaan. He held a shiny snake and stuck its fang into my arm. So this was the bite that had brought warmth to my fever-dreams.

'Will Snake-Killer come back soon?' I asked, my heart becoming heavy.

'All will be made known,' said Ravaan.

'Will I ever see Sett, your great Chief?'

'Close your eyes, Warrior,' said Askar, 'and sleep.'

I awoke, not knowing how long I had slept. My spear arm was well coated with the magic grease, and already my fingers could move as I wanted them to. I got up and walked around the closed cave. I could not fathom the shiny things I saw before me – I knew no words to even start to describe them. Askar came in and helped me back to the cold flat bed.

'You must lie all day like this,' he said. 'Tomorrow I'll show you the rest of our ship. And you will meet more of the gods . . .'

My eyes saw things for which there are no words as I scouted the shiny caves. Askar was by my side, letting me go where I wished. My spear arm was throbbing but anxious for revenge against Nima. Askar opened the mouths of small caves and I watched the gods inside making strange things happen. The gods looked me over then turned away back to their work. Some smiled at each other in a way that made me uneasy inside. Yet others spoke to me in the tongue of the Huanacs, wishing me good fortune in the fight against Nima.

In one cave two gods sat watching a frozen pond which held the image of my tribe. I saw Nima. I heard him telling lies to the warriors. He said that I, Boaz, had led the war party into the massacre. That he alone had won the battle. The Moon-Child, he said, had surrendered and was awaiting his commands. I heard women wailing for their men and warriors shouting in an unsure victory. I fought back the rage I felt for Nima.

As we left this cave a thought came to me so I spoke it to Askar:

'Why do the gods look just like the Huanacs?'

'What do you mean, Boaz?' asked Askar, smiling as one does to a child.

I spoke carefully: 'None of you wear the heads of birds, cats or serpents. It is only your Moon-skin that is different. That and your great powers.'

Askar lost his smile and thought for a moment. 'Yes. You are right,' he said.

'It is because we created men in our own image ... Look, this is where we train our bodies.' He stepped toward a wall and it slid open. Inside a large cave gods were lifting rocks, running without moving and clashing thin slabs of thin, shiny stone until sparks flew.

They turned at once to look at me. A giant huge and mighty stepped quickly forward, with puma eyes about to pounce. His face grew a line of hair beneath his nose and around his chin. I knew him immediately to be a god of war. He wiped the sweat off his brow and roared gruffly:

'Your arm is ready to fight the Chief?'

'If it is half as strong as my rage – yes.'

The giant's huge eyebrows raised to his hairline as he laughed in surprise; 'Hah! A good answer for a native of this world.'

'A good answer for any man,' said Askar, guiding me past the giant.

'I ask again if your arm is ready to fight?' said the giant as his fingers wrapped around my other arm like the loops of a boa.

'We shall know soon enough, Mahala,' said Askar.

'You are right, Askar. Come, we shall play a game, this Earth-man and I. Boaz ... you put your elbow on that table, as shall I. Then we'll grasp hands and try to push the other's hand down. We'll see if you're ready to face the enemy.'

'He needs his strength to fight Nima,' said the healing god, but I had already pushed past him and had my elbow on the table.

'I will do as Mahala says. Only I do not wish to cause him harm.'

31

A great bellowing laugh burst from the giant as he pulled off his outer skin. His body was the same dreadful white as his face and hands. But his body looked as if it could snap a tree in half.

His shoulders glistened, rippling with powerful grace. My blood-pump beat fast as many questions ran through my thoughts. I licked my dry mouth and waited. Fingers as thick as vipers wrapped round my hand and the giant made one plunging move downward. I could not stop him until my hand was a finger's thickness from the table.

My humbleness before this man-who-was-not-a-man suddenly vanished as my warrior's instinct flared. This was a game I had often played with Olmec and my other friends. Slowly his arm retreated – pushed back to where we had started. Redness flushed the giant's moon-skin. The strength of the Huanacs surged through me. The puma eyes were staring into mine. The eyes were like Nima's and my rage brought spirit to my strength. I forced down his hand to the table. I saw smiles on a few faces but no one spoke until Mahala said, 'Ravaan is a good healer. Perhaps he put rocks into your arm instead of muscle.'

I stammered for a reply; 'It is a good game,' I said. 'But it is mostly played by children.' I tried to smile but could only wince in pain. My arm felt the bites of snakes, spiders and scorpions from my fingers to my neck. Mahala turned and walked away as Askar rubbed grease into my bleeding scar.

'It is ready to fight Nima?' I asked.

'It is ready to fight an avalanche.' said the healer.

I slept for a short space. Then Oraan shook me awake. 'We shall fly to the shore of the Huanacs. Follow me.'

He took me to a large cave where there were many small eggs of the Moon-Child. As many small moons as the fingers of one hand lay in the nesting cave each large enough to hold several men. A large hole opened in the side of the cave. The bright sunlight hurt my eyes, but the waves of the Sacred Lake gave me the sweetest music. I yelped in joy – I was still in the world of the living! And the gods had not been demons in disguise.

Oraan and Askar urged me inside one of the smaller Moon-beasts. After we had entered, the Moon-beast closed its mouth and jerked forward, spilling me back against a soft sitting pad. Oraan sat before an altar of smooth stones and shiny sticks against one wall. He barked commands to some warrior-gods who reported back over the hummings of insect wings. Askar tied a strap across me. When he saw me tense my muscles, he laughed.

'Relax your body, Boaz. Think instead of your battle with Nima.' His finger traced the scar and scowled. There was a red trickle flowing down my arm.

'Look, Boaz,' spoke Oraan while Askar rubbed more grease around the wound, 'you are the first man on this green planet to ride above the ground.' He pressed a stone and the wall opened into a hole covered with a layer of clear ice. The tips of trees flew below me along with cliffs and shores.

'Tiki!' I shouted. 'It's just as Tamba said.'

Oraan looked at me strangely and said; 'Others before you have flown in an air ship?'

'Tamba, our Spirit Catcher, caught the spirit of the Sacred Condor and rode on its back,' I whispered, awed by what I saw.

Askar laughed aloud at my words.

Oraan looked at him sharply before turning back to me. 'Vision-Catcher is in the land of the dead' he said, 'and can find no condor to bring him back. Who in your tribe ever saw the condor come to Tamba?'

'It was only his words which brought the sight.' I said, looking out through the clear ice. Below, I saw the tribal ground rushing towards me and my thoughts turned red with hatred of Nima. Oraan spoke carefully: 'Right now it is not a condor which the Huanacs see but a Moon-beast. And out of it will step not Tamba but Boaz.'

'You do not want to kill Nima yourself?' I asked.

'We will do nothing to take away your glory – if it is you who win.'

'I am thinking of how we can show my people that the Moon-Gods are our friends.' I said. Then I had a sudden idea: 'Will you smash the Chief's hut when I raise my spear-arm high?'

'If this will win your tribe's respect – yes. But we can do nothing more. It is you who the Huanacs must follow.'

Beneath us the women and children were plunging head-long into the woods. Warriors, urged by Nima's voice, stood

33

their ground, waiting to accept the gods' surrender. Nima himself crept off to hide behind his hut.

'Nima has spoken lies to the warriors,' I said, 'do not kill them for their ignorance . . .'

'There will be no more killing,' said Oraan. The ground rose to meet us.

The child of the Moon sank onto the tribal fire, spinning embers in all directions. The last traces of confidence vanished from the warriors and they scattered like the sparks from the fire.

A mouth opened in front of me and a shiny tongue flowed to the ground. I took one last look at the stone faces of the gods and stepped into the deserted camp. With a great rush of wind the mouth closed and the Moon-beast lifted. Within the blink of an eye it was as high as the first star after sunset.

'Nima!' I shouted, 'Chief of the sows! Betrayer of the Huanacs! Murderer of the bravest warriors! It is I, Boaz, returned by the gods from the land of the dead. The days of your power are gone!'

Silence was broken by murmurings amongst the hidden warriors. Then came a terrified shriek from behind the Chief's hut: 'Kill him!' Nima squealed.

I answered quickly: 'I was killed – I have returned. Nima will taste not the blood of the Moon but his own!' I stood tall, waiting for Nima or any warriors who still fell under his sway.

Then came the sounds of women behind the chief's hut. The wives of Nima nagged and prodded him to do battle. Olani's voice was the loudest of all. Nima's slaps and punches could not still their mockery. Warriors began to drift forward, their spears lowered, staring at my body of spirit made flesh.

'Yes, warriors, it is Boaz – Boaz the coward,' I shouted, 'Come to fight mighty Nima – but where is Mighty Nima?'

My spear hand pointed to the sky and the gods kept their promise. Nima's hut burst into flames and vanished within heartbeats. Nima was caught by the eyes of the tribe striking Bitka, oldest of his wives and mother of his three warrior sons.

Nima had a choice. Either he refused to fight or he met my challenge. If he refused, his body would be eaten while yet he lived. If he died in battle his body would be used as part of the rites for the new Chief.

Nima called for his bearers. Not one man stepped forward. I took my axe and broke it over my knee: 'I will fight bare-handed,' I sneered, 'since you fight bare-footed.'

Bursts of laughter came from the tribe. Then more insults from the women. It was more than he could bear. He shook his war-club and all noise stopped.

Bitka took Nima's arm and tried to lead him away into the forest. Nima was all she had and ever would have. Nima threw her to the ground.

He stepped forward, a great wad of coca puffing out his cheek, feeding his War-Glory. Nima was fat but his fat was firm, not slack. His body was as thick and powerful as that of a bear. He was once the greatest warrior and had easily killed the Chief before him. But that was before he used words instead of deeds to lead the Huanacs.

I braced myself for his attack, cursing my arm weakened from the game with Mahala. Then like a wounded cat he charged raising his stick high and swooping it down so fast it could hardly be seen. I sprang forward from my crouch, my hand chopping at his wrist. The war-club flew out of his hand, and lay quivering in the ground behind me.

My spear hand chopped at his stomach, my other at his face. We grappled for strangleholds. His arms closed round me, trying to crush my spine like a bear. As he squeezed he bit viciously at the join of my spear-arm, causing it to bleed and quickly grow numb. My feet struck his shins and soft toes. My elbows swung into his blood reddened jaw, so hard that he fell back. I landed on top of him.

Suddenly my sight went blank for a few moments as a gob of coca juice was spat into my eyes. Nima's knee found my man-parts and I doubled over in pain. He kicked at my spear arm – a kick which sent black clouds across my thinking. He dived for his battle-club and swung it at me. It chopped off the hair close to my scalp. I clutched it and as he backed away I hurled it into the forest.

We circled each other for many pumps of blood, lashing out and kicking. No one gained advantage.

I knew I must finish Nima quickly, for his kick had made my spear arm almost useles. Nima saw this and sprang for it. I stepped aside and crashed my other fist into his nose. Dazed, he staggered. I jumped high into the air, twisting

35

my ankles around his great neck. It was a move that Snake-Killer had shown me many years before. I locked my ankles together and twisted my body as we both fell. Before he hit the ground I heard his fat neck crack like a branch.

Nima glared hatred, coughed blood, then departed his body.

THREE

Nima was dead. And I felt near to it, so great was the pain in my shoulder. But the rite had to continue. I grabbed a battle-stick from my friend Olmec and severed the dead Chief's head. Great cheers hailed me from the tribe. My tribe. Sticks pounded against gourds as the joy was felt by all. All except Bitka and her three sons.

A new Chief had conquered the old. The strength of this joy gave me ancient powers which numbed the pain and restored my spirit. I held up both arms and there was silence.

'The ways of the Dead are no more. First Tamba – Now Nima. Their ways are the ways of the dead. And my tribe is alive!' I let them cheer. 'I, Chief of the Huanacs have brought with me the ways of the living. The gods themselves will live among us!'

I pointed to the bright star overhead and it descended with the sound of whirling winds.

'Stand proud,' was my first command as Chief and one which tasted as sweet as honey on my tongue.

Only the children disobeyed, setting up a wailing and clutching for the softness of their mothers.

Oraan and Askar stepped down the shiny tongue which folded to the ground. The paleness of their skin frightened the tribe. Oraan's look was as cold as moonlight, but Askar was smiling.

'Be not afraid,' I reassured my people. Then to the gods I said: 'The tribe of the Huanacs welcomes you!'

Cheers and chants and drum beats bade them welcome. Askar took out a black, four-sided stone and pointed it at us. I froze. The stone made a clicking noise but no one fell dead.

Smiling Askar lowered the stone.

Oraan held up his hand when the cheering waned;

'Greetings,' he said in the tongue of the Huanacs, 'May

36

you live as long as the lake.' Joyous cries followed this sacred greeting of our tribe. 'We come not to harm you,' he continued. 'We killed your brave warriors only because we were attacked. But Boaz knows this. He knows also that with our coming we bring great changes. Mighty deeds will be done – great battles will be won! Deeds and battles which will make the Huanacs honoured amongst the tribes of the earth.'

As he spoke, Askar was walking in and out of the Moon-beast, carrying things I had seen inside the mother-ship. Things so mysterious they were stranger than the Spirit-world; I saw the rocks which the gods called boxes. These boxes remembered sights and sounds for their eyes and ears. Then there were strange gourds made from the smooth ice which was not cold. The gourds were filled with a liquid which we were soon to know more about. Things of the shiny rock which the gods called *metal* were put in a pile. These things would dig up our earth and cook our food better than tools of stone or bone.

The words of Oraan continued; 'We only ask that you join us in the glory that we offer. Boaz will tell you later of the mighty plans we have. But now is not the time for plans, or even duties. Now is the time to rejoice!'

At my signal the tribe let out a roar of agreement and broke into preparation for the festivities. Some women carried off Nima's headless body while others roasted deer, parrots and roots. It seemed many ages ago that Boaz the hunter was stalking the land for food. Truly a whole life-time had passed, for who would have known then that the gods would come from the sky. That Boaz the hunter would be Boaz the Chief.

Surely not Tamba – or Nima!

As maize was pushed into the glowing embers the tribe started their dancing. Askar placed his seeing-box to his eye many times. An old god with no hair on his head or face carefully watched the women preparing the food. Some warrior-gods whose names had not been spoken walked out from the Moon-beast drinking from clear gourds. They were offered wads of coca leaves to chew upon. Only Askar took the leaves, for he seemed most interested in the ways of my tribe. Soon after I noticed him secretly spitting them out.

It was not coca that the warrior-gods wanted. Their eyes

37

were already caressing our young virgins as they painted sky and fire colours on each other. The girls held their hands over giggling, whispering mouths. They knew that none but the ugliest would be virgins before the night was over.

Reed mats were placed on the ground for the gods to sit during the feast. They invited me to share it with them. I called for food and we stuffed our bellies with the crisp meat, dipping the maize in deer fat. The eyes of the deer were offered to Oraan but he did me great honour by passing them back to me.

When the feast was over, the rites for the new chief continued according to ancient tradition.

Bitka stepped forward, tears streaming down her face as she held the roasted sex-parts of the dead chief. I took them and called for Olani, the girl I had stolen from the Jaguar tribe. Bitka stepped back to the circle of women and began to wail.

Olani's eyes sparkled as her mouth opened. Her sharp teeth were ready to devour the flesh which had so many times devoured her body. Chantings, drums and flutes called upon the Spirit-world to join the ceremony.

Oraan stepped between us and knocked the flesh out of my hands. Olani shrunk into a crouch.

'Stand!' I commanded her. She did so, and quickly moved away. The only noises now were the waves lapping on the shore. I stepped back. Rage roared through my blood. The ancient tradition, as old as the tribe, had been broken. It was only fear for the safety of my people that stopped me from attacking. I tried to find words;

'Great are your ways,' I spoke while my body trembled, 'But great too are the ways of the Huanacs. This is the way that all dead chiefs give their blessing to the tribe – a way which must be carried out. As it will when I am defeated.'

'The old ways are no more, Boaz – that you yourself told your tribe,' said Oraan slowly. 'But we do not take away power without giving something even more powerful.' He turned his back to me and walked over to the clear gourds that stood in rows. He picked one up and held it to me.

'Drink,' he said, 'for this is Sacred juice that contains the fire of the stars. Give some to your wives and warriors in place of Nima's flesh.'

When I hesitated to accept this replacement Oraan swallowed some himself and a low cheer came from the nameless gods. Then he raised the gourd in the air. 'To mighty Boaz of the Huanacs!' he shouted. Askar and the nameless ones rose as one and drank, 'To mighty Boaz of the Huanacs,' they repeated.

I took the gourd and swallowed. Fire leapt down my throat and I coughed and spluttered. Askar laughed – a challenge to drink some more. I swallowed again and this time the fire went down to join the warm glow spreading through me. I poured some into Olani's throat and laughed at her choking. One by one my wives drank, then my warriors. By this time the glow had come to be a friend.

I heard my voice speaking: 'the gods have honoured the Huanacs. Now we give as we receive. The warmest and wettest of the virgins shall be theirs!'

The fathers and would-be husbands of the virgins scowled as the nameless gods quickly selected the choicest of the virgins. Askar spoke a few sharp words to the gods but they did not seem to hear as they chose and fondled their brides. The virgins were frightened but excited to belong to the gods, and some drank deeply of the Star-Juice. Oraan sent the girls inside the Moon beast and had more Star-Juice brought out.

The fathers and disappointed lovers began to complain, so I ordered them to drink more. The best thing for the gods to do was leave with their brides. This they did, for as soon as Oraan stepped inside, the hole closed and the small ship rose in the air, to our wonder and worship.

The Star-Juice was mightier than the power in the dead Chief's flesh. Warriors were hopping in the air and falling to the ground like Tamba riding the Condor.

My dancing soon brought the Chief's wives around me. Their breasts and woman-lips rubbed against my thighs. Hands grabbed for my man-spear. That which made thoughts within me was stilled as my lust rose higher than the trees. The power of the gods seemed less mighty now that my own was bursting from my bark-cloth. I rubbed foreheads with Olani, then with other wives. Hands, fingers, lips and nipples fought for my touch. The tribal blood pulsed through drums and flutes as the fingers stripped my live flesh bare.

Olani lay with her legs spread in the sand. Cheers and drum beats accompanied me inside her. Then one after another the wives spread or kneeled and my man-spear pierced their open wounds. Soon I was back with Olani. My lightning flashed deep within her fertile sea. From this lightning would come a son, and I would be to him as Snake-Killer was to me.

I had performed the Sacred Duty of the New Chief. The Spirit of the Huanacs would continue – with or without the help of the gods. Had I failed to flash my lightning I would have been killed and a new Chief chosen on the spot.

I poured the rest of the Star-Juice into my warriors' mouths in the same rite as the passing-out of Nima's flesh. The juice of the gods made us forget the old ways and helped bring forth the new. A new way for the Huanacs – a new way for the tribes of the Earth.

We danced with great joy and coupled with strength and laughter. As the last of the fire surrendered to the re-birth of the sun, we knew not where the new way would lead. But in the coldness of the dawn I knew the change would be great.

And with the dawn came changes. The heads of my tribe throbbed as if they were hanging from the altar of the Jaguar-Tribe. Then in front of us we heard the roar of thunder. Our pounding eyes saw the great mother Moon-beast climb into the air, wobbling like a wounded bird. It was as big as a mountain, and it glowed a pale orange like the rising sun conquering the peaks.

Trembling fingers pointed to an egg spewing from its mother's womb. It shot towards the sacred cave of Kuelpa, where the roots of Swollen Breasts rise up from the water. The great Moon-beast flew into the cave-womb of Kuelpa whilst its warrior child hovered high above it. It seemed to be guarding its mother, but from what I could not imagine.

The Mother ship disappeared beyond the rocks of Kuelpa's bay. Then the thunder died in bursts of echoes.

I reached for my war-stick and ran to the top of a nearby rise. The gods had flown into the cave of Kuelpa, drawn to the protection of its great Spirit. The small moon was coming for me.

The tribe watched as the shiny moon hovered over me and unrolled its metal tongue. I did not fear to climb up and be swallowed. The giant Mahala stood before me as the tongue folded back into place.

'We have need for you, strong Chief,' he smiled.

40

'This is good,' I answered, trying to clear my head from the Star-Juice. Askar came from behind me and rubbed my shoulder.

'The wound's been opened, Boaz,' he said, 'we'll put you under the healer in the mother ship.'

'No, Askar, it is well. It was well enough to kill Nima and keep me astride my wives.'

'Is it well enough to wrestle again?' asked Mahala, grinning.

Before I could answer the Moon had already landed on the bay and a magic sight appeared before me. The mother Moon fitted into Kuelpa like a man into a woman. Only part of it was not covered by the great cave.

We walked toward it, but not before I had bowed to the spirit of Kuelpa, for she was held very sacred to my tribe. Mahala waited until my reverance was finished and then spoke:

'There is much work to be done. And it is I who will see the work is done. It is to me you and your tribe will answer if you fail to do your Sacred Duties.' I looked into his eyes – the same puma eyes that challenged me in the strength-game. But I no longer felt the fear I had before. Oraan joined us, together with another god, the same hairless god who had studied the women making food at the feast.

'Boaz, this is Looth, a friend of your tribe. It is he who will feed the Huanacs.'

I looked at the man-god. His skinny shoulders seemed not built for the hurling of spears.

'We have many good hunters,' I said.

'Your hunters will be workers,' said Mahala. Oraan motioned him to silence.

Looth said:

'In the great mountains and plateaus grow sacred plants which will give the strength of warriors even to the children of the Huanacs. These plants will be brought to the tribe. Also llamas, vicunyas and deer can be made to stay together in herds so it will no longer be necessary for them to be hunted. The work is such that the women and children can do most of it, while the men do great deeds.'

I liked the look in the skinny one's eyes.

'We will watch and listen, Looth.' I said. Looth extended his hand and gripped mine with great strength. This was not a challenge but a sign of friendship. Oraan spoke:

'Boaz, Mahala will instruct you with the protection of the mother ship against the Serpents.'

'The Serpents?' I asked, feeling a stab of fear.

'We will talk of this, and much more, after your tribe has disguised our ship.' He and Looth walked off, their hard hoofs crunching over the small stones of the bay. Mahala pointed to the exposed part of the ship:

'That must not be seen by the flying Serpents. We must build a shell of trees and branches over the corner and cover it with rocks to make it look like a cliff. Do you understand?'

'I understand.'

The small Moon-beast picked up four hands of warriors and flew them back to the bay of Kuelpa. They stumbled out, wide-eyed and terrified, but they were thankful for the protection of Kuelpa. While they huddled together on the beach I flew beside Mahala, showing him where the tallest trees grew. They were in a valley in the land of the sunrise, where I had once gone with Snake-Killer.

We flew over sharp ridges and steep valley walls. The flight was smoother than that of a condor. I pointed out below me, in the land of the dreaded Falcon Tribe, the tallest trees I had ever seen. Mahala snapped an order in Moon-tongue and we descended towards the grove. As we hovered over the largest of the trees a hole opened in the floor.

One of the warrior-gods strapped a large black box on his back. He held a pointed rod in one hand and a metal vine in the other. The vine was woven finer than a bird's nest. Then he stepped into the air. Invisible wings stopped his fall halfway down the tree. He tied the vine around the strongest branches, then landed gently as a squirrel on the ground. He pointed his rod to the tree. I shrieked and nearly fell through the opening. For a red tongue of death, the same one which had killed many men of my tribe, was licking a line across the trunk. The tree was cut from its stump faster than Nima's head from his body.

The tree stayed upright, held by the claws of the Moon-beast. When the god had flown back in through the hole the ship sped off, pulling the tree with it as if it were a feather.

I could not help but laugh when I beheld the terror of my tribesmen as they saw us coming toward the bay. Some scattered over the rocks while others jumped in the water. The rest prayed to Kuelpa for a speedy death.

Slowly, the tree was lowered over the exposed part of the mother Moonship. Then the vine was untied and we were off again for more.

When a hand of the giant trees were leaning against the opening of the cave, I led my tribesmen in the carrying of rocks to place among the branches and trunks. By throwing small rocks over the large ones we had helped to build the mountain that would guard the ship of the gods. The Spirit of Kuelpa was happy.

We finished as the sun died in the great salt waters beyond the high plain. Then the gods flew us back to our shore with many gourds of Star-Juice. My painful limbs were soothed by Olani, her caress having more power than all the healing boxes of Askar and Ravaan.

Looth walked into the camp as the food was being cooked. He bowed to me and smiled at the children. Then he told us not to be bothered by him while he once again looked over the food. He scratched a small rod over white leaves as we ate.

'The gods play many children's games,' I said to Olani, who giggled.

After the food we drank the Star-Juice and forgot our weariness. My other wives were nagging me for attention and I danced and coupled with them all, coming back to Olani for sleep. Looth had curled up asleep beneath the stars, his shiny outer skin keeping him warm in the frozen night.

Looth woke me early and laughed when I gruffly pushed his hand aside. He went outside my hut and I heard him pacing in the rocky ground. Olani wrapped her limbs around me to keep me in her warmth of sleep. Each pacing in the sand made me more awake. Each pacing pounded in my head. I was in an angry mood as I slipped from Olani and stepped outside. I bowed slightly to Looth.

'The Star-Juice is good but it brings a sickness with the morning,' I said.

Looth laughed and slapped me on the shoulder;

'That is because it is sacred to the Moon – and hated by the Sun. Come, let's walk into the forest and I'll show you a pepper that takes the throb away.'

In the forest we came upon young Curu emptying his

belly behind a tree. Looth seemed delighted and called for the boy to bring the smelly earth-food over and place it in a small clear gourd he held out. Once covered, it was put into a large pouch he carried about his shoulder.

Curu and I were puzzled.

'Tiki!' said the brash boy, 'What would the gods want with my earth-food?' It was a good question and I did not slap him.

Looth answered slowly, 'We must see what you eat and how your belly makes this earth-food. Then we can make sure the right food is being eaten to make you strong.'

Curu wanted to join us and Looth agreed, seeming to show a fondness for the boy.

Further on, Looth picked a small pepper that our tribe knew to eat if the hunting was not good. 'We must dry these and pound them into a powder,' he said. 'That will be the cure for your pounding head.'

A guinea pig wandered across the path. Looth sprang forward and captured it without breaking its neck.

'We will make great huts for these,' he spoke, his eyes twinkling, 'then they can be bred and slaughtered without trouble. Boaz, I must have a good man from your tribe. One who has a spirit for taming things. He need not be a good warrior. Do you know such a man?'

'There is Shomu, son of Vision-Catcher. It is said that he can speak with the lower animals.'

'Good,' said Looth, 'I shall work with this man while you lead your people in more important things.'

'Curu would not do such women's work,' said the lad boastfully, 'Curu is made to kill enemies – like Chief Boaz does.' He swiftly dodged my kick while Looth laughed, picking more plants and putting them into clear skin pouches.

'With these plants we will kill many sicknesses,' Looth said. 'With other plants we will feed your strength. And with this . . .' he held up a tall plant, 'we can even make Star-Juice.'

The walk with Looth and Curu made me happy. It was the old and new walking side by side. And together it was the spirit of the Huanacs. The Spirits of the Lake, the Peaks and the Trees had accepted the coming of the gods. But not without change.

44

When we reached the camp I called for Shomu. He came wearing a frown. I could tell he did not want to work with the beings who killed his father. But Looth spoke gently with him. He told of the great changes that would be made. How the rivers feeding the lake could be twisted to water the ground for planting. How the llamas and guinea pigs could be housed and cared for. The light from Looth's eyes soon brightened those of Shomu. But I could still see that the loss of his father had turned the boy's mind in a way that I did not like.

Above a sudden burst of children's yells I heard my name called from the shore. There Oraan was waving from a boat made of reeds. I looked on dumbfounded. In the past our tribesmen had sat upon floating logs to fish in the deep waters. But never had I seen a craft that was hand-fashioned to float upon the water.

Two nameless gods held long branches within the boat and seemed more tired than Oraan. Oraan jumped to the shore and waved the children away with a small flick of his fingers. It needed nothing more than that to turn their delight into a howling run back to their mothers. To me this craft was a miracle as great as the Moon-beast. For it was simply made and I knew my tribe could make another like it.

'Sett has designed this boat from reeds that grow beside your sacred lake. It will carry many men or many rocks, and it will stay afloat for many snows,' said the sharp-faced being.

'Great are the wonders of the gods,' I said, prodding the reed-bundles with my chief's mace.

'Great are the wonders of the fingers and thumbs,' said Oraan, stretching and spreading his pale hand outward. 'For these alone can build. We need many hands to build and work these boats. And many more for digging and building. Great are the wonders that our hands shall build together.'

'What digging – what building do you talk about?'

Oraan turned his smile into a frown. 'Very well, Boaz, the time to tell you more has come.' He spoke in a low, even voice: 'This world balances on the edge of the avalanche. For the sky is alive with Serpents.'

I pushed back the shiver these words brought with them. I said; 'I have heard talk of these Serpents before. Boaz can kill the greatest of Serpents, as could his father before him.'

'I know that,' said the god, 'that is why we brought you back from the dead.'

'But why do *you* hide from them?' I asked.

Oraan stared darkly at me; 'Great wars are fought between the stars. This is but one of them. Unless we stop them the Serpents will consume this planet like a giant boa swallowing a baby deer. Slowly, while all tribes of the earth scream with the same terror!'

My blood pump was racing as I asked: 'What can the Huanacs do?'

'We need more than just the Huanacs. All the tribes of the lake, all the tribes of the high plains must come together.'

'Tiki!' I cried, 'this can not be done – for the wars of these parts are as fierce as any that rage in the stars.'

'It will be done,' said Oraan. 'And you will lead them all.'

'Into battle?' I eagerly asked.

'Not at first. Before the battle we must be prepared. There are two islands on the lake of the Moon. A great temple will be built on the larger of the two. Then we will dig in the land of the Jaguar people. For the ground there is rich in the sacred rock which will feed the God of the gods in the temple. With this Power shall the Serpents be crushed.' As he spoke he ground his heavy hoof into a crab that had strayed too close.

My tongue could not find the words my mind was thinking. I stammered out a series of questions: 'A temple on the Island of the Demons? Digging in the land of our enemies? To feed a Great Spirit with rocks that hold much power?' I watched as the Spirit of the dead crab twitched its legs and pincers.

Oraan seemed to ignore my questions. 'First you must send runners to every tribe within two sleeps from here. A great many of them have seen and heard our Moonbeast so the message shall be clear. Join us or leave the high plains! We come in friendship, but our Great Plan must be followed, as we ourselves follow it.'

I forgot for the moment about the Island of the Demons. Calling three hands of young Huanacs, I told them to run to all the tribes on the lake and the high plateau with the news. The rest of the tribe helped with different tasks.

While some of the tribe were put to work on the building

of reed boats, others helped Looth and Shomu in the building of wooden pens for the animals. It was Olmec who led the raft builders, and I who led the pen builders.

Using metal cutters and shapers, supplied by the gods, we formed the wood into four sides that joined together. Then with one side open, we watched the gods in three Moon-beasts as they swooped low over Swollen Breasts and the land of the Falcon Tribe. Soon we heard a thunder of hooves and a herd of llamas, as many as the leaves on a coca plant, were frightened into the pen. Looth quickly closed the open side and we then had enough meat to feed the Huanacs for many snows. But there would be barely enough to feed the other tribes – if any came at all.

Olmec told me how Oraan had them working on the boats. Groups of reeds were bound tightly together using the tough parts of plants woven together to make rope. Then each bound bundle of reeds would be placed together and formed into the shape of the Moon on the wane. One long rope was then bound around and between the bundles. The water swelled the reeds and held the rope fast.

Those who thought the hard work was over were mistaken, for after these tasks there were many more to come. Great spaces in the forest had to be cleared of tree stumps and rocks so that plants could be tended as easily as the herd of llamas: plants to eat, to heal and to make Star-Juice. After that would come the changing of the mountain streams which ran into the Sacred Lake. This water would feed the plants and the plants would feed us. Under Looth's guidance the tribe worked with joyful spirits, for a full belly during the deep snows was a thing we had only dreamed of before the coming of the gods.

Four sleeps after they had left, all of the runners had returned. All except Curu and the runner to the Jaguar Tribe. Most tribes had listened respectfully and were heading for the lake. Two had turned the runners away with angry threats.

Curu came back the next day. He had been captured by the Chivas who were allies of the Jaguar Tribe. Before escaping from the back of a Jaguar hut, he had seen the clawed head of the runner I had sent to the Jaguars. The head of his friend now hung on the altar of the Sacred

47

Jaguar – his headless body being gnawed on by a mighty jaguar kept in a pit below the altar.

I had Curu repeat his story to Oraan. The god cursed beneath his breath and sent the lad away;

'We must have the Jaguar Tribe and their land,' he said, 'but we cannot afford to kill more of their men.'

I spoke quickly, for my hands were sore with the day-long work and my thoughts yearned for excitement : 'I will go to them alone. Will you destroy their altar if I signal as before?'

'We will,' said Oraan, 'but you shouldn't go alone.'

Without answering I called for bear's blood and sacred mud. My mind was filled with thoughts of revenge for the young runner whose flesh filled the belly of the mangy cat-god. The hatred that I felt for the Jaguar Tribe darkened my mind like a storm cloud. The runner was a child of Olmec, the man who might be chief if I failed with our ancient enemies. I had Olani paint emblems of the Jaguar Tribe on my skin.

I plunged into the thick forest. The first thing to do was kill a jaguar.

I crept to a spot sacred to the Jaguar Men – a grove where many cats made their homes in caves. I lay down and slashed my arm so the smell of my blood would settle like fog over the grove.

There was not long to wait. No noise, only the bending of branches alerted me. The jaguar watched me where I lay with flies settling on my wound.

With a high-pitched roar it sprang . . . I was ready. I rolled under its leap, and by the time it had landed and whirled around to attack, my spear was already stuck through one eye and out of its neck. I skinned the jaguar and rubbed dirt in the wet skin to lessen the stench it made when I put it over my head.

I crept deep into the lands of the Jaguar Tribe. Soon I saw their huts.

No one noticed as the Huanac with the jaguar's head slipped in amongst the crowd of warriors. They were all listening to Chief Aroona stirring up their War-Glory. His necklace of jaguar fangs rattled as he waved his arms and spoke. Behind him the shaman known as Dream-Speaker was bending backwards to the ground, shaking his mace whilst his shoulders heaved in a trance. He wore the whole

48

skin of a giant jaguar and aroused fear deep in every man. Aroona shouted to the men of his tribe and the Chivas who had joined him:

'Those who burned away the very bones of my father the Chief, those who join with the Huanacs to plot our massacre, those that now want *us* to join the devil-gods – So shall they all die!'

Fearful murmurs arose in the two tribes. I worked my way forward. Aroona, lover of Olani before I had stolen her from him, moved his wirey body to the pit of death. Above it was the altar of Jaguar skins worn by the bravest of the dead chiefs. And the heads of enemies. Dream Speaker thrust his Spirit stick in the ground by the altar and wrestled with it. He was calling up the protection of all who had died in battles against enemies. I glanced up to the sky for the bright star which shone even in daylight. It was there.

'Sacred spirit of the Jaguar, Sacred Chiefs of the Jaguar and Chiva tribes,' spoke Aroona, every word screaming from his mouth, 'bring us strength to defeat the monsters from the sky and the Huanacs they enslave.'

The murmurings began to change into war cries. I knew I must act now, before the frenzy of War-Glory closed the eyes and ears of the warriors.

I broke through the crowd yelling, 'Surrender to the gods!' I jumped clear over the pit and landed on the altar. 'Surrender now and join us, enemies of my tribe. Or leave this land forever!' I pulled off my jaguar head and jumped clear of the altar. 'Surrender now and join us as brothers, or beware the fire of the gods!' I held up my spear arm and the red fire-tongue sent the altar crashing into flames. A cinder hit the jaguar in the pit and with one great leap it jumped free and charged headlong towards me. I stepped aside, expecting to be killed for sure. But the cat kept on running, screeching into the forest.

The tribes were frozen stiff. Only Aroona reached for his spear. His hatred of me was stronger than the wrath of the gods.

I flung my mace at his spear, and both weapons splintered.

'You are surrounded by the fire of the gods,' I shouted. All the men in both tribes looked up to the bright star floating in the blue sky. They bowed in surrender.

All except Aroona.

'A stealer of wives shall not lead my people,' he challenged.

'I will fight you,' I said, 'but I will not kill you.'

'Then die, Devil-Slave!' Aroona sprung at me with the strength of two jaguars. The gods' red tongue licked at the ground between us and the forest of warriors. We fought long and with all our skill. He was faster than Nima, but not as powerful. His sharpened nails drew blood from my face but my kicks and punches made him weak. He threw dust in my face and knocked me into the pit. He jumped on top of me then gripped a dead man's leg and flung it at my head. It knocked me down but now I was fighting with the blood of two Huanacs. My kick caught him in the groin and sent him sprawling. I drove my forearm into his neck until he rolled his eyes upwards, his body becoming slack.

I threw him out of the pit and jumped up beside him. I spoke to the tribes:

'I am here to offer friendship. Friendship and peace, in the name of the gods. You will worship these gods, yet the Jaguar may remain your sacred Spirit. I know not what the gods want but I know we must listen – and obey!'

There was a silence until the first warrior started to cheer. Then all joined in. But not Aroona.

He flew on my shoulders from behind. We fought over the still glowing cinders of the altar. Four fists, four feet, kicking, jabbing, grabbing, twisting. I felt in him a man of my own courage.

We fought until we could fight no more. With my last surge of strength I kicked at his chin. He clutched my ankle and we both fell down.

We looked at each other. Slowly our hatred vanished and frowns were replaced by smiles of respect.

'We will join you,' said Aroona. 'But may Olani poison your food and come back to me.' His smile disappeared and so did mine. Yet I saw in him a man like myself; brothers of the high plains, two brave Chieftains who together might conquer the Serpents.

Dream Speaker had not stopped shaking and rattling during the long fight. And now he broke out in a flurry of cat-like noises and movements. He thrust his stick into the ground and growled:

'Sacred Jaguar bows to the Gods from the sky. Jaguar

will outlive them all but bows, for mighty is the Power of the Sky Gods.' He shook and stretched his jaguar claws, then leaped high in the air; 'I see a new altar. The Jaguar shall serve the Sky-Gods on the island in the lake. The island where the first rays of the sun touched when the world was born. The island where the first people-who-thought-like-man were made and live still. The waters of the Sacred lake shall sing to the temple of the Sky-Gods!'

FOUR

The shores of the Huanacs swelled with the tribes of the high plateau. One by one came the Bear, the Puma, the Crab, then all the rest of the tribes that lived on the distant banks of the Sacred Waters. They came with their weapons lowered, ready to receive the gifts of the gods. Only the fierce Falcon tribe refused to come, along with two smaller tribes who had joined them.

Oraan met each chief alone. He told them of the greatness of their tribe and the part that they would play in the Great Plan. He spoke of the age after the defeat of the Serpents. Then all tribes could return to their lands and live with the full blessings of the gods. There would be no wars, no starvation, no frozen bodies in the great snows. And there would be Star-Juice flowing like bubbling streams into the Lake.

When the Jaguar and Chiva tribes came, a great feast was given by the gods and the Huanacs. For two passings of the Sun and Moon we danced, sang, ate and drank. Not a word was raised in anger, and women and men from all tribes mated with laughter and joy. If this was what life would be like under the Moon-Gods, we were ready to have it last forever.

On the third sunrise the gods announced that the Duties must begin. The Chiefs were gathered together in a council with Oraan, Mahala and the strange-faced Chiruwi, who wore sparkling frozen ice before his eyes. Different chiefs were given different jobs to do. We were all eager to please the gods and listened carefully to their instructions.

Many of the tribes were taken to a part of the Jaguar lands at the roots of Tall Feather. Later Olmec told me of the first day's work. They saw a small moon hover above

51

a cliff, then fly away faster than a stone from a sling. A blast smashed a hole at the bottom of the cliff. More moons came, each one blasting a bigger hole.

Mahala told the tribes to clear the rocks away for the next blast. By the end of a hard day there was a hole that went into the cliff farther than a stone's throw. Mahala worked with a tall god with a square face called Vakal. Each time the tribesmen had carried out the rocks from the hole, Vakal would walk inside carrying a box which clicked like the cicadas. As the sun was setting he emerged smiling from the hole carrying chunks of a sticky black rock.

Mahala's face shone with joy and the promise of revenge. He lifted the rocks high, roaring in a harsh voice:

'Hear me, weary tribesmen. This is the Sacred food that the God of Power will devour. The more He eats, the bigger He grows and the more He'll want. The God of All-Power will live on the Island of the Sun in the Great Lake. He will receive many boat-loads of these rocks each day. The work will get harder and harder as the God demands more and more. But we must defeat the Serpents, and only this great God of Gods can help us!'

I had not forgotten the demons of the Island of the Sun. As the tribes were joined with ancient enemies to work together, I found it impossible to forget the demons. For they hovered in the stories told at night by the old men of all tribes. Tonopec, my tribe's Story-Teller, had long made our hair stand on end with tales that had frightened our ancestors.

Oraan wanted me and Aroona to head a party of conquest to the Island. This would bind our old wounds and bring our War-Glories together. Or else it would prove who was stronger. The Moon-beast would not help, said Oraan, for this was to be a test of faith and cunning. Aroona and I grunted at each other, recognising the joy of battle in each other's faces.

I called for Tonopec and listened carefully to the stories. One told of a race of apes from the far jungles beyond the Great Peaks who had climbed over them to pay homage to the Sacred Lake. There they had profaned the Spirit by capturing women of an ancient cave-tribe. In his anger, the Spirit of the Lake had put the apes, the women and the monsters they had fathered to live on the island, and taken away their power to swim.

Another story told of the first tribe at the beginning of the world, when the Sun and Moon were first born from the Sacred Lake. From there the first tribe spread out in all directions across the world. They had brows shaped like horns and bodies like great, stooping hairy apes. They buried their dead with flowers and red powder covering the corpses. They worshipped the night and all growing things. They had the power to snap trees yet tried to live peacefully, eating only greens, roots and berries. But then came the hairless tribes that now peopled the earth. They made great sport of killing the man-apes. All had been slaughtered except those remaining on the island.

Other stories told of how the apes could make their bodies vanish. They would swim ashore and play tricks during the night. They would grab the breasts of women and make love to them as if they were their husbands. Many a woman swore this had happened to her.

It was then that I remembered a tale told to me by Snake-Killer. A young warrior, who had chewed too much coca, swam all the way to the island. He never returned, but his screams had carried across the water for days.

After the Sun was swallowed by the night we put a hand of men into each of the four boats that had been built. Our spears were tipped with the shiny metal stone. There were warriors from most of the tribes under my command. Together we pushed off from the shore and landed before sunrise at the island of demons.

Wisps of fog covered the crags and high places of the island. The warriors broke apart into three groups led by Aroona, the chief of the Chivas and myself. As we walked inland a strange stench filled our nostrils. A stench that awakened an ancient dread. We made no more noise than the fog rising to the brightening sky.

In the distance was a sudden sound of a man choking on his blood. Then a flurry of snaps were heard as if large branches were broken off a tree for a fire. Before my fear could stop me I was charging toward the sounds.

I heard Aroona's men ahead murmuring in broken gasps. Then we broke into a clearing, the fastest of my men just behind me.

Some of Aroona's men were retching from the sight and the smell. I ordered all to keep silent whilst my eyes swept over the carnage.

53

The snapping sounds had not been branches but spines. The warriors were like broken tree stumps, bones sticking out from their bodies. Their faces were set in bloody masks of terror. The Chief of the Chivas had chopped off the hairy inhuman arm of a demon. It still gripped a stone axe that dripped with the dead Chief's brains. There were heavy, bloody tracks where the wounded demon had been dragged away.

Above all rose the stench of death and horror.

A warrior from the Bear Tribe lost his mind to the terror. He ran off into the bush screaming like a monkey with a scorpion still hanging from its bottom. I took this to be an omen.

'Quickly – we must follow him!' I ordered. Forgetting the nightmare behind us, I led the men out of the clearing and easily followed the madman's trail. Soon his wild path led to one used often, and I felt the close presence of the demon creatures.

I held my hand up and my men fell silent. The trail wound around and down a large outcropping of boulders. Climbing to the top of one I saw the frenzied warrior running beneath. The trail led into a series of caves on either side of it. The madman gave a slow rising moan as he saw a line of demons blocking his way.

There were as many of them as fingers on one hand. Three males and two females. A small one held onto its mother.

Pink eyes glared in their hideous faces. Their lips snarled with the fury of all hunted animals. They towered at least one arm's length above the warrior. He sank to trembling knees and awaited his death.

I motioned my men to join me with spears ready to throw. Below us the largest of the beasts stepped forward. Now something inside the warrior snapped and his courage returned. With one last effort to remain alive he sprang for the demon's throat. The beast grabbed his hair with one arm and screamed a single sound of rage and sorrow. It was a sound that rose in pitch until it seemed to gnaw away our ears with pain. Then he swung the warrior like a snake and heaved him against a thick tree. The Bear Warrior curled around the trunk and fell to a heap at its roots.

It was then that I ordered the spears to be thrown. The

metal points were well-aimed and killed a male and a female. The remaining demons pulled free the spears and flung them to the ground. We jumped down from the rocks to meet the enraged creatures. They lowered their heads and charged, butting two men dead against the rocks. Another was snapped in two, but not before he had slashed open the beast's stomach. More bodies flew like leaves before the snow. The ape with the slashed stomach came towards me, screaming his awful cry. He lifted me up but my mace crushed his skull before he could crush my bones.

My men were fighting bravely, but only weapons could hurt the beasts. Not the mere muscles of men.

The child ran into a cave in the rocks and the remaining male and female moved to guard the entrance. More spears were picked up and hurled into their bodies. The female slumped back into the cave as Aroona charged the male. He was the last demon, or else others would have come to the attack. Aroona sank his blade into the monster's side as it flew for his throat. The creature's fury knocked Aroona to the ground. Clawed hands seized his throat to tear his head from his body. At the same moment my war-club shattered the creature's skull.

Aroona rolled out from under the quivering corpse and gave me a look of thanks. Together we warily entered the cave. The child was nursing at its dead mother's milk sac. It made the same whimpering noises as the children of the hairless tribes. Aroona reached for a spear and slew the small one through the neck.

A hairy hand grabbed for his ankle and pulled him down. The beast who had lost his arm to the Chivas' Chief now crunched his teeth into Aroona's leg. I leapt towards the beast. My war-club found its skull tough, but breakable.

'You saved me twice, Boaz,' said Aroona as I dragged him out. 'I have fought like a child.'

'You have fought like a Chief,' I told him.

Half of our men were killed and more were injured. But we had conquered and slain the demons. A cry of victory arose from our dry throats.

Then a Moon-beast descended from the sky.

Oraan stepped down with Chiruwi. The strange god looked with pleasure through his eye-discs at the corpses of the demons, his snowy great eyebrows the only hair on his face or skull. In one hand he carried a rod made of

Sun metal. We had often found pieces of this metal and given them to the children.

'Where this rod sinks into the ground,' his high voice sang, 'There we will build the temple.' He looked up to the sky and made some secret signs. Oraan watched, his stone-face revealing nothing.

I supposed Chiruwi to be a great shaman of the Moon-Gods, for then he walked past the bodies, paying them no heed, and threw his rod toward the ground. It hit rocks and fell flat. Then he picked up the rod and walked further down the trail, disappearing beyond the rocks.

Oraan poked at a dead beast with his stick. The body was that of a demon, but its frozen face gave forth knowledge and sorrow. Oraan spoke Moon-talk to nameless ones. They carried Ardoona into the ship, his foot hanging to his leg by skin alone. Then they covered the body of the demon-child and carried it inside.

The warriors had all followed after the Temple-Finder. I stepped toward Oraan but he moved to one side.

'Back, Boaz. Bathe in the Lake for you smell like the monsters that live no more.'

'I am sorry they live no more.' I spoke as though to myself but Oraan heard me, and replied harshly:

'You are mistaken. The demons had to die. They were enemies of the Plan.'

'I do not understand. They lived in peace before we came.'

'They worked for the Serpent. And their bodies shall be given back to the Serpent.' He pointed a rod at the corpses. I knew its meaning and jumped aside as the bodies smoked and burst into flame.

Oraan and I followed the trail of the Temple-Finder. My mind was asking more questions but my mouth would not speak them.

Suddenly we heard a cry and cheers from the high ground before us. Both god and I ran toward the cheering, Oraan bounding ahead of me like a young stag. I reached the top of a rise and saw the crowd of warriors surrounding the Shaman by the banks of a large stream. His golden rod was sunk to its tip in the ground.

The old god cried out as fire flashed from his eye-disks:

'I, Chiruwi, set this place as the site for the great Temple. May the God of All Power bring blessings to the builders of His temple!'

56

Above us roared four of the Moon-beasts, circling the spot that Chiruwi had found. 'Step back,' Chiruwi warned, pointing to the rise where I was standing. He broke into a run towards me, the warriors following with curious faces. Reaching me, Chiruwi whirled back to face the chosen spot and held his staff up high.

'Behold,' he said, 'for the Spirit of the Temple is with us, now!'

Before our eyes appeared a mighty mountain. It did not flow like the great peaks but stood even and square, like Askar's sound and picture boxes. I knew not what to compare it with, so I sank to my knees and bowed with the others. Suddenly the roar of the Moon-beast disappeared, and with it went the vision. It faded away like smoke into an empty sky.

'You have seen the temple you will build. May you work for the Glory of the Lake and the Moon,' said the old god. He turned and walked silently to Oraan and together they headed for their Moon-beast.

As silent as were the gods, so were my men as we walked over the island. We followed the stream plunging towards the Great Waters. Halfway to the shore was a small altar where the beasts who lived no more had worshipped. There were flowers and tiny vines growing within a sheltered hut of reeds and grass. There were no weeds now, but there would be soon.

I felt I knew what the demon's ear-shattering scream had meant. It had howled the question: *'Why?'*

We worked the rest of the day wrapping the dead warriors in leaves and vines and throwing them into the sacred waters. We slept overnight on the island. But few men slept well.

FIVE

One of the reed boats took me back to the shore. I expected the tribes to welcome and praise our first battle in the name of the Sacred Duty. But only the children ran to our boats and tried to climb aboard. Olani ran to me outside the Chief's hut. Had I not taken Oraan's advice and bathed a long time, I doubt she would have hugged me so hard.

57

'Where are they all?' I demanded to know.

'The Chiefs were given Star-Juice last night. Today they have taken their tribes to where they are needed. I saw you save Aroona's life.'

I looked at her hard.

'Explain,' I said.

'Last night Oraan gave the drink to the Chiefs, as I have told you.'

'So you have. Go on, woman.'

'Well – then he pointed up to the sky and said "Behold your leaders as they fight to clear the way for the Temple."'

'And you looked too?'

'How could I not look, my brave, handsome Chief,' she said, her hand reaching inside my bark cloth. I slapped it away:

'Tell me what you saw!'

'It was the battle you led against the demons. Everyone saw it – even those who had not drunk. We saw the greatest of the Chiefs save the life of his old enemy. And for that I thank you and wish to show you my thanks.'

'You will, Olani, but first answer a few more questions.' Olani pouted.

'Where are the Huanacs?' I asked.

'Most of them are gathering reeds where the river Xilli feeds the Lake. They are to build many flat boats which will carry the black rock to the Temple.'

'And the rest of the tribes?' I snapped.

'Some have left to change the course of the Xilli. Many have already been flown to the island to start work on the temple. Others go with the gods to pick roots which Looth and Shomu found. These roots he calls potatoes and says they will nourish like meat. They will also bring back grass for the llamas and greens for the guinea-pigs. Still more have gone to dig the black rock. There, I've told you enough.'

'Tiki!' I said, feeling dizzy with the meaning of her words. These changes had caught me like a swollen river when the snow melts. The snow had once stood firm on the peak of my glory. But now the Moon was melting away my power. I was caught in the overflow and there was no turning back.

Yet it was I the Gods had saved from death and chosen to be Chief of the chiefs. Surely the gods had chosen wisely – for I felt myself to be a good leader of my people. Once

58

again I brushed aside Olani's warm hands as I pondered the words of my thoughts. They were gods, to be sure – but why would they build a temple to honour themselves?

'I have not seen the gods eat the black, sticky rock. Have you?' I asked Olani.

'No, Boaz,' she said, shaking her head. 'They eat meat – and lots of it.'

'Come with me, Olani. I want to look over the llamas and see how many are left.'

As we walked towards the herd of llamas, I saw the worry-lines in Olani's pretty face.

'What is it?' I asked.

She spoke her fears with difficulty:

'Many of the Huanacs have been asking . . . about the virgins the gods took to their Moonchild.'

'What do they ask?'

'Why not one has come to visit, not one sent a message that she is well.'

'I will ask about it. Tell my people they need not fear.'

As we reached the enclosure of the llamas, I saw Vakal and a hand of warriors come towards us from the direction of the mine. 'Hail, Boaz,' he shouted, then sprang forward and gripped my shoulder. 'That was a splendid battle,' he praised, smiling. 'You must feel proud that you killed them all.'

'I did – but not so much now.'

Vakal laughed, 'You've proven that you can fight. You could battle with the strongest and ugliest creatures on any world!'

I smiled, but then remembered Olani's words.

'There is one thing I must know. The brides of the gods are still Huanacs. The Huanacs want to hear and see their children and sisters.'

Vakal's smile fled his face.

'I will ask Mahala about it,' he said. 'Or better you speak to Oraan.' He led the warriors into the enclosure and put twisted vine around the necks of three hands of llamas.

'You take that many llamas for meat?' I asked.

'No. Just two. The rest will be taught to carry loads of rock from the mines to the shore.'

'But can they be taught such a thing?'

'Look how much we've taught you,' he laughed in a way that I did not like.

That night a boat came from Kuelpa. In it were the brides, let out from the Moon-Child for the first time. They were smiling and tearful as they embraced their tribe. They told stories of the great shiny caves and of the Star-Juice and the ways of the gods. Only when the loving of the gods was asked about did their faces lose their smiles. They spoke quickly of something else.

There was no Star-Juice that night. There would be only Star-Juice one night out of a hand of nights. This was the order of the unseen Sett, and was not well accepted. Without it stiff muscles hurt and the men fell asleep ignoring their women.

Aroona returned from the healing box the next morning. He entered my hut and kicked my shoulder.

'Look, Boaz,' he said, 'my foot grows back into place.' Olani opened her eyes and the two gave long looks to each other.

'Come,' said Aroona, 'we go to the mines.'

'You are ordering *me*?' I said as I rose to the challenge. Aroona only smiled.

'Oraan orders *both* of us.' He looked at Olani and spoke softly; 'Greetings, Olani. Does the Chief of chiefs treat you well?'

Olani looked down as blood flushed her face.

'Yes, Aroona. I am happy.'

Aroona grunted and stepped outside to wait for me.

We walked in silence to the mines in the land of Aroona's tribe. I marvelled that less than a Moon-change ago we were two warriors creeping along these trails in pursuit of each other's blood. It was good that our strengths had been tested in battle and friendship. Fighting over women was one of the ways of old.

We saw a line of llamas as they walked toward us bearing heavy pouches of rocks. Vakal was leading the train forward, whipping the llamas for better speed. 'Hail the conquering heroes!' the young god greeted us as we stepped aside. 'Mahala will speak with you both. The Plan is going too slow.'

We saw tribesmen lying exhausted in front of the mine at the cliff. Mahala was shouting at them as we came closer:

'On your feet, laggards! You've rested for minutes already!' The men got up and began to stumble inside except one young warrior who had fallen asleep. Mahala pulled out his rod and pointed it at the boy's hair, which burst into flames. The boy ran screaming towards us. Aroona caught hold of the boy then grabbed some leaves and smothered the fire with them. I threw my chief's stick quivering at Mahala's feet.

The giant whirled his weapon towards me; 'Be very careful, Earth-man,' he said, raising his rod in my direction.

'You have hurt a boy of my tribe,' shouted Aroona, veins bulging from his forehead. He moved menacingly towards Mahala. 'We were told that this would not happen.' Many tribesmen had gathered at the entrance to watch.

'Good. Then it *did* not happen.' Mahala turned to the crowd. 'And it *will* not happen as long as the sacred rock is kept moving fast to the temple. Which it is not doing now. So *move*!' he shouted, and the tribes silently turned and disappeared into the dark pit, lit only by strange spots of fire without flame.

'Aroona,' Mahala barked, 'take the boy down and show him how a demon-killer works.' Aroona put his arm around the lad's shoulder and trudged towards the hole in the Earth.

'Oraan will hear of this,' I said, following Aroona into the pit to inspect it and listen to the feelings of the people.

In the days that passed, Mahala worked the miners hard yet there were no further cruelties. I told Oraan of the incident but he said nothing more about it, nor did Mahala. The giant watched carefully whenever I returned to the mine. Even though he was a god, I could not mistake the look of hate that his puma's eyes gave me.

The nights of Star-Juice came and went many times. By then the tribes had assembled together as bees in a hive. Under the direction of the gods the many different parts of the Plan were fitted together. Around the Queen Bee within Kuelpa buzzed the gods in shiny skins. They gave directions to us, the workers, and we obeyed. I was surprised at the way the tribes obeyed. Perhaps it was because of the Star-Juice. One tribe even came from the desert near the Salt Waters just to join with the drinkers of the Juice. They were the red-skinned Seal tribe, with slit-eyes and wind-hewn faces. Signs of the Seal were tattooed on bodies and they had beautiful women they would not share.

The Temple to the God of gods was to be the honeycomb to which the workers brought the black rock honey. The workers dug the pollen from the dark cave. The llamas brought it to the reed boatmen. Once on the island, the black rock waited in great mounds whilst the Temple was being built.

The temple-builders under the guide of Chiruwi were different from those on the mainland. They worked silently and with few smiles. The stench was still there to remind them of the sad-faced demons. Their shrines had been destroyed by Oraan. Scorched away into smoke.

The Temple's form grew steadily, for Chiruwi was a god who inspired fear. He was not like Mahala and never even raised his voice. But no one dared to slacken the hard pace. The stories of what he would do to them kept the workers in line. Whispers abounded in the work-camp, whispers of dark magic powers: 'Chiruwi writes the names of those who will die and be fed to the Condor's young,' 'Chiruwi is the spider god who spins the web of water ripples on the lake when the wind blows.' Such stories kept the stones moving.

Sometimes Chiruwi came among the workers dressed as a straggler. He would put on another face and he would test them. He would say that the gods were no more than sand crabs and listen for laughter. They did not laugh for they knew only he would say such a thing – aloud anyway. Then he would disappear inside a Moon-beast and spread out his writing sheet. He would draw and measure and be such a man as his straggler-self was not. Thus the men worked well for him, gathering great rocks after the Moon-beast had cut them into slabs with the red tongue of fire. The large rocks were carried by the Moon-beast to the temple site and then cut into smaller slabs by a god who directed his rod over them. Then the workers put the small rocks on a land boat which used round rolling stones instead of oars. These so-called 'wheels' carried the rocks to the place where Chiruwi would point. Flat wooden paths let the wheels run upwards as the Temple grew like a child into a man.

Everyday we worked, making solid the vision we had seen on the day of the conquest.

The black rock made its own mountain by the side of the growing Temple. It was then that many men were brought from the mine to help finish this Hut of huts. It was so big that it could be seen from all the distant shores at the end of the Sacred Waters. Some over four sleeps away.

Then we built stone lines around the Temple. We enclosed it as we had done with the llamas and guinea pigs. A great rock was rested at the top of two columns. On that rock were carved the visions seen by the Dream-Speaker of the Jaguar Tribe. Chiruwi had called for Dream-Speaker and spent much time with him. It seemed as if the Shaman of the Gods was telling Dream-Speaker of their Mysteries.

Little by little Dream-Speaker began to serve the gods. Better than he had ever served the Jaguar Tribe. And the shamans of the other tribes found that their Spirits could not heal the sick as well as the strange metal boxes and powders given by Ravaan and Askar on the great mother Moonship.

The mine and Temple broke and crushed the bones of many men. The tribal shamans were brought to the bay of Kuelpa so that they could help the healing miracles of the gods by calling on tribal ancestors. Some men were crushed so badly that they did not heal and they died.

Dream-Speaker was allowed to go everywhere, spreading the visions he had seen. He cried that the Temple was the greatest place of Power on the earth. Mighty was this God of Gods. The Destroyer and Creator as One. Soon the wrath of the God of All Power would destroy the Serpents who wanted to swallow the earth. Dream-Speaker had seen visions of the Serpents too, and when he saw them we could all tell. His body went stiff; he would scream with the cries of a wounded jaguar. His tongue would writhe in his mouth like a Serpent. It would shoot out and strike. Then he would roll on the ground as if snake-bitten, as if in death agonies. He screamed to the God of Gods for help. Then, mouth-frothing, he described great battles where the Serpents died under the hail of fiery stones. He saw the Serpents' eyeballs melting and their fangs turn to dust as they struck at each other in terror.

Every tribesman who saw Dream-Speaker's agonies was frightened. When I myself had seen him my belief was complete. I pushed the tribes harder to build the Temple. I ordered my men about like Mahala. And when the night of Star-Juice arrived the men would drink more and more. They wanted to shake themselves free from the terrible strain of their work.

The women and children worked as hard as the men. They tended the animals and the plants. They placed the flesh of slaughtered animals on the roof of a stone-built hut. Smoke from saplings rose from the floor of the hut and made the meat last longer. The meat and the plants would be sent to the mines, the Temple and the bay of Kuelpa.

The reed boatmen were the happiest workers, for they soon began to invent ways of their own to make the boats faster and stronger. One of these men was Pica of the Kutcho tribe who came from another lake many sleeps away. This man came to be well-liked for his songs and stories. He worshipped his boat so much that he slept in it, along with his three wives. His songs were about the glory of serving the gods and the troubles of mating in a wobbly, narrow boat. He was soon put in charge of the boats.

The Temple was not finished until many hands of men had hauled strange metal boxes into its centre. A hole was left in the roof above the boxes. Great pipes sucked at the water of the stream and spat it out into the lake.

The gods held a ceremony when the Temple was completed. Warriors of all tribes were ferried across the waters and shown the wondrous building. Dream-Speaker went into a trance and poured out his visions of conquest. The throats of many vicunas were slit by the gate of Carved Visions and the gods' red tongue of death turned the bodies into meat within a few pumps of blood. It was then shared by them and the tribesmen alike.

Much Star-Juice was drunk. As we were staggering and stumbling Oraan pointed to the stars with his rod and we beheld the very images that Dream-Speaker saw. Giant Serpents as large as the largest mountains opened their venomous mouths wide and came slithering towards us. Then the Mother Moonship swooped down, blasting them with a white pillar of fire that made our eyes turn away.

We were thankful to the gods for helping us. And thankful when the vision was gone.

The next day the warriors were told to carry the black rock into a pit by the Temple. A Moon-beast flew above the pit. Its red tongue soon melted the rock into a bubbling stew. When the stew had hardened, we took great metal points and broke it up. This was then melted again until the only thing left was a very small pool of white metal.

Wearing thick outer skins and ice-bubbles over their heads, the gods carried the glowing metal inside the Temple. Only the gods and Dream-Speaker were allowed inside the Temple.

Few tribesmen stayed on the island after the ceremony. These few were needed to move the rock from the pile to the pit. The rest of the men were put into the mines.

With Looth and Shomu I inspected the changed course of the Xilli. Instead of falling straight down from the mountain, the river now split into small streams pouring off to the fields of plants in the land below. Great sweeps of land had been stripped of their forests. The wood from the trees was used for bracing the mine shaft and feeding the many fires needed by the makers of the Great Plan.

I saw below me the small temple for the making of Star-Juice. The dots near to it were women who sat all day chewing the manioc plants and spitting them into a giant metal pot.

Next to this were the coca fields. Looth had instructed that the Seal Tribe return to the coast and bring back many llama-loads of shells. These shells were placed in great fires and then ground into powder. The powder was then added to the dried coca leaves. The workers who chewed this had little need of sleep or food, so great was the power from the bulge in their cheeks.

I saw the lake spread like the sky below me, and beheld a strange sight on the Island. A Moon-beast hovered above the centre of the Temple and spat down its red tongue of fire into the hole in the roof. Flashes of lightning and great noises echoed all the way to the mountains. Looth grew excited at this, but his own deeds were more important to him than all the noise-making below. His long finger pointed out the crops of potatoes, beans, coca, manioc, peppers, corn and quinoa.

'All this is for you,' he said, putting one arm around Shomu's shoulders and the other around mine. 'For you and your children, for the Xilli will flow thus until the end of time.' I followed the river with my eyes as it wound back to its old course. I looked at Looth, then at Shomu. Both were grinning and proud. I performed a dance of celebration, joined soon by both god and Huanac. Great were the

65

deeds of gods and tribes. But inside my thoughts I yearned for the miracles to pass, the battles to begin.

I looked again at Shomu and saw a strangeness in him that made me uneasy. His mind was still twisted somehow. He saw my look and avoided my eyes. He is no longer a Huanac, I thought. He wishes he was one of the gods instead of a man from a proud and strong tribe. A sudden darkness clouded my spirit as I said goodbye to the two of them.

SIX

I went down the hills filled with questions that I asked aloud to the ground and mountains. 'Why all this toil and sweat? If there are no battles, what do we live for? If there are no hunting parties will not the people weaken? Is Star-Juice the balm for this time without Wars?' The one question I wanted to ask most of all I could not say. Nor could I allow my thoughts to dwell on it for long: *Are the gods really gods?*

I passed by the temple of Star-Juice. The old ladies looked carefully at me as I filled my gourd. One hag from the Chivas flew at me, yelling that this was not allowed. I pushed her aside roughly and she fell – not even knowing who I was. The other ladies knew, however, and begged me to spare her life. I cursed the lot of them, taking long gulps as I marched off. I felt that something mighty was about to happen. I prayed to Viracocha to speed up the journey of the Sun so it would come to pass.

Aroona came to my hut that night and sat. Olani faded back into the shadows. One of his eyes was puffy and black.

'Mahala drives the miners too hard,' he said, his muscles bursting underneath the black rock dust on his skin. 'He is not like the other gods – for he is cruel by nature and spirit. He takes the wives of those who do not respond to his lashes.'

'He uses a lash?' I said, Star-Juice making me slur my words.

'That and more . . .' He pointed to his eye. 'This he gave me after he used the wife of one of my brothers.'

Looking at him through Star-Juice, I saw a weakling who deserved his punishment.

66

'You are too head-strong, my friend,' I said, offering him my gourd. He pushed it away.

'This is not the night,' he said, looking at me carefully. 'How did you get hold of it?'

My voice rose in drunken anger, 'You speak to Boaz, not your son. I am the favoured of the gods. They do not tell me what to do.'

'Oh, yes they do!' Aroona's anger rose with my own. 'They keep you drunk so that you'll stay by your women and forget about your people.'

'The gods are good and just,' I said controlling my voice. 'They do not wish us harm. Mahala is cruel because he has to be cruel. His spirit lashes out, like the Jaguar.'

'Better than the Condor who pecks out the rotten eyes of the dead.'

I stood slowly, as did Aroona. Ancient streams of hatred poured between us. We looked at each other long and hard over the small fire. Finally Aroona smiled slightly and sat down.

'The words I spoke were from anger,' he said as a friend. I let my tottering knees collapse and returned his smile.

'We have fought well, side by side,' I said. 'And I see some truth in what you say. I will speak with Oraan. But it will not stop the cruel god.'

Aroona listened in silence. Then he got up to leave.

'Stay tonight,' I said, 'and we will go for my wives together. I cannot do more for a friend.'

Aroona's eyes sought out Olani's. Her eyes shone with expectation.

'Even Olani?' said Aroona.

'Both of us – together,' said I.

Aroona sat down and took a long drink from the gourd. Then he held it out to Olani as my other wives giggled in the back of the hut. Olani crawled forward, white teeth shining in her smile. She took a drink then tore off both our bulging loin cloths at once. We each entered her body by different gates and the other wives came forward to lick and caress us. Olani's long, low moans and laughter gave strength to our movements. And thus did we move till the dawn.

After a short but restful sleep we all got up to bathe in the ice-cold waters. For the first time I saw a bulge in Olani's sleek belly.

'Is this the bulge of child?' I asked. Olani looked down and nodded. I said nothing more to her. I was deeply happy.

Aroona and I walked to the mine. He asked me if I looked forward to the battle with the Serpents.

'Does the son of Snake-Killer fear Serpents?' I replied. Aroona laughed.

'Do you know where the battle will be?'

'If we can see it in the sky, it could be anywhere,' I said.

We walked silently past Vakal and Mahala and went into the mine. There I heard that Aroona had spoken the truth. The coughing and sneezing echoed to us as we climbed downward. The pit was now deeper than three arrow-shots. Spitting llamas led by choking tribesmen passed us as we pressed against the sides. At the bottom of the hole the workers struggled to swing their metal points against the powdery rock. All had two cheeks of coca leaves and bags of the leaves hanging around their necks. Some had red lines across their backs and large patches of black bruises as fearsome as Aroona's.

'Does Mahala not come into the hole?' I asked.

'Never,' said Aroona. 'Just Vakal and some nameless gods who tell us which way to dig. My men long for freedom.'

'We are all working for freedom,' I said.

I worked with the miners all day, but could not go long without coca. Meat was brought to us by two old women.

'You don't eat in the fresh air?' I asked Olmec.

The strong man looked at me and laughed bitterly. 'We are too far down the pit to waste time – or so Mahala says. So we stop long enough to cough some more and then start again.'

That night I ordered Pica to row me to the bay of Kuelpa. I lay back on the bottom of the boat – my body more stiff than after the bloodiest battle. I listened to Pica's haunting songs of the coming of the gods. I chewed fresh coca to keep my eyes open and gave some to Pica to see how much faster he would row.

Oraan stepped towards us as we floated into the Sacred Bay. Around us the night was as black as the mine. Soft waves moved the pebbles gently. Oraan asked us both into the Moonchild. He had heard of Pica's songs and asked him to sing for the gods. Pica trembled a little, but the coca gave him confidence. I waited my chance to speak about the giant.

Once inside the great home of the gods we were taken into the large cave where they relaxed. Some gods were playing games with square pieces of paper, or stones on a board. Others were playing with moving pieces of metal. Some threw small spears into many rings of circles. The floor was covered with strange coloured furs from beasts of distant stars. On the walls hung the heads of fanged creatures and huge-tusked monsters. My hunter's eye brought shivers with thoughts of meeting those beasts in battle.

Pica gathered his wits and sang a song of honour to the gods. Some of them stopped the games they were playing and listened, while others paid no attention.

I ground my jaws impatiently while Pica sang with great spirit. The gods roared with laughter at his song of mating in a narrow boat. He was given Star-Juice and asked to play his flute. I could wait no longer and took Oraan back into the hallway.

'I did not come here to sing,' I said.

'No,' spoke Oraan, 'you came to ask about Mahala. So let me tell you of him. He is the last of a race of gods from a part of the Heavens that was devoured by the Serpents. He has killed many Serpents and is eager to kill many more. Sometimes his passion for revenge gets the better of him.'

'But he must know that my people are not Serpents.'

Oraan's face grew cold as he looked beyond my eyes. 'Without Mahala the God of Gods would not have enough black rock. You will tell your tribes to obey and work harder. That way they will not suffer.'

'My people can work no harder than they are working now.'

Oraan fought back a surge of redness to his face and tried to smile; 'Great deeds can only come through great actions, Boaz. If you hold your world precious there is no other choice.'

'I have nothing else to say, Great One. I will give you my trust, as I have in the past. This trust is also that of the Huanacs and the other tribes that you have summoned. Great are your promises to us, and great is your power. But mark that we are proud and simple people. If you can heal my peoples' suffering like you can cure the sick, I pray that you do so quickly.'

'We will do our best,' said Oraan. He called for Pica to join us.

Oraan waved goodbye at the opening. Pica was glowing as much from praise as from Star-Juice as the two of us walked down the metal steps that led into the blackened night.

Then suddenly it was no longer night.

A bright flash outshone the stars. Another sun had been born on the sacred island. On the spot where the Temple stood.

The metal tongue lifted up so fast that it threw Pica and I to the ground. A wind blast blew rocks against our bodies and the wall where the opening had been. From the Moon-ship came a high-pitched sound and then great thunder roared around us. Although my eyes were closed, the light still shone in my head.

The night soon conquered the Sun. As I looked up I saw a part of the brightness hovering over the island. It became a distant star. Or was it still the flash in my eyes? The door opened and Oraan and Chiruwi ran down to look. From the side of the cave shot out a full hand of Moon-beasts growling as they leapt into the sky.

Chiruwi's hairless face was blood-red, lit by a last flickering flame from the Temple. He shouted at Oraan in Moon-tongue and Oraan shouted back. A nameless god carried forward the box that made the noise of the cicadas.

'Get back to your tribe,' said Oraan as Chiruwi ran into the ship, 'Tell them that the Serpents have attacked but have not won their attack. The Temple will be rebuilt on the other side of the island. The mines will be worked throughout the days and nights. That is all.'

He turned back and walked up the metal tongue. Pica watched him carefully, then looked at the Temple where two Moon-beasts had already landed.

'The gods are strong,' he said as we ran to the boat, 'but there are others just as strong.'

I got into the boat and Pica pushed us from the shore. The mixture of feelings inside me made my head spin. The battle had begun, and this made my blood swell. But how can I fight against a flash in the sky? This attack would be good for my tribe and the tribes under my command. It would make them work harder, for now they had something to fight for.

Halfway from Kuelpa to the Huanac shore we heard cries for help alongside the boat. Two men were pulled aboard.

Their arms and bellies were red and sore.

One man was a boatman from Pica's tribe. He had been asleep in a cave when the attack came. The other was a mover of the black rock. They had both leapt into the water when fire flowed over the island. Now they grew sick and shook with fever as Pica rowed us towards the shore.

We reached the fires of the Tribes. A crowd of warriors cheered when they saw my boat.

'I have come from Kuelpa with words from the gods,' I told them. 'It was the Serpents who attacked the Temple. We will rebuild the Temple in a spirit of War-Glory. We will mine the Sacred Rock until our bones crack. The battle has begun, and the glory shall be ours!'

The assembled tribes broke into their own war chants and dances. Once we would have danced to kill each other – now we danced together to keep the world alive. The two sick men were taken to the hut where the women go during their time of bleeding. We waited for a Moon-beast to carry them away. None came that night.

Dream-Speaker and the Shaman from Pica's tribe shook their rattles and called to the Spirit world to halt the sickness in the warriors. Even after many swallows of Star-Juice the men still screamed in horrible pain.

Dawn saw the two men dead, their faces and bodies flowing with yellow water. The poison in the fangs of the Serpents was strong and deadly.

The children were the first to see the white bellies of the floating fish. Then the tribes gathered silently as they beheld the waters, white with dead fish.

Women gathered the fish.

A Moon-beast came from Kuelpa and landed by the shore. Askar ran out and shouted at the women and children not to touch or eat the fish. Oraan came later and took me into my hut. He said:

'The venom of the Serpents has reached the water and the air. The fish are full of the venom. They are all to be collected and taken far away. There they will be burned and buried. Those of your people who have eaten the fish or die from the venom in the next few days will also be burned and buried there.'

'Why cannot they just be burned?' I asked.

'Because their ashes will still be poisonous.'

'*Tiki!*'

71

'All men who built the first temple will build the second. Go only from the stone pits to the site of the new Temple – keep away from the old one. Mahala will take complete charge of the mines.' Oraan left my hut without waiting for a reply.

The boatmen rowed the temple-builders to the island. This time there was no stench and no Temple. Nor was one single plant or tree left alive. Chiruwi was already there, giving instructions to the nameless ones.

Work began as soon as our feet touched shore. Bags of coca were shipped to the island so that work would be faster. Already some miners had started to shake when they awoke and only a mouthful of coca and burnt shell could cure them. The temple-builders chewed and worked at the quarry for days and nights on end. When a worker collapsed with sleep he would be taken to a cave and left with a bag of coca and a piece of meat ready for his awakening. I spent my time keeping peace within the tribes so that we could fight our common battle.

I learned that some miners were digging a red rock at a mine higher up in the mountains. This was shipped to the island where gods would melt it with the red tongue of fire to make another kind of metal. They shaped this metal into strange-looking boxes, joining the sides together using white sparks as bright as a comet trail. Askar told me that they were making big boxes like those in the centre of the destroyed Temple.

I had told Oraan that we were simple people but proud. Under this new work the strain soon took its toll. Some men went mad. They lost their minds to the Serpent and their Spirits ran away like a wild creature in the night. These men were quickly taken away to the healing centre. Most returned soon, able to work but not remembering even their own family.

One day a boy was taken sick. He admitted that he had eaten a bite from a poisoned fish. Askar took him to the Moonship. The boy came back more sick than before. His belly was puffed out and his skin was covered with bites of the Serpent. The tribesmen were frightened; for here was a sickness even the gods could not cure.

The child was a son of Olmec. It was he who had lost a virgin daughter to the gods, it was he who had lost another son, murdered by the Jaguar Tribe. I went to get

72

Olmec from the mines to be with his dying son. Vakal let me take him away without challenge. The child was covered now with blood spots and did not even know his father, who cried tears of outrage and helplessness. The boy died soon after and was taken where the ashes of the fish lie buried. I made Olmec return to the mines as soon as his boy was buried. I saw the once proud and joyful man turn bitter and sullen. The coming of the gods seemed to be a curse on him and his family.

That night I had a long quarrel with Olani. Her blood did not feel that the gods were trying to save the world. She felt them as beings who used us in the same way as we now used llamas. She said that Aroona had agreed on this with her, as did most of the women who saw their men turning into ghosts before their eyes. My mind was in the Star-Juice trance and I threw her out of the hut:

'Go find Aroona in the red rock mine so you can agree with him for ever! Go gather the women and agree with them. Get out and stay out!' I shouted at the height of my voice. She huddled by the entrance and wept all night. But I would not let her in. I seized a gift-wife from one of the tribes and thrust my man-spear into a woman whose words could not hurt. It was in the middle of our heat that a Jaguar warrior ran into the hut screaming:

'The mine has been struck by the Serpents! Many hands of men have died!' He collapsed at my feet and begged that I save him.

I sniffed some pepper powder to clear my head and took a hold of my mace. Overhead a Moon-beast thundered towards Tall-Feather. 'Tell me more,' I said, offering the man water.

He had a long drink and then spoke: 'I was loading the black rock onto the llamas when I heard screaming from deep inside the pit. Then many hands of men came running out. Mahala was there, and he ordered them to stop and go back.

'Some kept running,' he continued, 'and were eaten by the red tongue. Others stopped and screamed that the mine was on fire. Mahala and Vakal used lashes to drive the men back inside while more ran out. I broke away from my fright and ran to you. The man I was with has gone to Aroona.'

'Ha! Aroona cannot help. Come with me back to the mines,' I said, but the warrior was exhausted with running and would not respond to my kicks.

I tumbled into the forest, letting my foot-pads find the shortest route to the mines. I covered what remained of the forest and broke into the fields leading up to the mine.

Bodies of warriors and children lay on the ground in front of the mine. Oraan and Vakal were ordering those that remained of the workers to sit in one place and await their orders. In the sun's first rays there was a red glow seeping from the opening into the cliff.

I was about to shout to Oraan when a hand grabbed my ankle. It was Olmec, who was badly hurt with a hole in his side. His face was a mass of drying blood.

'Listen to me, Boaz. Listen to my last words.'

I leaned down to listen, but Olmec had passed out.

'Is that Boaz?' called Oraan.

'It is I,' I answered, running to him.

'The Serpents have struck again. They did not destroy the mine but killed many men. They even entered the mind of a warrior and caused him to attack Mahala.' I noticed for the first time that Mahala was not there. Oraan continued: 'Do you know a warrior named Olmec?'

'Yes – He is a Huanac and one of my finest men.'

'He is an enemy,' said Oraan. 'If he still lives.'

'What has he done?' I asked as Aroona came running up to join us.

Oraan did not answer, but said instead, 'If he is alive then I want him found and murdered by your own hands. If he is dead then he shall be fed to the worms and the wasps of the forest. Take Aroona and find him!' Vakal was holding the clicking box to the head of the mine. This time it made little noise.

'Do you know why the gods want Olmec?' I asked Aroona as we left.

'The runner who came to me saw Olmec fighting with Mahala,' he said. 'Perhaps the cruel god is alive no more.'

'Then you *are* a traitor – like Olmec!'

Aroona grabbed my shoulders and shook me, 'Boaz, you fool, open your eyes and see with the rest of the people. Olmec was the bravest in all the tribes, for he fought against the giant who had killed and maimed his people – *our* people.'

74

I saw truth in Aroona's eyes. 'Olmec is not yet dead,' I whispered. 'He lies in the fields.'

The Jaguar Chief brightened; 'Now we will know what really happened. For Olmec has always been a man of high honour. Let us find a body and name it Olmec so the gods can do what they want with it. We will take Olmec back to the shore and listen to his words.'

I found the body of a Huanac and raised a great cry as I smashed the skull and severed the head. Oraan came running.

'This is the man Olmec?' he asked.

'This was the traitor,' I answered. I spat on the severed head, as did Aroona. I said, 'May his Spirit never find the home of his ancestors.'

Oraan seemed satisfied with this. 'I am flying all those still alive to the healing place on the mothership. Work will continue. By mid-morning the mines will be cool enough to continue work. We must not stop. You, Boaz, must help all you can by your deeds.'

'None of the dead need have died,' spoke Aroona. Oraan's eyes flared but before he could speak I slapped Aroona sharply across the mouth. 'I will handle this woman-thinker!' I spoke with confidence and pushed him away. 'The tribes on the shore must know about this,' I said to the god, 'I go now.'

SEVEN

'Fool!'

I lashed Aroona with the word when I found him awaiting me beside the motionless body of Olmec.

'I could not stop my tongue,' he protested, 'from telling its thought aloud.'

'That is what makes you a savage,' I said contemptuously, 'and makes me closer to the gods.'

'If those pale-skinned creatures really are gods, I am happy to be far removed from them. But you did right to strike me,' he said. His tongue washed blood from the corner of his mouth.

Olmec's eyes were closed as if in death yet life still beat in his body. We carried him through the waist-high manioc plants and into the forest.

We laid him in the hut of his sister. The plants Looth

75

had told me to use on wounds stopped the flow of blood from the gash in his side. He lay peacefully upon a reed bed, nearer the land of Spirits than his tribe.

I was anxious to hear his words yet knew he was too ill to talk further that night. I ordered that no one approach the hut except his sister and her children. Her man had been one of those killed by the monsters of the island. To her I said: 'Look after him well. If he dies, you die.' I cautioned Aroona not to speak one word about Olmec, even to Olani.

When I told the tribes about the attack on the mines, their fear was great. Men who would be proud to give their lives in battle trembled at the horror of a slow death beneath the ground, scorched alive by the breath of Serpents. I used all my powers to still their fears. But there were too many widows weeping for the dead. Too many sons and daughters with no fathers to tell them stories of courage and initiate them into the duties of their tribes.

Dream Speaker kept up his visions with a frenzy. His eyes rolled back into the Spiritworld when he shared with us his terrible dreams. He shook and flung himself to the ground as the Serpent struck. But the Condors gripped the demon in their claws while the Jaguar ripped open its head. Then he went to the Bear tribe and saw the Bears destroying the Serpent. He went to every tribe and showed them the vision. And the tribes felt gladness as each heard how their totem helped destroy the greatest enemy the world had ever known.

My own strong words gave courage to the greatness of the tribes. They were spoken not from dreams but from the world of flesh. After a long day my throat was sore with shouting words of strength. I stepped back into my hut and sank into the softness of Olani. The warmth we felt for each other was greater than our fight of the night before. Those moments of warmth and peace did not last for long. A son of Olmec's sister came running. The wounded man was awake and able to speak.

'You know me well, Boaz.' Olmec spoke in a soft whisper which caused him much pain. I was alone with him, having dismissed the family.

'You know that I have fought well by your side and followed the gods without question. I lost two sons and

76

stood silently while the gods removed my daughter from our tribe.' He coughed up black blood before he continued: 'I knew Snake-Killer well and say now that he is proud of you. Already I feel myself slip away from my flesh and see the spirits of the dead hover around us.'

'May you live as long as the Lake,' I said, wiping his brow, 'But tell me why you angered the gods so greatly.'

'I endured the wrath of Mahala when his lash made bloody my back and the backs of my tribesmen. His power was driving us to work. And work had to be done. In this way I could respect him – even worship him – for it is said that the gods are just like men, yet more so. Men can be cruel but Mahala was more cruel. He was the god of cruelty.' He stopped to cough some more, and I wiped away the blood.

'You speak of the god as if he is dead,' I said.

'Let me tell so you can fully understand. When I came back from watching my last son die, buried with the ashes of poisoned fish, Mahala saw me coming and whipped me without mercy. Even though I left at your command and with Vakal's permission. Even then I did not speak out.'

'What happened last night?' I asked, bending my ear to his mouth.

'First came the sweat from our bodies. Our bodies were the first to know that something was wrong. Then we felt the heat coming from the walls, the floor and the ceiling. Quickly the heat became such that the desert sands of the coast would seem to be like snow. The weakest ones collapsed. I saw the walls becoming red as fire. Men were running, choking, struggling over other bodies. The fire glow spread up the shaft, setting alight the wooden braces. The Sacred Rock was falling around us, knocking down those who were fleeing upwards. In the scramble to save my life I found the boy Curu and scooped him up. Then another boy fell before me and I picked him up too. The workers halfway up the mine were able to outrun the fire glow. Only I of the many diggers at the bottom escaped – with the help of Viracocha!'

Olmec's eyes closed as his mind wandered. I called for Shomu to gather more leaves and roots. Shomu looked with shocked and angry eyes at the man who was supposed to be dead. He brought the healing plants and left quickly.

77

After many moments Olmec came back from the Spirits and whispered:

'Men were streaming out, yelling in terror. But above all other noises were the screams of Mahala as he turned people back and pushed them towards the mine. As I came out his fury exploded. He seized me and pushed. I then became the warrior I used to be. I set down the boys in my arms and kicked at Mahala's face. The crack I heard from his jaws was not that of one who lives forever. He blasted me with his weapon. But I fell on him and wrestled him for it. Suddenly the red tongue tore apart his blood pump and he was dead.'

'Dead!' I echoed, hardly able to believe it.

'As dead as my sons – as dead as Nima. With my last strength I dragged the corpse into the mine, where the walls glowed white like the sun. I threw him over a burning brace. As I left the mine I saw his body burning to the bones. I went to find Curu but could not find him. Is the boy safe? Does he still live? . . .' At these words he sank deeply into sleep and I left.

Shomu had betrayed me. The tribes on the Huanac shore gathered together to speak their fright to each other. Suddenly a Moon-beast appeared above the hut where Olmec lay and let loose the red tongue of fire. Olmec, his sister and her children vanished like the morning shadows.

Dream-Speaker fell to the ground with a vision: Olmec had been captured by the Serpents. They entered his body after killing his mind. Olmec's body was used to set fire to the mine and to attack the giant Mahala, their mightiest enemy. Olmec, using the words of the Serpents, won the trust of Boaz and Aroona. Shomu the gallant hero told the gods where Olmec lay. And Mahala, who wrestled the Serpent in the pit of fire and won, was back in the Mothership, planning the final victory for the Moon-Gods.

After speaking this dream he collapsed and let his many wives comfort him. He had already picked the fairest of the widows left by the dead miners to add to his cluster of women. I walked away enraged and confused. I knew this was not a vision but merely a story told to him by the gods.

I felt the whole of my work and my power crumbling

78

around me. Sitting in my hut, drinking my Star-Juice, I could do nothing but wait for the gods to come to me.

I did not have to wait for long. When I heard the thunder of the Moon-beast above my hut, I told my wives to run. But the red tongue did not destroy my hut and the ship landed. Oraan appeared in the opening of my hut and motioned for me to follow him. His face was tight, his mouth silent as the Moon-beast flew us to its Mother.

I walked along the shiny entrails of the Mothership with my fists clenched tightly. Oraan paused as a wall opened into a giant cave filled with many buttons and strange shiny riddles.

'Wait here, and do not move,' Oraan ordered, leaving me alone. I looked through a large sheet of clear ice which showed me the inside womb of Kuelpa. I defied Oraan's orders and wandered about the cave. But I knew better than to touch anything.

After a while Oraan came back – this time with a tall, thin being with hair as white as llama's milk. His piercing eyes went through me like a splash of cold water.

'I am Sett,' he revealed, 'the leader of the gods. And friend to the Huanacs before I was betrayed. Why did you betray me?'

My voice spoke without trembling. 'Olmec was a brave warrior and friend of my father's. He had long won the love and trust of my people.'

'Yet you gave him refuge – and lied to Oraan – even when you were told the truth.'

'Of what truth do you speak?' I asked.

'The truth that Dream-Speaker saw in his vision,' said the father of the gods.

'It has always been my duty as Chief to listen to the truth,' I said. 'And I have been taught by my father that truth can be seen differently from different eyes.'

'You have disobeyed and lied,' spoke Oraan. Sett motioned for silence.

'It is my first duty as Chief to protect my people,' I said. 'I am not afraid to die for this duty.'

'This is as it should be,' said Sett, 'but even as we speak the Serpent waits to strike again. Next time it could be Kuelpa or your tribal shore.'

'I stand ready to fight the Serpent – as always.' I said.

'And that is what you will do. There is only one way you

79

can win back our favour and the love of your people,' Sett said slowly, fixing me with his eyes. I thought of Dream-Speaker spreading the gods' stories as if they were his own visions. I knew how easily he could turn them against me.

'I will follow the commands of the gods,' I said.

'Good. We shall call a council of all the tribes. They will hear of our plans to defeat the Serpents.' With this, Sett turned his back on me and, with Oraan, briskly left the room.

Askar took me back to the shore.

'You have angered them greatly,' said the young god.

'Yet you are not angered, Askar. Do you think I did wrong by listening to Olmec before he died?'

'I can neither say yes or no,' said Askar with confusion in his voice. 'But know that I will always try to be your friend. And hope that you will be mine.'

Pica was there to row me back to the Huanac shore. Once we pushed off I fell into a tremble and a sweat.

'What is it?' asked Pica with a gentle smile.

'I did not know that even I could be so brave,' I said. Pica laughed putting his shoulders into the rowing.

As we neared the shores two Moon-beasts landed amongst the clustered tribes. The tribes watched me land without cheers, without hatred. They were simply waiting – waiting for the next thing to happen. Their faces were tired and worn. For some this was the first rest they had had since the Temple was attacked.

The crowd cleared a path between me and the Moon-beasts. As I walked toward them, metal steps unfolded from each beast. Oraan descended from one and held his hands high for silence.

'Tribes of the High Plateau,' he began, 'listen well for the Serpents have attacked twice and twice have they done great damage. Both times we have turned them back yet still the Serpents remain poised to strike their venom into your hearts. Through terror they seek to frighten you from worship of the true gods and turn your thoughts to evil . . . Peoples of the mountains and the plains, you must show your faith is strong and not so easily shaken. You must meet the challenge of the Serpents! A group of your mightiest warriors will find the nest of these vipers and trample them beneath their war-dance!'

80

The force of Oraan's words caused a great roar of cheering. Pleased, he waited for the noise to die before continuing.

'This will be a battle such as no man in your small world has ever imagined. Already our scouts have discovered their nest. It lies far beyond the land of the sunrise and will take many changes of the Moon to reach. Only the bravest of warriors could ever reach it. Therefore, so that he may regain the honour he has lost and prove himself once more a brave and worthy chief, the expedition to the land of the Serpents will be led by Boaz!'

Again I felt the joy which fed the roar of the tribes. It gave me much pleasure. I knew I had not lost their trust.

'But Boaz will not lead alone,' Oraan shouted, 'for the gods will be with him. A fierce Moon-beast will follow the warriors over mountains, rivers, jungles and seas greater than you have ever dreamed of. It will guard the war-party against attacks by the Serpents. But all other dangers must be overcome by the warriors themselves for they must prove themselves worthy of being champions of the gods...'

Oraan's arm swept over the heads of the massed tribes: 'Those of you who remain can also help win the great battle. By your labours you will bring about the defeat of the Serpents who would swallow your world as the anaconda swallows an egg – You will continue to dig the Sacred Rock to feed the God of All Power! With the aid of Boaz and his men we will use this mighty Power to slay the Serpents. The god who will watch over the war-expedition and unleash the mighty Power against the slimey ones is He whose name has been defiled by the lies of unbelievers...'

At these words, a familiar figure descended from the Moon-beast. Surprise rippled through the crowd as the god stepped forward. Surprise and terror for the god was Mahala. His mocking laughter trampled the sudden deathly silence of the Tribes.

Part II

INTO THE LAND OF
THE SERPENTS

EIGHT

In the next few days time passed as fast as the changes. The gods said little to me except that Aroona would be second in command of the war-expedition against the Serpents and that no women could accompany us. The warriors of all the tribes wanted to join the war party. They fought amongst each other to escape the crushing work demanded by the Moon-skinned gods.

I was offered every wife in the tribes for a chance to join the expedition – even women of the Seal Tribe. There were so many who wanted to join the hunt that I had to devise contests of skill and strength. I could take only the best fighters, climbers and runners. By now many warriors were stooped as old men from digging in the mines. These quickly found out that they were doomed to live underground until the God of Gods had eaten his fill of black rock. Sometimes the gods would fly from Kuelpa to watch the contests. They enjoyed the tests, cheering and urging on their favourites.

I picked men until the gods told me to stop. In all there were as many men as in two handfuls of coca leaves. Those who were chosen were the envy of all tribes. They would be the ones who would fight the great enemy. But they would be free to worship the mountains and waters of Viracocha – free to feel the joy of the hunt and the glory of battle. And, if they lived, the triumph of victory.

Shomu and Dream-Speaker now took my place as speakers for the tribes. They were well liked by the gods, for they had been the most helpful and the least complaining. I had become something apart – a Chief without power. The gods now shunned me, all except for Askar. He brought me happiness when he told me that he would ride in Mahala's Moon-beast.

Olani was furious that she couldn't come. She swore she could kill as well as any man. I laughed and told her she could kill any man who tried to take her from me. I pointed to the ripening bulge in her belly and told her to keep the future Chief safe and in good health. Besides, I would be back before the melting of the next snows, I laughed. Yet deep inside I knew I might never come back. For I did not even know where I was going, or from where I would return.

All the gods had said was that we were to follow the Moon-beast, that it would lead my war party over mountains, jungles, rivers and great salt oceans.

If we had not fought the Serpents when we reached the end of the river, we would sail across the great Salt Waters to attack their nest inside the Secret Temple of the Serpents.

On the day of departure I called for Shomu to tell him of the duties of the Chief. He would not look me in the eyes so great was his disrespect.

'Shomu,' I said, 'do not forget the people and their feelings. The gods are great and powerful, but you are not one of them. Your father Tamba watches you from the Spirit World. Beware the power you will have over others.'

'Your men await you, Boaz,' he said as he stood with a twisted grin. 'To be Chief of the Dead as you were Chief of Traitors . . .'

My hand shot out for his neck. I could have snapped his frail body in two with pleasure.

'I say again, do not forget that you are a man. You owe much to your people, who are also men. Men are not meant to be like llamas – nor like gods. Let the Great Spirit of the Huanacs speak through you.' I let him go. This time he

83

looked me in the eyes and his were full of fear. 'The women and children will have much need for a strong Chief,' I continued. 'Even though you are built like a sapling, I know your thoughts to be strong. Be careful of Dream-Speaker, for he is tied to the gods even tighter than you.'

Shomu rubbed the red marks around his neck; 'I will do what I can, Boaz,' he said grudgingly.

I sent him out and called for Olani. We did not speak as we mated. When my lightning struck she cried many salt tears. I rested my hand on her bulging belly and felt my son kick strongly, like a brave young warrior.

'I will return,' I said, 'before my son can walk.'

Olani watched silently as I grabbed the Chief's mace and took my place at the head of the war party. There were many many hands of men and each warrior's face was filled with quiet excitement.

We filed onto the reed boats and their large flat carriers. We would be many days on the Sacred Lake, following the ridge of the mountains to our right. Few warriors with me had ever been from one end of the Sacred Waters to the other.

We pushed off from the Huanac shore. The tribes stood alongside it as the forest had stood before the coming of the gods. Only a few were cheering. Soon they looked no larger than guinea pigs. I watched Shomu leading the people back to work and I wondered about the ways of the living and the ways of the dead. Perhaps the New and the Old were not as different as I once had thought. Above us, the Moon-beast led the way. We followed, Pica guiding the lead boat.

Sometimes the Moon-beast swept off over the range of sacred peaks and disappeared for many hundreds of breaths. Pica held the course steady and the Moon-beast always returned to the same point before us. Had I killed Olmec I would be riding in the sky-craft too. But I felt happier to be with my people.

Pica interrupted my thoughts: 'I will come along with you to battle the Serpents,' he said, his face set in a determined grin.

'Why?' I asked. It had been decided that he remain with the boats when we marched inland.

Pica shrugged his shoulders: 'It could have been myself asleep on the island when the Serpents struck. It could have been me who died of their awful venom. But it wasn't. It was a brave man, my friend since we were both peeing on our mothers. I would like to kill the Serpent who killed my friend. But there are more reasons. Should I go on?'

'No,' I said, 'save them for the long journey.' I looked ahead at the Sacred Waters. They were a colour all of their own. Bluer than the skies, greener than the spring leaves. Shinier than the skin on Olani's breasts. I let my fears settle themselves in the ripples and waves.

We camped at night along a sandy shore. The muscles of my warriors ached as they stretched from sitting in the narrow boats. What a mighty army, I thought. Together we could conquer the fiercest tribes in the world – as long as they were flesh and blood.

We wolfed down our meat and huddled against the frozen air in our sleeping furs. Looking back in the direction of the Island of the Sun, I thought I could see flashes. Perhaps they were the white sparks that flew when the gods forged their metal. Or perhaps something worse. I thought of Olani – of all my wives sleeping alone. Or were they? I stayed up most of the night thinking more than I should.

When I woke, the Moon-beast was already roaring overhead, eager to press on.

The far end of the Sacred Waters loomed ahead. A vast, barren land stretched before us, where the skeletons of trees had long been forgotten by their spirits. Even the shrubs and plants seemed tired and hostile, already brown from the oncoming Winter. Soon the snows would come – we had to be out of the mountains by then.

Food and supplies were carried on llamas. We gripped our metal-pointed weapons and blades proudly as we moved beneath the Moon-beast. Occasionally small families of nomads appeared on the rises and disappeared as quickly. A few times I heard taunts echoing down from the foothills for me and my army to join tribes united against the gods. The Moon-beast was now over the mountains of the fierce Falcon tribe.

Gradually the slopes grew higher and sharper, the valleys narrower and harder to climb. We were now sniffing at the roots of the mountains which towered before us. Strange shrieks and yells echoed from the valley walls. They became louder and more numerous as we headed into a great pass between the trunks of two mountains.

The first sling-stone broke the skull of a llama. Then an

arrow pierced the neck of its leader. We looked for an enemy to fight but saw only rocks and mountains. The Sky-God was sending forth whirling mists spilling down from the peaks.

The llama was quickly skinned by a nervous warrior. Its flesh and supplies were carried by the other llamas. I had the men stick close to the rocks and be ready for any attack – whether by man or Serpents.

Two hands of warriors ran ahead to scout on either side of the pass. They faded quickly into the landscape ahead, as silent as a fawn awaiting its mother.

It was not long until there were sounds of fighting. They ended as fast as they began. Soon Aroona and three men came back swinging human heads for us to see. Large nosed and sunken-cheeked, they wore Falcon feathers through their ears and noses.

'How many are there?' I asked Aroona.

'Not more than ten hands altogether,' he replied, 'but they guard the place where the pass becomes no wider than the width of a llama. There seems little to do but attack them directly or find some other route.'

'I did not ask your military opinion,' I chided him. 'Do not cloud my mind with your fears.'

Aroona paid little attention to my words. He knew me as a friend, and as a friend knew my many moods. This was the first battle – but it could well be the last.

My eyes searched the sky. There was no sign of the Moon-beast. Then I knew this was my first test as war-leader.

'How far ahead is the narrow part?' I asked.

'About three twists in the trail, little more than an arrow-shot.'

'Good, now your words give me direction. How are their men placed?'

'Most of them stand before the pass. One on either side hides behind the boulders high above in the mountains. I know their ways – they are there to cause a rock slide.'

'I also know their ways. My father was killed by this tribe.'

'Forgive me, Boaz, but . . .'

'Forget it, Aroona. We must pluck these human birds who would flood the pass with rocks.'

'Noam and Saloona – two of my best climbers are already at the task.'

86

At first my pride flared at Aroona who dared outguess me. But I knew that he had acted rightly. Aroona smiled when he saw my face turn many expressions.

I returned his smile and ordered my men to advance beyond the next twist of the trail. I ran ahead and scuttled up to the top of a rocky ridge.

Below me, over a lower ridge, I saw the scene as Aroona described it. The Falcon tribe were holding their ground in a deep gorge, blocking a crack in the cliffs which led the way to the jungles below. My men were silent and still as they advanced, not yet within sight of the defenders. The Falcon Tribe chanted their War-Glory, led by their old Chief.

I climbed back down and said:

'I want every man who carries bow and arrows to climb to where I've been and fire when I signal. Every arrow shot must sink into flesh.'

'But that's over half the men,' Aroona questioned. 'We will lose many men if we attack with only half our power.'

'It is our only chance,' I said, 'they have no defence against a flying arrow. And we do not know if your men have killed the rockslide makers.'

'You may not know – But I do.'

I led my men around the next turn while the archers took up their positions. Then I climbed a tall tower of rock and stood tall as I shouted to the Falcon Tribe: 'What does the Falcon Tribe want of the Warriors of the Gods? Let us pass. There will be no bloodshed if you stand aside.'

The old Chief put an end to his warriors' chanting with a wave of his hand. He stepped forward. His rough hewn face stretched with hate as he yelled in reply:

'Long have I heard reports of your devil-gods. Long have I grown sick to my Spirit as I heard how the plains tribes let themselves be made slaves of those who poison the Sacred Waters, who torture the men and abuse the women – who drive the llamas from our hills. Now the hills are bare and the forests are vanishing. And the island of the First People becomes a temple of death. You have grown weaker in spirit than earthworms. You do not deserve to live.' As he shouted this last judgement, he held high his Chief's mace.

An arrow sank into my shoulder. A Falcon Warrior on the rocks above was notching a second arrow to his bow when he felt the sharpness of Noam's hunting blade. I pulled the arrow from my shoulder and gave the signal for my archers to strike.

Within heart-beats half the warriors lay still or twitching on the ground. Then my men attacked and after a brief, fierce battle the pass was ours. We had lost but a hand of men. The Falcon Chief was still alive as I approached to claim his head.

'Beware, son of Snake-Killer,' the old man laughed, 'for there are many traps ahead . . . I have told the women and children that if we lost this battle they must join the slaves on the Huanac shore. Otherwise they would not live through the snows. We are both fools, Huanac. I defended my land as you defend the gods of the Thunder-Moon. Because of them we will all die. But we will both be long remembered by our people.' With this he died. I cut off his head and ordered his body to be thrown to the falcons.

It was not a great battle, yet it served to spark the fires of conquest. I knew that these fires had to be kept ablaze.

Falcon women and children were found huddled in the pass. To my men's dismay, I ordered them not to be touched. The warriors had gone many days without the taste of women. They grumbled against me, but I did not care. It was good for them to dislike me – as long as they still feared me.

After covering the corpses of their husbands and sons with the rocks of their native land, the Falcon women and their children retraced the tracks of my army. Silent and without tears, they went and soon were gone from sight.

Above us, the Moon-beast reappeared, bright and cold, neither approving nor disapproving.

Once through the pass we started a steep climb that led past the camp of the Falcon Tribe. I thought once again of the shrines of the Man-Apes, dwellings that would live only in dreams and nightmares. The fire still smouldered where the tribe had cooked their morning food. On an altar of stone rested a long perch. Sitting on it were a hand of the sacred falcons.

In respect of the tribe that was no more. I let loose the leather thongs which held the birds. They flapped away, spiralling into the freezing mist. They drove their wings strongly to conquer the pull of the mountains.

Soon we were far above the dead camp. Alongside the

trail stood the thatched huts of the Shamans, with bales of coca leaves inside. Each of my men was able to fill his dwindling shoulder bag and the remainder was put on the backs of the llamas. There were also gourds and sticks which the Shamans rubbed together to invoke the Great Spirit. Next to them were many bones and feathers of the falcon. Lying in one corner was an old Shaman who had taken his life as he saw us climbing towards him.

NINE

The trail led up a craggy brown mountain and spiralled away towards the distant snow peaks. Tired, the warriors wanted to stop and rest but the sight of the grey, low sky urged me to use all the daylight. The wounded were helped up the steepening slope by their comrades, who themselves were helped by full cheeks of coca. Soon the llamas would go no further. They hissed and spat as the rod lashed them on. Finally they sat and defied my anger as no warrior would ever dare.

We roasted the llama whose defiance had been cut short by the Falcon sling-stone. Its brothers watched and learned as we ate and put healing leaves on the wounds of the warriors. My own arrow wound was only remembered as I lay down to sleep. A layer of coca paste cooled away the pain.

Halfway up the mountain the trail wound around and down to a further pass. The going was slow, for our muscles soon ached as much as our strained lungs. Strange horned creatures shied at our approach. Some of them were slow enough to make more meat for us.

The Spirit of Viracocha in these mountains was mighty. These peaks which we had looked on only weeks before as distant points on our horizon now held our very lives to their Power. The Sky-God hurled lashes of wind around our eyes and ears. All our extra furs were used to cover our hands and feet and hairless faces. Life by the Sacred Waters was harsh but these mountains were not for life at all. No more enemies appeared to spark our War-Glory; no miracles, no surprises came to stop the aching of our muscles and blood-pumps. The ridges and valleys seemed to endlessly surround us.

The snow started as a single scout-flake which landed on Pica's nose. He began a song about the death of a snowflake. Then the attack came on full force. Soon even the boatman's face turned grim as the whiteness overwhelmed the mountains and the sky. Before we knew it our footsteps were crunching on a finger's width of snow. I drove the men and beasts through the crevasses and valleys. Even the furs that we quickly tied around our feet could not keep out the freezing cold.

The Moon-beast had been gone for days, although I told the others I had seen it during the nights. I myself was not frightened, for I felt I no longer needed the watching eye of the gods. My strength as leader had become as natural as breathing. Somehow the force of my spirits saw the way forward. My eyes showed me the mountains as a single living Being whose spirit told mine which path to take.

At night the men slept together in piles of naked bodies surrounding a fire made of shrubs gathered during the day. In this way, they were able to forget about women. Soon even the youngest of the warriors had their special favourites.

After two days and nights the snow ceased and the sky became a deep, dark blue. The Moon-beast was hovering once more to our left, over a high join that ran between a cluster of great peaks. Now the world itself was whiter than the teeth of children – the Moon-beast as blinding as the sun.

The climb up the join of the mountains was the hardest climb of all. Two scouts fell through a crack in the trail. We heard their dying screams as we circled around the gorge. They begged that we should kill them there in the dark, snow-filled crack. I had members of their own tribes tumble rocks into the gorge to still their agonies. A llama stumbled off the path and dragged its leader with it. The man's frozen fingers could not let go of the rope in time and they fell to their deaths together. We had killed many llamas for meat and fur. The remaining llamas except for one stopped and refused to continue. They quickly became more weight strapped to the backs of the warriors.

Whilst we climbed up a narrow ravine to its summit the Moon-beast appeared suddenly close to us. It thundered above our heads, then swooped off suddenly back in the direction of the Sacred Lake. Its fading roar gave birth to another, from the deepest throats of the mountains.

From high above came a wall of snow springing down towards us like a jaguar on a wounded fawn. But for a feeling I had the men would all have jumped to their deaths in panic. I ordered that the last llama be sacrificed for the forgiveness of Viracocha. As the red blood spurted into the snow, the Spirit of the mountains answered. We watched the moving wall hit a hidden ridge of the mountain that turned its anger away from us. The sky darkened with rising powder as the avalanche crashed into a valley on the other side of the ridge.

'Great are the tests of the gods,' I said, trembling but proud.

'Why do they test us at all?' asked Aroona. A murmur of agreement came from the men.

'You all know that it is Mahala who rides the Moon-beast,' I said. 'His ways are cruel – more so since he returned from death.'

'The gods use our lives to play their games,' said Katupo, the strongest of Nima's three sons. His two brothers added their scowls to his words.

'The test was a good one,' I said, 'for the sacrifice of our last llama saved us from death. For this we should feel thanks – not bitterness. Now move quickly forward. There cannot be far to go.'

The warriors picked up their packs and weapons and continued the climb. Pica started a song that we all joined in, for it helped us to forget our pains. As we reached the summit between the many peaks our singing gave way to shouts of joy and conquest. Far beyond and below us, over many snowy ridges and lesser mountains, lay the smooth green fur of the jungle.

I allowed the men to camp at the summit for the night, Pica told us that seeing the sunrise from such a sacred spot makes all men strong. 'It is the closest they will ever be to Viracocha,' he said.

I doubted his words. For only I had ridden in a Moon-beast. And yet it was as he said. When the Sun rose we silently watched. There were no words to say about the colours, the sights and the feelings we tasted. We gaped as the orange-blooded globe raised its head from the distant jungle green. Soon the blood had spread out to the shiny snake-like rivers that curled their way from the mountains to the Sun. We were wrapped in the Sacred Spirit – even the toughest of us.

The enemy, whoever or whatever they might be, held no more fears than the sweetest thoughts of our wives and children. We watched the mingling of colours from the land, Sun and sky. We forgot that we were men on a quest, prepared to do battle to the death. We knew the unknowable. But not for long.

'On your feet,' I yelled as the colours faded like a dream upon waking. 'The Serpents who would swallow this earth have yet to be slain!'

We climbed down the ledge of snow-covered rocks that led to the valley below. The ledge soon became so narrow that had it not been for rocks and roots to cling to, we would surely have fallen. Climbing down into the valley we heard another rumbling, and the men looked in fear to see if the gods were testing them again. It was like an avalanche but not a frozen one – for the rumble was made by a great stream as it plunged downward into the jungle below us. It spilled down from a blue-green gemstone of ice that stretched high above between a range of peaks. It was a sight such as none of us had ever before seen. The blue-green gemstone seemed like one alive, and the stream was part of its life blood, rushing to the land of the sunrise.

'This is the very water that will take us to the Serpents,' said Pica, rushing over and cupping the ice-clear liquid to his mouth.

'Yes,' I said, 'but not yet. We have many more days of following the stream before the land levels out.'

'Reed rafts will pass over the worst of it . . . Aiee, it is cold!' he cried as he jumped in to know it better.

While Pica splashed about like a madman I turned to Aroona. 'We must look for food as we follow the water,' I said. 'Already what little we have left of the llama meat grows alive with worms . . .'

'Let us hunt together when we reach the jungle floor,' said Aroona, clasping my shoulder like a brother.

'That is good, Aroona my friend.' I answered wondering if any hate still lurked in the heart of the man who had been my fiercest enemy.

Pica came running up, his bark cloth and black hair dripping and his skin the colour of the sky. 'We must start gathering reeds,' he said as he slid shivering into his furs, 'for we cannot attack the enemy by floating on our bellies.'

We had thought that the going would now be easy. The gods fated otherwise. It began to snow so hard that we only knew the right direction by listening to the sound of the water. One after another, we stumbled sideways along a ledge no wider than the spread of thumb and little finger. Twice I heard the death-screams of men who slipped on the freezing trail and dropped onto the foaming rocks of the stream far below. The trail wound around the humps of peaks, steep as the fangs of a puma. Yet another warrior tripped and fell into the snow-sky which swirled around us. We had to keep going even throughout the darkness, for there were never places wide enough to pause and rest. Those who fell asleep never woke again.

Then the sacred moon conquered the clouds to give her gift of silver light. As the sky grew lighter we could see a deep valley below us. The precious stream was now closer and many times wider than before.

We reached the banks of the stream and collapsed as the Sun rose above the fang-like hills. I allowed my men a short sleep before we pressed on. We were able now to follow along the side of the stream as it plunged ever downwards over huge boulders.

Green shrubs began to press their heads above the thinning snow. Some men crossed the swift waters to hunt and to gather reeds that grew on the far bank. A few goats and monkeys were found, but not enough to fill the bellies of my hungry army.

Soon we could look back at the peaks we had crossed. We wondered how we had done it – and how we would cross them again on our return.

The stream was soon joined by another, twice as big. Pica climbed a great rise and told us to gather reeds and wood. For now we would begin to travel with the fish.

The same clouds that gave snow to the mountains now gave us rain. This rain fell like a waterfall out of the sky. It did not stop for the many days it took for the boats to be built. Tall vines from the trees were used instead of the rope spun from plants. The reeds were shaped together in the manner of the boats on the Lake, but larger. Pica warned me against this shape, but I insisted. I knew I could trust the way that Sett had designed them. For did he not design the very ship that travelled the blackness beyond the sky?

The rain finally stopped and the air hung warm and stale around us. We could see that the mountains were now a solid crest of snow and ice. We had truly travelled with the blessings of Viracocha. He had held back the storm so we could live to fight the enemy of all men.

My reputation as a ship-builder lasted only a short while. At the first plunging-down of the waters, nearly half of the boats collapsed and those who could not swim were seized by the Spirit of Death.

I tried to blame the gods but Pica would not let me. He took me aside as the men pulled in the boats and the mangled bodies. In some of the corpses not one bone was left uncrushed.

'I speak as a friend, Boaz. These deaths were caused not by the gods but yourself.'

'You speak as a friend about to get his head severed.'

'Do what you will. But first listen to me. Now we will build the boats my way. You may be the Chief of the army, but I am Chief of the waters. The boats will be torn apart and put together again. They will not be curved, narrow boats but flat rafts, many of them. They will all be loosely tied together so that we will look like a snake of many parts travelling down river. As I say, each part will have a flat bottom and top, so that even the steepest plunge and the sharpest rock will not turn us over. I know now that this must be the way.' At this he kneeled down and motioned for my blade to strike his neck. I raised my war-club and brought it down. Gently so it but brushed his skin.

'I am weakened by your smile and your confidence,' I said. 'Get up and follow your vision.'

I had noticed a change in the land. The bare rocks and craggy ravines of the foothills were suddenly devoured by the misty jungle. Even the cliffs of the mountains grew trees from their roots to their sharp peaks.

With the deaths of many men weighing down my spirit, I approached Aroona and silently motioned him to follow me. I took a spear and a blade. Aroona did the same. Together we entered the dark green jungle.

It felt good to be scouting over solid land like a hunter

again. We chased and caught an animal as big as a deer but with a snout more like a condor. For a while I forgot that I was the Chief of chiefs and that my mistakes had already lost the lives of many men.

As we carried back the animal Aroona tried to lighten my spirit.

'May our tribes never be enemies, Boaz.' he said. 'For we will always have songs in common from now on.'

Then, as if to challenge his very words, a jaguar appeared. Aroona quickly dropped the pole on which hung our catch and sank to his knees. Here was the Sacred Jaguar, the only true god of his ancestors. He could do nothing but kneel as a worshipper before his god, and let the god feast if he wished.

The great cat accepted the sacrifice. He sprang for Aroona. But he was not my god. I leapt in front of my friend and took the impact on my blade. The beast turned full force and sprang for my throat. As his claws slashed for my neck my metal blade entered his. We flew to the ground together. His claws ripped into my back. Turning, I gripped his head with both arms and snapped it back. His neck broke, ending his snarl with a crack.

I staggered up to meet Aroona's glare of hatred. The point of his spear was aimed at my chest.

'Make a paste of coca leaves for my wounds,' I ordered. He did not move. In my anger I rushed at him but fell as he quickly stepped back.

'You have destroyed the guardian of my tribe,' he said through clenched jaws.

'I saved the life of my friend,' I calmly answered, 'so that the jaguars will still have a world with tribes to guard. Help me, Aroona. Look past your tribal laws. We are all of a bigger tribe now.'

Slowly he lowered his spear. I lay there whilst he straightened out the body of the cat and cut out its blood-pump from its body. This he buried as he chanted ancient words. Then he made a paste of leaves and jaguar blood and smoothed it over my wounds.

'The blood of the jaguar will save your own,' was all he said as he helped me up and walked me back to the camp.

The warriors crowded around us as we returned. I shook off Aroona's help to show my strength.

'The jungle has put your Chiefs to its test,' I said, 'and

the Chiefs have won the jungle. Two men will collect the game we left behind. The jaguar will be left where it lies.'

Pica's rafts were ready to go. There were now two giant snakes as Pica had described. Each of their lengths was as big as a hut, with many loops to hold on to and through which to stick our oars. The men carried their weapons and provisions strapped beside them. Every section of the snakes held a hand of men, and each was joined loosely by vines to the next.

We pushed off from the shores after each man said prayers to the gods and to the totem of his tribe. Pica played his flute to a race of giants about which he had often sung.

The totems worked their blessings as we were swept into the swirling torrents. Very soon the first rapids could be heard as a deep rumble beyond the rising mist ahead of us. The rafts tumbled downwards, but Pica's vision held true. If the small boats had not been tied together to stop each other from overturning, it would have been the final battle. But it was not. The warriors used their poles to balance and adjust. All day we battled the furious waters. At the end of the day the warriors were shaken – but alive.

We pulled into the bank and slept after drinking the last of the Star-Juice. A steady rain guarded our sleep from the flying-needles humming angrily in the trees.

The next day the current was slower. Pica had the men gather poles to push us faster. The river twisted and turned like a snake and many times our rafts ran aground on sand or mud along the banks.

The furs that had saved our hands and feet from freezing were soon damp and falling apart. And the insects – surely messengers from the Serpents – never left us in peace. Often the river became a thundering torrent of rapids and whirlpools to throw us from its back. But by now we were experts at keeping ourselves afloat. Pica's voice grew hoarse from shouting directions above the roar of rapids. Other times the water spread out into shallow lagoons, where shiny rocks glowed and the fish bubbled like a boiling cauldron. We had only to tie a string to an arrow or spear, close our eyes and shoot. We pulled in more fish than we could eat. But these quickly became foul, unlike the high plains where meat would keep for many days.

This was a different land from any we had ever seen. The

joy of conquering the mountains soon gave way to a quiet time when each man was left alone with his thoughts. Each turn of the river brought the same, flat jungle, now with monkeys looking at us and laughing, then with parrots bursting in colourful groups overhead. At one point Pica shouted for us to pull ashore, for the next turn was a waterfall which no boat could travel. Sharp rocks cut our feet as we hoisted our heavy rafts onto our shoulders. One man brushed aside a leafy branch and found it stuck to his arm with poisoned fangs. We buried his body after crushing the green snake to death. I silently prayed the Serpents would be as easy to kill.

After the man's death a nervous silence settled on us, The river grew wider and from then on we had to pull hard on our oars to keep ahead of the sluggish current.

No sign of man had been seen or even felt. Only the birds and monkeys who mocked the chosen Warriors of the Gods.

TEN

One night we came to a halt as the river widened to the greatness of a sea. Had we already conquered the jungle, with no sign of man and only one small serpent? Surely that was not the Serpent who writhed through the sky – this one small snapper with only enough venom to kill a single man? But there was no further time to dwell upon the thought, for as we landed the bugs fell on us like rain. It seemed as if every tiny bug in the jungle had heard about us. Pica thought of sleeping under a tent of twigs covered with leaves. He and those who followed his example were only half eaten in the morning. The rest of us had lumps from our feet to our heads.

We rowed to where the clear water of our river poured into the yellow-brown sea, with only a faint line of trees on the far shores.

Tamtanamka of the Seal Tribe dipped his hand into the water and tasted it.

'This is not the great Salt Water,' he said. 'Nor are there waves as come crashing to the desert shore.' His small black eyes and hooked nose looked out across the great expanse of quietly moving water. 'But yet this cannot be a lake like the Sacred Waters . . . Look how that tree glides on the swift current in the middle waters.'

'No, it is not a sea, nor a lake,' said Pica. 'It is the river of giants. An old song says they made a river big enough to bathe and swim in fresh water all the way to the Ocean of the Sunrise.'

'Then let us follow in their wake to the ocean,' I said.

Pica spoke: 'Boaz, I am concerned about the rafts. The many rapids have taken their toll. They already ride a hand's length lower in the water.'

'We can no longer waste time,' I said 'We'll keep close to the shore in case of trouble.'

'All the easier to get an arrow in the eye for our caution,' said Aroona. 'Let us push into the middle waters where the current is swift. Where the bugs and arrows cannot find us.'

'First we will do it my way,' I said, eyeing my second-in-command narrowly.

We pushed our rafts into the water. It was now the colour of savage storm clouds. Muscles strained at oars as the jungle banks went by. During that long day of blinding sunshine many men took ill. Some passed out only from the heat, and they were soon brought to life with splashes of water. Others had a deeper sickness. Many who had been badly bitten by the flying needles began to turn pale and shake. They tried to row but could not keep up their strokes for long. Coca was given for them to chew, but soon they had no strength even to chew.

I would have pulled in sooner but there was no place to land. The very roots of trees reached out into the water. Finally when there was only a blood-red glimmer of light remaining we saw an outcrop of boulders and brought the sick ashore. The bugs were not as bad here but the moans of the sick needled our sleep.

We woke with the screams of dying men in our ears. They were being clawed to death by a host of jaguars. Aroona bounded forward, stopping suddenly as the jaguars stood up and became men. I could see that there was an arrow pointed at us from behind every leaf of every tree. The jaguar men screeched as they severed the heads of my warriors. I drew back my arm to throw my spear. Aroona held my arm. He thrust out both his hands like claws. Then, stepping forward, he kneeled and made a long set of motions. He slowly took his blade and slashed his arm.

98

We watched numbly as the tallest of the Jaguar Men did the same with his tusk-pointed spear. Aroona drew close to him. They held the slashed cuts together, and then embraced. Bows and spears were lowered.

The tribe stepped out from behind the trees. They were a short, thick-set people with blazing eyes and sharpened teeth. In their hands they held long, straight sticks with a hole running through its length, and short but powerful bows.

'Boaz,' called Aroona, 'slash your arm like me and step forward.' I did as he had said and the tall Jaguar Man met me and our arms touched. His mouth opened in a pointed smile.

They had killed a hand of our men. The Chief barked in an unknown tongue and a hand of his own warriors were slain before our eyes. Their bodies were put with those of my tribe.

Although they could not speak together, Aroona and the Jungle Chief could make their hands say what their tongues could not.

My warriors were led an arrow-shot inland, where a great open hut contained the whole tribe. Mountains of fish were fried along with pigs and deer. A Jaguar altar in the middle of the great hut looked almost the same as the one the gods had destroyed. Plants were rubbed over the bodies of the sick men and a strong brew was given them.

Aroona talked with his hands for a long while with the jungle tribesmen. At one point the Chief grew very angry and pointed his spear at Aroona. But Aroona pointed up to the Moon-beast floating like a second moon in the sky above.

The Chief and his tribe shrank back with wonder and with fright. The Chief wailed an order and those with the long, hollow sticks pointed them upwards and puffed their cheeks. The Moon-beast remained where it was and the Chief and his tribe threw themselves to the ground.

After this the Chief treated us as if we were gods ourselves. We were offered food and healing medicines for fever, for wounds and to keep the insects from our skin. The Chief told Xinu, one of his own sons, to join our war party to make up for the men his tribe had killed. And to help the Sacred Jaguar defeat the Sky-Serpents.

We pushed off once more into the river of the giants. I could see many women weeping at the departure of Xinu. The young warrior waved happily and played his pan-pipes in a farewell song.

'Did you know that there were other Jaguar tribes?' I asked Aroona.

'It has been told over campfires that the realm of the Jaguar worshippers stretched from the ocean of sunrise to the ocean of sunset.'

'What did you say to make the Chief almost kill you?'

'I told him that now there were other gods as mighty as the Jaguar – and if the Moon-beast hadn't been there when I pointed . . .' He scratched at my eyes with his hand as with a claw. He did not have to speak further.

The Chief's son stood next to Aroona and I, learning the language of the high plains. He had brought a hand of hollow poles and many wooden darts. He showed us his skill by pointing the pole upwards and puffing out his cheeks. A white bird landed by our feet with his dart in its breast.

He pointed out strange sights. On a sandy shore we saw countless numbers of creatures with round green shells and wrinkled legs. They were laying eggs in the sand, climbing over each other to get to a bare patch. Soon there was no sand to be seen. Further on he pointed out a great monster nibbling at the weeds which grew by the banks. With our arrows we killed the monster, which had the face of a nightmare and the tail of a fish. The Chief's son told Aroona that they were monsters born of the Yamaricumá. These were a tribe of women who only used men if they felt lust and the need for children. When they could not find men they mated with the dolphins further down-river and these monsters were their children.

We munched on the monster's raw flesh as we moved along the great river. There was enough meat to feed my whole army.

'Tell me more about the Yamaricumá.' I asked Xinu. He now knew enough of the Huanaca tongue to make himself understood.

'Sometimes our men are captured,' he nervously laughed, 'and taken to lake two sleeps inland. Men made drunk and find woman flesh all around. Loin-clothes ripped off – the lust of the women makes men glad they captured. Ceremonies last for many passings of Sun and Moon. Our warriors kept very busy – get very tired,' he laughed again. 'They have great temple where they worship Father Sun. Temple has just parrot feathers for roof. The inside of temple lined with Sun-metal. But men not allowed inside. Their Chief called Conyori. She watches over everyone.' Now his smile quickly turned to fear. 'Then one night a warrior tried to go inside Temple. They strung him up by loins. Blindfold the rest of my tribe and take them back to our lands. After many changes of moon our tribe find two hands of boy children. Their skin paler than rest of the tribe. That is the Yamaricumá.'

Something struck me about Xinu. His own skin was half as dark as his father's. He saw my look and grinned knowingly.

'Yes, I one of them. And the Chief pick me as his because I the bravest already. The monster we just ate – who knows? – might be my own brother!' This made him laugh like a monkey. He stopped to look around the group of men listening to him and burst into laughter again; 'And now you all grow pale as I,' he said 'Are you my brothers too?' We all roared with laughter.

Droplets of rain began to speckle the yellow brown water pulling us to the sea. Soon the drops turned to spears of water, winding down like snakes from the sky. A mood of gloom settled over all but Xinu, who didn't seem to notice. Instead he pointed to the bushes. 'Look,' he cried, 'the naked form in that tree. She is of Yamaricumá. Now they will all know.'

'Will they attack?' I asked.

'They love to attack, but I do not know,' he said, 'there has never been so many warriors on the river as this.' Xinu wiped the black oil off a dart and brought his weapon to his lips. Before I had time to stop him he had puffed his cheeks. A woman's scream followed the sight of her dropping from the tree. Xinu jumped into the water and soon dragged her body to the raft. She was pulled on board by eager hands and the dart taken from her shoulder.

'I don't think there were more,' said Xinu, shrugging off water, 'but it was best to stop her tongue.'

I held back my anger. 'You have done right,' I said. 'But never act again without orders.' Xinu smiled and cocked his head at me. He nodded.

I looked at the woman who was now awakening. The only

101

thing she wore was a slender thread around her waist which held a small patch to her woman-parts. She was strong and full-bosomed. Her skin was the colour of the river and her long hair was tied like twine and wound, dripping, around her head.

She opened her eyes and spat at me. She tried to jump overboard but I was on top of her, and this first touch of woman flesh inflamed my sex. She let out a high-pitched scream as I entered her. She chopped at my sides and scratched at my face with the fury of a wounded puma.

This only served to excite me more, and once again I forgot the duty of the Chief. Thunder shook the jungle – or was it the ship of the gods?

The attack came at the next curve of the river. The Yamaricumá charged us in hollowed trees, coming towards us with the speed and surprise of lightning. Arrows rained out of trees along the shores. At my first glance upward the woman shot her knee into my loins and dived into the water. She escaped our arrows and sling-stones as her tribe's weapons struck amongst us with the raindrops. Their canoes quickly surrounded us. Were it not for the narrow ledges which stopped many arrows, even more of my men would have died.

The woman who had felt the thrust of my man-spear swam to the first canoe and was dragged aboard. Now she aimed her spears at me and me alone.

Our own weapons proved true, and soon long scaley beasts with many teeth came to tear the flesh off floating bodies of men and women. The women fought fiercely. Had there been a lesser leader than me they would no doubt have conquered us.

The rain stopped and our two armies fought until the setting sun made the water as red as the blood from our battle. Sensing defeat, the women withdrew. Except the one who was mine. Alone, in a boatful of corpses, she charged the raft and jumped aboard. Her bone spear flew at me, followed by a many-spiked club. Both weapons splashed into the water. My fist sought her jaw and she was down.

No longer would we laugh at the tribe of women. They had killed more men than all the dangers of the unknown before them. In the quiet darkness after the battle we heard fearful noises. Wild grunts and furious splashes made us shudder as the demons of the river ate the dead.

We lost as many warriors as the fingers and toes of two men. Fortunately many who died were those already faint with fever. Pica had a bad wound on his thigh. Xinu set about applying leaves and roots to our wounds.

We remained adrift all night. When we awoke there were skeletons dangling in the water. Only the hands which grasped onto the boat had any flesh left at all. When we released the skeletons, a flurry of silver slashes fought over them.

Within blood-pumps the water was still.

The Yamaricumá woman was tied up strongly but the hate in her eyes conquered all looks of lust – even mine. She had eyes the colour of the jungle and muscles to equal the strongest of men.

We cut loose three of the rafts. They could carry nothing but the Spirits of the dead.

The river wound on, revealing more wonders with every bend. Giant trees now appeared, looming high above the rest of the jungle. They were covered with vines and moon-white blossoms. After the fierce battle, some feared that the very trees would uproot and hurl themselves at us. For if a tribe of women can be so deadly – why not trees? Why not the water itself?

Both these fears were soon proved to be real.

The sky turned the colour of the water and hung over us for half the day. Even Xinu looked to the clouds and trembled.

'It is because of the battle,' he said. 'The Father Sun is angered at the loss of so many of His worshippers.'

But I did not tremble at the darkening sky. It was the woman that made me tremble. Here was a female made for the mightiest of Chiefs. Her long limbs were able to fight against the bravest warrior, yet they were as smooth and lustful as those of the sweetest virgin. I sat down beside her and tried to tame her savage hate by smoothing her hair and smiling. Her jungle eyes narrowed in anger. Her teeth sank into my wrist with the fury of the flesh-eating fish. Would Olani dare do that? Olani, who had never killed a squirrel, did she have the savage beauty of this Yamaricumá? I made up my mind to defy the warnings of Oraan. Let us both die together, this woman and I. I would turn her hate to lust before we died.

103

The damp, heavy air gave Spirit to my thoughts. When the thunder and lightning started I did not notice. I stroked her skin, now dripping with streams of raindrops. She looked to the shore in despair. The thunder clapped around us with the sound of an avalanche and a sudden wind turned the water into small mountains.

Men held on to the reed loops for their lives. For in the crests of the waves were the killer-fish, flashing their silver scales and snapping their pointed teeth at us. The woman huddled into a ball while many men grew sick and gave the fish something to still their hunger for a while.

We watched as the rising water tore chunks from the shoreline and swept them into the current. Trees crashed in front of us while we struggled to keep afloat. Spiders large as a spread hand floated by, along with writhing water-snakes.

It was almost dark when Xinu pointed to a small channel leading off the river. Pica understood and guided the rafts into its mouth. There we sheltered where there were no waves and slept as the rain soaked through to our very dreams.

We awoke to strange beauty. The morning mist hung over the water. It looked as if the tree trunks were rising out of a cloud as they met each other overhead. There were flowers growing from the upper branches, as blue as the waters of the Sacred Lake. I climbed up a hanging vine and plucked the largest bloom, then climbed down and hung it in the woman's hair. She looked quickly away, but did not shake it out. Above the trees the sky was blue. The air was still and suffocating.

We pushed back onto the river, with countless white butterflies accompanying us through the rising mist. Xinu had gathered more plants to aid the wounded and bark for the feverish ones to chew.

The river was settled once more but the shore had changed. Floating islands now attached themselves to solid banks and great holes appeared where shore had been. I could see the weariness in the face of every man. They longed to be rid of the jungle. They longed to fight the great enemy and be done with it. I saw them thinking of the Sacred Lake and the women left behind. I saw their looks of envy as I dallied with the Yamaricumá. I heard the mumblings of Nima's two sons – they had lost a brother to the fierce tribe of women. I ordered their silence. They looked me over, then turned away. Aroona, too, seemed changed in mood since the battle.

Although the juices of the leaves kept away most of the bugs, other enemies would not let us rest. Blood-sucking demons attacked us by night. Men woke feeling weakness, their necks covered with the red bites of the leathery-winged beasts.

Giant whirlpools spun us round where a great river hurled into the brown waters and we barely escaped being sucked to the bottom. After that we had to row through the long scaley beasts which littered the water like a forest of floating trees. They snapped at our oars, biting them to splinters.

We pushed through this river of enemies, ever wary of attack. But there were no more human enemies so long as we stayed in the middle of the water. Whenever we strayed too close to the shore a flurry of arrows greeted us.

Those settlements we saw on the shore were always deserted when we passed. But food still cooked on newly-fed fires.

'The news of our might travels fast,' I said to Aroona.

He shrugged his shoulders, swatting at a cloud of flies. 'Perhaps they lie in wait around the next bend. Ready to watch the demons drink our blood. Perhaps they, like the gods above, laugh at us as they see the limbs ripped from warrior after warrior. Only the foolish women dared to attack face to face . . . The tribes led by men are wise enough to stand back and watch this cursed river kill us one by one.'

'You speak with the words of one who has fever,' I said, reaching out to touch the skin of my friend. He pushed my hand aside.

'My mind is clearer than yours, Great Chief. Go touch your killer-woman instead. Have your pleasures as we're sucked into the teeth of the Serpent.'

I looked around. Too many men had heard Aroona's words. I held back an urge to lash at him. I saw him doing the same.

At this time an excited shout came from Tamtanamka.

'Look!' he cried, his narrow eyes ablaze, 'there are high water marks on the shoreline. We are near the Great Salt!'

The shore reached high above us now. Muddy banks

were alive with frogs and grubs. Yet the river was still so wide that the other side could not be seen at all. We saw only islands in the distance. The Moon-beast slowly shifted position to the opposite side of the River of Giants. I threw an oar at the woman and pointed to the far shores.

'We follow the Moon-Gods!' I roared. The woman put her oar through a loop and heaved her shoulders as she pulled with the rest of us. Her look was dark and resentful.

We rowed out into the deep current and slowly forced our way across. Some men fainted from the ripe sun's heat. But we pressed on until we had made the crossing.

Near the opposite bank were many islands, floating and solid. These passed swiftly by. Aroona and I pulled our oars together, forgetting the bitterness between us.

We stopped to rest where the shore made a broad bend to the left. Beyond us lay white-capped mountain waves stretching to the sky. The yellow-brown river pushed half-way to the limits of sight before it was swallowed by the blue-green sea.

The cheers of my warriors were not to last for long. A sudden wave of darts bit into the throats of many men. They stiffened at once into death. I ordered my men to charge into the jungle, rather than be targets on the shore. Fierce cries carried through the trees, and soon my men were running back to the boats in defeat. We were surrounded by the unseen enemy. And then the gods did as they said they would not.

In the red glow of sunset a single comet streaked towards us, like a fire dropped from the furnace of the gods. From this fire shot the red tongue of death. It crashed trees over and spilled out the smoking bodies of golden-skinned enemies. The Yamaricumá clung to me for protection.

The single flare circled above us, lashing the forest with its red whip of flame. Then landed with a roar by my side. Askar pushed back an ice-bubble over his head and raised his palm at me in greeting.

'I had a hard time doing this,' he said, lifting off a box of fire from his back, 'but I couldn't lose you all so soon.'

'We would have won without you, O god-man,' I said for my leadership through so many dangers had given strength to my spirit and to my tongue. The Yamaricumá slunk back into the shadows, her face a strange mixture of awe and contempt.

106

'Maybe yes – maybe no,' said Askar with a smile, 'In any case your army still survives. How are you my, friend?'

'We have done the gods' bidding and followed the trail that leads to the land of the Serpents.'

'Ah yes. But the trail leads on, Boaz. You must cross the Great Sea to find the nesting place of the Devils. Your reed rafts must give way to larger craft.'

'We are tired of these endless tests,' shouted the older of Nima's two sons. 'When will we fight the Sky Devils and return to our sacred land?' Murmurs of agreement echoed amongst my men.

'Soon. Soon enough, brave warriors. Do not forget the importance of your mission.'

These words did little to stop the angry mutterings 'Now I want to speak with the boat master, Pica.' said Askar.

Pica stepped forward, and Askar hailed him: 'Greetings, singer of songs and master of the water. The crafts that you will build will again use the reeds of your rafts.' He handed Pica a white leaf with a drawing of a huge ship. Its front and back were raised high so that the craft looked like the sliver of moon before it changes into blackness.

'The reeds are water-logged,' said Pica. 'They cannot be reshaped.'

'Yes they can. Strip the reeds of all your rafts. Rebuild so that the dry reeds go below water. The sun will soon dry the rest.'

Tamtanamka interrupted in a gruff voice: 'I have lived all my life in the ocean of the sunset. Such ships could not stand the terrors of the deep waters.'

'Ships of timber would be better,' said Askar, 'but there is no time to spare. Pica, you will follow the drawing as best you can. Boaz, push out into the waters, rowing along the great paths of the fish. You will be carried past many islands up the coast of this land before you catch the great river within the ocean. Memorise the stars at night and set your course by them. We will be there to guide you.'

'Where do you go when you leave our sight?' I asked.

'We go many places, searching for signs of the enemy. We return sometimes to the land of your people,' he said, strapping on his flying box. 'I must go back quickly. Mahala did not want me to come down at all.'

'But wait,' I shouted, 'What of our wives, our children? Why have you let so many warriors die?'

107

Askar's flying box shot him upwards. 'All is well,' he shouted back. 'All will be well.'

There was silence in the camp as sharp thunder heaved Askar back towards the sleeping Moon-beast. The first noise to be heard was howling laughter from the Yamari-cumá. I went over and shook her till she stopped. She spoke a stream of words I could not understand.

'What does she say?' I asked Xinu.

'She says the Serpent swallows its own tail,' he revealed softly, 'and the blood of the Moon is our own.'

I grabbed her again. 'What do you mean by that? What do you know?'

The woman only spat at the ground where Askar stood, his shoe-prints still visible in the damp ground.

'Ah, stupid woman,' I said, shoving her aside. 'I should have fed you long ago to the jaws of the river demons.' Xinu repeated these words in her language.

She slumped to the ground and shivered as the coolness of night crept over her. She said a string of words, almost in tears.

'She says that she, Conyori, has lost the best part of her tribe to the fire-god. They had lived proudly after their men disappeared long ago on a hunting trip. They had learned to be warriors and live in peace amongst themselves. And now all is lost, for the fire-god leads us into the mouth of death.'

'Let's get some fires going,' I said. 'Tomorrow we will start the great reed crafts. And we'll need many animals to smoke for meat and timber for long oars. Xinu, I do not want to hear another word she says, this Chief of a band of women!'

'Why don't you sacrifice her,' said the youngest of Nima's sons, 'and be done with her?'

'Yes,' said his brother. 'The blood of a woman would be pleasing to the powers that protect us.'

I saw in both of them the same savage stupidity of their father. 'You, too, will cease to speak your words of challenge. Unless you want to challenge me here and now!'

They lost their savage looks at once.

'Both of you! Both at once. If the fat spirit of Nima comes stumbling back from the Otherworld, then him too!'

They turned away and walked into the midst of the wounded and exhausted. With our coca bags now empty, the rain, the bugs and dangers of constant attack had nibbled away our War-Glory.

After eating, Pica sat studying the drawing whilst playing the pan-pipes lent to him by Xinu.

I seized Conyori and put strong thrusts of manhood into her. For the first time she yielded like a woman, her tears mixing in with our sweat.

When I awoke in the morning she was gone, her tracks leading off beyond the broken trees.

ELEVEN

Pica did not have to study the drawing for long. By the time the sun was high we had stripped the reeds and started rebuilding. The new boats were like great wide hollowed logs, both of them large enough to hold more than twenty hands of warriors. The ends of each boat curved upward like a scorpion's tail.

Tamtanamka convinced Pica that the boats should at least have timber braces within the hollow. The Seal man had some men strip the bark from the trees felled by the red-tongue and shape them into planks. Wedges made from a hardwood tree were used to join the braces. The reeds were gathered into round bundles and fashioned around the braces.

In the hard work that followed over three days and nights, all bitterness was again forgotten. And the disappearance of the Yamaricumá also seemed to bring smiles back to the faces of all except me.

There were few large animals to be found in this part of the jungle. But Xinu brought down many monkeys and pigs with his darts. Other men brought in deer and large snakes. The smoke from our smoke-house devoured a forest of trees.

We watched the high waters surge up the mouth of the river. As they were going down again we pushed off the muddy banks with great joy. The bottoms of the boats were packed with dried meat and many skins of water. The craft balanced evenly in the strong waters.

Heaving on our oars, we watched the clearing that had been our camp become one with the thick line of jungle in the distance.

Pica called me aside after many hours. 'We are not going in the direction that we should,' he said. 'We are still being

109

pushed out by the great river. Taste the water. Even out here it doesn't taste salty.'

I wiped my finger along Pica's steering oar. 'You are right,' I said. 'Look! The Moon-beast lies far away, still above the coast line.' Panic grabbed at my heart but the leader in me took over—

'Turn the ships about!' I ordered. 'Oarsmen on the right, raise oars!' Though we sweated long and hard the ships would not adjust. As the land finally faded from sight the men began to show open fear. The Moon-beast still hung on the twilight horizon like the first star that follows the Sun's death.

All night we kept trying to turn the boats. Suddenly a mighty storm lashed in with the sunrise. Bursts of wind shot waves high above our prow. Pica again took over the orders, not trying to alter course – just keeping the boats pointed into the waves. Tamtanamka and Aroona were copying us in the other ship.

Great bursts of lightning flashed from the direction of the Moon-beast. Flashes even brighter than lightning followed. Then a great clapping roar reached our ears. After that we saw nothing except the clouds and rain. Heavy drops struck like arrows. The waves soaked my men many times over as we were hurled down the walls of deep blue-green valleys.

The storm did not cease until late next day. When the last clouds let the sun soak up steam from our ships there was nothing to see but sky and water. With us in the centre of both.

There was no land. No Moon-ship. We were lost on the naked waters.

The boats had sunk a hand's width into the water. But they had ridden the mountain-waves well. Though to me this was a sign of good, the rest of my men did not think so. On my boat the men talked darkly to each other as we rowed on.

'When will we catch the river within the ocean?' I asked Pica. He knew no more than I, but his gentle voice gave me comfort:

'Very soon, Boaz. We can only trust in Askar's words. If we were truly lost, the ship would appear, as he said it would.'

'Fine. But what were those flashes we saw last night during the storm? They were too much like the great white flash that destroyed the first Temple on the island.'

110

'The Serpents have struck the Moon-ship!' said Nima's oldest son. 'We are lost and at their mercy.'

I ran to him and slapped him back to his rowing place. 'If you truly believe that then your body will be the first to please them.'

'My body will not be the first. How many men will have died before me? One out of every three who joined the warriors of the gods is dead!'

'You will row!' I shouted at him and all men, 'Row with all your strength. The course is straight. The gods will protect us for the final battle.'

The ships pulled alongside each other. Aboard the other ship Aroona was having his own troubles.

'The men have lost their faith, Boaz,' the Jaguar Chief shouted.

'And you too, Aroona?'

The younger of Nima's sons stood beside Aroona on the other boat. 'The dead and dying amongst us long to go back. We must reverse our course now and get back to the Sacred Lake. The gods have deserted us.'

Anger raged in me like a wounded puma. These were taunts from a member of my own tribe. I took a running start and leapt from my boat to the other. My hands squeezed the life from Nima's son. Fighting broke out all around me, and on the other boat. Those who were faithful to me fought against those who listened to the poisonous tongues of Nima's sons and those who had lost friends and brothers. Aroona stood aloof, until a warrior spun his sling, about to let fly a stone at my head. Only then did Aroona step in and break the man's neck. On the other ship, Pica, the gentle boatsman was now in a fight for his life. He fought like a savage against Nima's remaining son.

Many bones were crushed, and the bodies in the water were devoured by huge yawning monsters that circled swiftly around the boats.

'Look! Look!' We stopped fighting for a moment to hear Aroona's cries. He was pointing off to the side at a distant shoreline, 'We have merged with the Great-Salt river!'

The fighting continued for a time, for there were many personal blows to be struck. But soon the men were silent as they watched the distant coast slide slowly by. Ahead of us were great green islands.

'The gods have answered our senseless fighting,' I

111

screamed. 'Now get back to your oars and steer to the outside of the islands. All men who fought against me are forgiven. For we are but men who know not the ways of the gods.'

The men looked again at the coastline then moved slowly back to their oars.

'Why did you save my life?' I asked Aroona as the two boats moved alongside each other.

'I owed it to you. Now the debt is paid.' He walked to the steering oar at the back of his ship and I leapt back aboard my own. Luckily the deadliest weapons were stowed in the hollow of the boats. Otherwise there would have been many more deaths. The grey monsters circled around our boats for many days thereafter, awaiting a further taste of our flesh.

After the great fight amongst us, the men settled down to steady rowing. We cut up leather for the men to wear around their wrists which chafed against the sides of the boats. Nights were a time of collapse. The men were so tired that they did not bother to lie down, but fell asleep across their oars. Pica soon learned the secret of the stars. He said that we were moving very fast – wherever we were going.

Then one day the coast was gone from our left. Again we were the centre of all horizons. The smoked meat was running out, but Tamtanamka showed us how to catch fish by trailing a piece of meat in the water on a bone or metal hook. We had not to wait many breaths before a fish would be caught.

The grey circling monsters vanished as the water and weather grew colder. In their place came other wonders. A flat, moon-shaped demon as wide as the surface of our ship reared out of a wave and flopped back with a sound of thunder. A demon with many great legs and a parrot's beak began to climb up the steering oar of Aroona's boat. A spear in its side released a gush of blood black as night and the demon vanished back beneath the waves.

Playful beings leapt from the surface of the ocean, seeming to smile as they twisted in the air before splashing down again. Xinu said that these were dolphins, the fathers of the river beast we had slain before the battle with Conyori's tribe. Fish with wings would dart out of the waters and flop against our backs and necks. They made very tasty eating.

Pica announced that we had changed direction yet again – that the coast was now directly behind us. The water lost its vivid colour and became a dim grey, like the mist on the river of giants.

Many sleepings passed.

Days turned into weeks. The lure of the Great Salt and its uncountable mysteries was felt by all. We were happy then, enchanted by the vastness of the waters.

Gradually the flat surface gave way to rolling waves. Then the waves grew into mountains as black clouds lined up on the horizon. It seemed as if the clouds were rumbling towards us like an angry avalanche. The seas rose higher and we rode on the backs of moving mountains. The black clouds trampled the Sun and soon the waves hissed with foam and exploded over the boats. The waves were sucked into the reed and given back to the ocean. Strong winds came which flattened the crests of the waves. We struggled to keep pointing into the waves. Had we allowed ourselves to be forced otherwise the mountains would have crushed us beneath their weight.

A wave leapt over us, bringing aboard a host of pink, shiny demons which stung many men before the next wave washed them overboard again. Those who were stung became paralysed. Great red sores appeared where the long pink arms had stung. The boats rolled with the waves, unsteady from this loss of oar-power.

The waves peaked high above us, then hurled the ships downwards. But Pica had followed Askar's design faithfully and the boats held firm. Many men were washed overboard. The lucky ones were tossed back on the following wave.

In the blackness of night we struggled against death and madness. Only the reeds kept their steadiness. The timber braces soon worked themselves loose from the rope which bound them together. Yet our ship sank but little and held us bravely afloat.

In the darkness we lost sight of Aroona's ship. Suddenly above the hisses and cracks of the waves we heard a low-pitched roar that ground into our ears with sickening terror.

It seemed to be coming from a living thing.

Then from the Spiritworld itself came a wave as high as the stars. Riding it was a sight to make the bravest man quake. A long neck stretched out from the crest and the face on the end was that of indescribable horror. It loomed above us, its roar greater than the waves. I heard my voice screaming before the full force of fear struck me:

113

'Each man take a spear! Xinu, smear your poisons on every one!'

'The men must not leave their posts,' Pica shouted back. 'The waves are more dangerous than any monster. If we turn broadside we are lost.'

As we plunged into the next deep valley, the monster charged. It was like a worm, bigger than the tallest tree. I saw many spears bristling from its humped body.

'It has already attacked Aroona's ship!' I shouted. 'All men stay at your oars. . . . Xinu, give me two spears and have your blowpipe ready!'

Xinu did as I bid whilst the monster thundered down the wall of water. The jungle man shot a dart into one of the beast's eyes. It screeched with the voice of a whole tribe being slaughtered. Its forked tail hammered against our boat. The reeds absorbed the blow. Again the monster snapped its tail and this time the whole boat was wrenched round slightly. Enough to cause the next wave to crash dangerously against us. My spear lodged deeply in the creature's neck. It moved as if it had no bones, and no blood dripped from spears nor darts.

'That much poison would kill all the beasts in the jungle,' cried Xinu, 'yet the monster feels nothing. We are finished!'

'Hold tight and keep puffing. The beast must not reach us with those teeth! . . . One by one every man bring in his oar. Xinu will strap a blade on each oar. We must keep rowing!' The great beast circled our bundles of reeds yet only knocked us further off course with every giant slap of its tail. Blades tied to oars cut through its skin but the demon-flesh closed back again instantly. Then, suddenly it dived and seemed to be gone. A cheer burst from every man's throat.

But the next thing we knew our stern lifted high out of the waves and came down with a terrific crack. Both steering oars were snapped, along with one of Pica's arms.

Pica could not think about his pain, for the craft was turning broadside to meet the next wave.

'Four oars must take the place of the steering oars. And drop the anchor-rock into the water!' the boatsman yelled. Quickly four men brought their oars to the stern and bound them with rope. A mighty wave swept two of the men overboard as they dropped the heavy rock. But the repairs were made. The ship turned smartly to plough straight through

114

the waves, which seemed to be getting weaker with the rising of the Sun.

Then the monster reappeared. This time it struck with savage fury. Its tail whipped at us and its head came alongside and roared a roar that raised our hair. I jammed a whole oar down its throat to discourage it. We heard the oar being broken up inside the monster.

The reeds had taken a mighty beating, but the craft was still sound. Not so the timber braces which were swinging freely, crushing any man who got in their way.

I seized two more spears and waited for the next onslaught of the monster. The men strained at their oars, united in their effort to survive. The sight of the monster in the brightening sky caused them to close their eyes against the fearful vision. Its dark brown skin, its worm-like movements and the fierce, evil look of its eyes were thus avoided as it attacked. It battered the front of the boat, rearing it halfway out of the water. I could see that the ropes binding together the bundles of reeds had been snapped. But the reeds were swollen enough to hold the split ends in place.

The monster seemed to be playing with us, as a puma plays with a rodent before he bites off its head, would dive, stay submerged for minutes, and then reappear, smashing its tail against the ship.

And then came the end of our chances. For over the flattening waves rode more monsters. There were three of them, each as big as the largest boulders of the sacred mountains. Their flashing teeth were big as a man's head. Their shiny black bodies leapt between the valleys of the waves, coming straight towards us at the speed of falling stars. They were shaped like the dolphins, yet many times bigger and broader. When they leapt in the air they showed us their white underbellies, as white as bleached bones.

Now even I was sure the Serpents had won. 'Gods of the stars,' I prayed, 'we have failed you.'

The writhing monster had dived once more but this time none of us moved to repel the next attack. The new monsters could crush our craft with a single flick of their fish-like tails. As they crashed towards us, spray spewed from their heads like fire from a volcano. Each man left on board made his peace with the totem of his tribe and waited calmly to die. All fear had been used up doing battle with the many-coiled demon.

115

The three monsters dived under our ship. Seconds later the worm flew up from the depths. We waited for it to crash down on us with its fellow demons to overturn the boat. Now I knew why Aroona's ancestors had fallen down before a hungry jaguar. There is no use in fighting forces that make men seem like bugs ready to be squashed.

The Serpent arched high in the air, giving out a stench of death along with a scream that almost stopped our blood-pumps. Then suddenly it shot backwards, as if being dragged down by its tail. It splashed back down into the water and was pulled struggling beneath the surface. For a long time the water thrashed and bubbled. Then the black monsters reappeared, each holding on to a piece of the Serpent's trunk and tearing away at it as a Condor tears at the entrails of the dead.

Those who still had their eyes open shouted to the others to look. We all stared in wonder – the monsters were battling each other!

The Serpent lashed at one of the boulder-monsters with its tail, coiling itself around it. The shiny black monster screamed in a series of high squeaks as its body was squeezed in two and red blood splurted from mouth and body.

The other two rushed at the Serpent's neck, sinking their teeth into the flesh of the great worm. They churned circles in the water as they ripped out great chunks of muddy brown flesh. A last thunder-growl erupted from the Serpent as a black monster clamped its jaws around its face and closed its teeth together with a sickening crunch. They did not stop, even when the humps flattened out and the body became slack. They continued to tear it to pieces before our disbelieving eyes and frozen voices.

And as if this were not enough mystery to confound the All-Knowing Viracocha Himself, a series of even stranger things happened. From out of nowhere a fast moving cloud appeared which dipped low and enveloped our boat in its whiteness. The air about us tingled in a way that made us feel as if all the gods and spirits hovered inside our bodies and minds. A noise of many musical notes was heard, all played at once. Yet neither Xinu nor Pica had touched their instruments. But there was yet more:

Red flashes crashed around us. Sparks as from an exploding sunset rained down from the heavy clouds above.

We watched them fall beyond the monsters and the blood-less meat of the worm.

After the red flashes vanished, the bright cloud hovered around us for a moment longer. Then it, too, faded away to nothingness.

Now the floating chunks of worm-flesh became a bubbling scum that seethed the waters.

The monsters who had saved our lives did not hear our cheers of thanks. They swam to their dead brother and made sorrowful squeaks as they tried to nudge it back to life. It lay with its white belly turned upward, blood darkening the water around it. Then smaller grey monsters appeared and darted in to bite off chunks of its flesh. The two monsters tried to chase away the circling forms, but finally gave up and raced off towards the horizon.

We gave thanks to the gods for answering our pleas and took count of the remaining men. We had lost nearly half of the warriors. But the rest of us had been spared once again to fight the final battle.

In the calming seas we searched for signs of the other ship. But there was nothing to be seen. 'They are lost,' said Pica while Xinu was binding his arm, 'I will sing a great song to their memory.'

'No,' I said, 'not yet. The Serpent may have only over-turned their ship. And the reeds do not sink. There might still be warriors clinging to the hull.'

Many of the provisions had been washed overboard, but there was enough dried meat for all the men to share and enough rain water to quench our thirst.

With our bellies full and our blood-pumps calmed, we gripped our oars with renewed strength. The Sun came out and outlined a shape denting the horizon.

'The ship!' I cried. 'Row fast!'

It was just as I had said. The ship lay capsized in the water with two hands of men waving wildly as we pulled closer. My blood-pump sent a surge of gladness through me at the thought that Aroona was amongst them.

When I saw my friend on board I could not contain my joy. I jumped in the water and swam to him.

'No, no!' he shouted. 'The Serpent! The Serpent!'

'Shit on the Serpent!' I replied as I clambered on board.

'This battle is over. The gods sent their monsters to attack and destroy the Serpent.'

Aroona's forehead wrinkled at my words; 'Would that they had saved us,' he said, 'it was like fighting all the evil spirits the world has ever known.'

'I know,' I said. 'I saw your spears in its neck. Even Xinu's poison could not stop it. Nearly half my men are lost!'

'You see what I have left? Even Tamtanamka is dead.'

'Let us give thanks that we are alive,' I said, hugging him and rubbing his cold skin. 'We have seen the spirits of evil but we've also seen the spirits of the gods. You should have seen them tear the Serpent apart!'

'Has the Moon-beast returned?' asked Aroona, not ready to share my joy.

'No – not unless the gods were in the bellies of the giants.'

'Then how do you know it was the gods who saved you?'

'What's the matter with you, Aroona?' I looked at him as at a stranger for he seemed to have lost much of his former spirit. 'You must have drunk too much sea-water.'

The men were hoisted on board, and we took great bundles of reeds of the capsized boat to repair our own craft when we reached land. If there was any land ever to be reached.

Strong shoulders bent with the pulling of the oars. Brave hearts listened to Pica's songs as his one arm kept the boat on course: 'With the help of the Gods,' he sang, 'we shall fill the emptiness. With the strength of our muscles we shall build on the fullness. Not all monsters are our enemies. We mourn their loss with our own. Quickly take your stand, for the battles are not over. The battles won't be over till we laugh with our children again. . .

We raced along the shiny grey waters as the Sun sank behind us.

Once again the strength gained in victory faded into boredom. I was thankful that there was only one of Nima's sons left to cause poison thoughts amongst my warriors. We rowed the choppy seas for many days, then many weeks. Rain did not fall, neither did flying fish serve themselves for dinner.

At least on the great river there had been a shore to look at, and colours to amuse the eye. But now there was just water and sky. And the worsening moods of men who are lost.

Our moods did not improve when I allowed only two

cupped hands of water each day. The warriors needed more but there was nothing I could do. The few fish caught each day were devoured while still squirming. Xinu helped by gathering small yellow animals which attached themselves onto the bottom of the boat. Soon even the beetles which crept out of the reeds were fought over.

TWELVE

One morning a single, white bird flew overhead, cawing noisily. Xinu brought it down with a dart. The spirit of my warriors rose, for we had seen these same birds flying overhead as we reached the sea from the River of Giants. It meant but one thing – land could not be far away. Oars were pulled with all the strength we could muster toward the promise of land, food and shelter.

'Eeee-eee!' cheered Pica at midday. 'Either I see a monster as big as a coastline, or blessed land itself!'

My eyes strained to make out a green line on the horizon. More birds appeared, but I told Xinu not to waste his darts. Xinu told me he had never wasted a dart since he was four. I forgave him his impudence in the wave of joy that overcame us all.

The men now rowed as if with full bellies, for the green line did not swim towards us with monstrous teeth. It lay like a frightened virgin, waiting for our possession. I praised Viracocha, the Creator, for this, voicing his greatest blessing. The warriors followed in praise for the One who made All.

The land ahead of us was a vibrant green with rolling hills and many streams which poured into the Great Salt. There was no sign of man nor beast as we rammed our ship on the pebble shore and threw down the rock anchor.

My men charged ashore and plunged themselves into the nearest freshwater stream. A bank of clouds swept away the few remaining throbs of the Sun. We climbed up the shore and rolled in soft green grass. Pica played his flute and Xinu joined him on his pan-pipes whilst we ate the last of our meat, sure we would find more in the morning.

Although the sea still rolled and pitched inside our heads, the feeling of solid land was a pleasure. The men slept soundly as night devoured the day. The lone guard fell asleep early on, not knowing that we were surrounded.

119

We awoke to the sound of bones being crushed by stones rolled down the grassy hills. They tumbled upon us through the thick morning mist, killing the men who slept at the edge of our circle.

Fierce war-cries bore down upon us as we scrambled to get our weapons. I arranged my warriors in a circle until we knew the direction from which we were being attacked.

Strange men appeared swinging gnarled clubs. They came out of the mist then vanished again, so we could see only flashes of their features. Their skin was as grey as the mist, covered with hair the colour of a jungle sunset.

Our metal-tipped arrows and spears quickly cut the grey hordes down before many more of our men departed their bodies. Their fierce cries now faded in retreat as the mist lifted. My orders were to attack and destroy every living thing on this island of doom.

Chasing the grey men over the hills we came within sight of their camp on the bay next to ours. Weapons clashed as they regrouped to defend their women, children and meat. But the fury of my men was too great, and the sight of the women and food acted as a stronger force than coca leaves to feed the flame of War-Glory.

Grey bodies lay trampled under our advance. Those who escaped us threw down their heavy clubs, the better to run away. The women, too, tried to escape but my warriors forced them down and ravished their bodies. So many changes of the moon without women made the servants of the gods into creatures worse than animals. Some of my warriors were battling each other over the choicest of the women.

Those who had escaped inland had not run away in cowardice. In the distance I saw more tribes of grey-skins pouring across the rolling hills towards us. Surely these could not be slaves of the Serpents, I thought. It was not worth making a stand and battling to the death. I ordered retreat.

We quickly gathered furs, food and women and hurried back to our ship. My men laughed as they carried the struggling women to the bay where our ship was waiting. Surely we were protected by the gods, for they had sent us a bloody battle to restore our spirits and kept our ship intact. We would swim to the ship and be gone before the pursuing hordes could reach us.

But the gods gave the enemy one last chance. For we had forgotten about the tides.

120

When we ran down the slopes of the bay, we saw our ship stranded on the pebbles. The waters were many man-lengths beyond the craft. They receded more with each feeble wave. The grey-skinned women yelled for their men to hurry. We tossed them and the food on board and heaved the boat slowly towards its home in the sea.

The grey-skinned savages converged on us as we reached the waves, throwing stones and hurling wooden-pointed spears. I shouted for half my men to meet the attack while the other half strained to get the boat afloat.

The gods had scared us, but they were with us still. Our arrows and sling-stones kept the grey-skins at bay so they could only attack us with stones. But more and more were pouring over the hills to press the attack. Some of us jumped in the boat, pushing into deeper waters with our oars. Whilst we struggled, many women jumped overboard and escaped.

Finally the boat floated free and after a final flurry of arrows the last of us swam aboard. Few of our men were missing. But we had soaked the shores of the grey-skins with much more of their own blood.

My men were joyous. The battle had restored their purpose after many idle months on the sea of unknown dangers. The captured women were passed from man to man. Their green eyes filled with tears as their bodies yielded time after time to the mighty lust of the Moon-Gods' warriors. My commands had once again been proven right. I gladly took my choice of women.

I best enjoyed myself with the youngest of the savage women. But the sight of her skin repelled me. I longed for a woman of my own kind, Olani or the mighty Conyori. This girl was short and squat with sores on her skin. Only the green of her hate-filled eyes inspired my lust.

I let my men fill their stomachs and empty their loins as we drifted away from the coast. I half expected the Moon-beast to appear and guide our direction, or send down a warning about the women on board. We had not seen it since the white flashes when we first put to sea. Yet I felt sure I was following the right course. The sea itself knew where to take me. Was not the world itself helping us to meet and defeat the Sky-Devils?

We were heading past a sharp point of land when Pica saw a solid coast ahead. But then clouds obscured the distant view. The sea became choppy and the men groaned once again as their muscles strained on the oars. Yet spirits were high and the men laughed at the sickness of the women. One jumped overboard and swam towards the land. She had not swum far before we heard her screams. The grey monsters tore her living flesh to shreds within moments.

The river within the sea pushed us on. We followed the long, unbroken coastline, rowing strongly to keep from rocks.

We had no room for thoughts of doom. Even the bitterest amongst us was contented by full bellies and the touch of women. And the strength of combat gave rise to many versions of the battle with the Serpents yet to come. There was no force, god-like or human, which we could not defeat.

Toward the end of sunlight we found we were swept into a huge bay. No amount of strength could turn the boat back to the open sea, but a good sleep would give us the extra power.

We landed where a thin forest met the water. There we slept, though this time with many men on guard.

Only I, Boaz, let all the questions of my mind unfurl themselves. And as always there were no answers. How could a handful of men defeat the nest of the Serpents? There was now only one man alive out of four who had fought the Falcon Tribe. Words of the Yamaricumá woman stung me; 'The Serpent swallows its own tail. The blood of the Moon is the blood of us all.' What did the words mean? What did she know – the woman who worshipped the Sun? I tossed and turned all night while Pica tested the gentleness of his newly-mended arm on my grey-skinned girl. We were the playthings of the gods, gods who had wagered with each other when I held the fitness contests. Had they now tired of the game? Was it just a plan to rid themselves of those who might rebel against them? Now the gathered tribes at the Sacred Waters were led by a soft-muscled boy and a Shaman who spoke others' visions. But why then had they sent the black shiny giants to kill the sea-serpent?

I roused my men at the first signs of light. I was angry that they needed only to follow orders. That was the difference between their deep sleeps and my restless wonderings.

We followed the coastline towards a far distant point on the horizon. By the end of the day we were only half way to

122

our goal. We rowed throughout the night in turns. By the end of the next day we were out of the bay. The reed boat flowed swiftly past the cliffs and inlets of an unknown land. The climate had changed from the cool mistiness of the grey-skins' island to a land of warm dry air with the Sun playing happily in the sky.

The sandy beaches of the coast gave us safe camp-sites for two nights. The men gathered shells for themselves and the women. Far from being sad and frightened, the females by now had joined in the spirit of the warriors. They prepared the food caught by fishing and hunting parties and tried to learn our language. They fought to be next to Pica and sing their own strange songs over the pan-pipes. Had we lost our boat at this point, we could have lived well as a tribe amongst the white-sand beaches and forests. It was easy to forget about our purpose. The gods seemed already like a half-forgotten dream. So were the faces and sacred places of the far land from which we had journeyed.

THIRTEEN

Pica's face brightened as he felt a change in the waters:

'We're moving fast now, Boaz.' he said. 'Look how the beaches go by. Ah, but look again!' he cried, pointing past an outcrop of beach. There was no more land beyond it. 'We're being swept around, to our left.'

'Now the land turns inward?'

'Yes – and the ocean-river follows it around. Not even the giants could swim faster than this!'

Every pull of the oars swept our sagging boat swiftly along. We watched the water turn as blue as the sky. Then I saw a thin line of coast off our starboard side. The two coasts seemed to be converging together. 'The air is tingling with spirits, men.' I called 'We are getting close to the nest!' Eager white-toothed smiles shone in the warm sun.

'Then let Pica start a chant to speed our journey!' shouted Aroona.

Pica broke into a war-like chant which all the oarsmen took up. Soon we saw before us a giant mountain made of one rock. It overlooked the edge of the coast. The land on our starboard side was not joined to the land we were following after all. Between them was a narrow channel which the mountain seemed to be guarding. It was much narrower than the river of giants. We swept into it past the spirit mountain.

Presently, the land on both sides of the narrow waters curved away. We were in an ocean within the ocean.

The great spirit rock was far behind us when we saw a sight that iced our hearts. Weapons quickly replaced oars. Coming swiftly towards us was not a demon of the deepest seas nor a vision of the gods.

It was a ship of timber planks. Towering above was a great square wall of cloth which filled with the wind and pushed the ship towards us with great speed. It was manned by neither gods nor serpents – but by men!

Pica alone felt no fear. For he was lost in admiration of the billowing sail; 'Look how it uses the wind,' he said. 'It uses the power of four hands of oarsmen.'

'Never mind,' I shouted as the timber craft grew closer to us with every blood-pump. 'Turn the ship broadside so our men can take clear aim.'

I made out the figures of golden-skinned warriors on board who looked at our craft with as much surprise as we looked at theirs. The warriors had long, pointed jaws and noses. Hair grew from their chins like a puma's claw and their faces were curled in savage, mocking grins. They heaved to within range of our weapons. A man stood on its prow and shouted in a harsh and ugly language.

'Who knows what they say?' I shrugged.

Dana, the grey-skinned girl who Pica and I shared stepped forward and spoke: 'They are the Sons of Shem. Ships of theirs have landed on my island. I have learned some words from a captured man.'

'Stop telling stories, girl. What do they say?'

'They demand to know where we have come from, where we are going, what cargo we carry and what gods we serve.'

'Good, then my answer needs no words,' I said, hurling my spear across the gap between the ships. The spear sank deep in the man's chest. He toppled into the water while my men roared with War-Glory.

The timber ship turned to ram us as sling-stones, arrows and spears were exchanged from both sides.

'Push away from their ship with your oars,' I shouted. Xinu's dart caught the man on the steering oars and the two ships met broadside.

The battle was furious. The long-faced ones fought well with metal-tipped weapons that flashed orange from the dying Sun. But they had not reckoned with skills such as we had learned on our long, hard journey.

We did not even notice the other enemy ship until an arrow grazed the back of my neck.

'Ha!' I shouted, 'at last there is an equal battle. Kill the ones on the first ship. We say goodbye now to our own battered craft!' My men flung themselves aboard the first ship and steadily overpowered the golden-skinned men whose blood ran thick. We hoisted the women aboard as the second ship rammed our reed boat into floating bits of straw.

Pica quickly took over control of the steering oars whilst the men from the second ship tried their best to slaughter us. We had to pluck our weapons out of the corpses littering the deck to deal with them. The two timber ships clashed broadside. Before the long-faced enemy could act I led all my men headlong onto the attacking ship.

My men were weak, and the weakest were soon killed, among them Nima's last remaining son. But our fury and quick fighting were too much for the golden ones. Even the grey-skinned women killed their share. Our metal cleaved through theirs and into their bodies. And as the Sun set towards the land from which we came, their blood mingled with the colour of the sky.

Our reed boat lay overturned and breaking up. It had served us well through the mightiest of storms and battles. The corpses of the long-faced Sons of Shem were thrown into the Mother-Ocean.

The second ship was longer than the first, so I chose it in preference. From the stores of the first ship, we brought over stocks of food and water. There were even jugs filled with deep-red Star-Juice.

As we were about to sink the death-filled vessel, we heard a low cry. I jumped back with my blade raised to kill and discovered a man huddled amongst the dead. He was not wearing the clothes of the Sons of Shem and he did not carry a weapon. His face was badly bruised and full of fear. He grabbed my arm and begged for his life to be spared. I did not understand his words but I understood his trembling.

Since my heart was warm from my first gulp of Star-Juice I helped him up and prodded him to our new, timber-built home. The man was fat and thick black hair grew

125

from his jowls and skull. He had not the pointed savage features of those whose blood rusted our blades.

He swallowed many swigs of Star-Juice and watched my men as they explored the workings of the ship. Already I could tell that I would miss the reed boat. This wooden one rode the waves with too much pitch and sway. And if sunk – it would go straight to the bottom.

In the last moments of light the man stumbled over to Pica and showed him how the flapping square sail was lowered and raised. With the help of the grey-skinned girl who knew the fat one's words, Pica learned all he had not already figured out. There were also a few oars on either side of the ship. I gathered the women and proved once again that I was Chief of the chiefs.

I pushed away the hand that tried to shake me awake. Aroona's smiling face grinned heavily. I pushed aside the women from the night before and looked around. The land was still to our left. There was no wind in the sail, yet we were moving fast.

The fat man was wide-eyed in amazement as he tried to tell something to Pica. Pica was smiling and gently nodding his head.

'What does he say?' I asked Pica.

'I know not his words.'

'Then why do you let him speak?'

'I like him. His hands speak for him. They say he has many children, a wife fatter than he, and the gods are working a great miracle.'

My head pounded with the Star-Juice and the nonsense of the boatman's words. To shake the dizziness from me I jumped in the water. The fat man tried to stop me.

Suddenly I knew why. The river within the sea was carrying me swiftly away from the boat. Pica became a savage, screaming at the oarsmen to turn the boat round. I swam as hard as I could to keep in the same place. It was many moments before the boat reached me. As soon as I was pulled aboard the oarsmen relaxed. The ship drifted against the current that had carried me.

Now Dana was awake and she told me the fat man's words.

'He says it's a miracle.'

126

'I have known many miracles,' I said, reaching for the bottom gulp of a jug.

'He says the current you fell into was the right one. That which carries this boat is a miracle.'

'But why should this be?'

'He says that on the other shore of this sea the waters are thick with the Sons of Shem. Other ships from other gods fight for control of the shipping routes. There are enemies off these shores, but not as many.'

A roar of happiness rose from my battle-scarred warriors. Even though the gods had vanished from our vision they were still with us. They had even given us a taste of how these strange people fought. They had provided us with a ship of a well-respected enemy. Fewer warriors would dare to attack a ship of the Sons of Shem than a flimsy reed boat barely riding above the water-line. Perhaps the bundle of loose reeds was even now catching the river-current back towards the lands of the sunset.

The fat man laughed with us. He said his home was many days sailing from here. As he spoke I noticed that many words he used I could understand.

'Tell me your story,' I said slowly. The man's raised eyebrows told me he could understand. With the help of Dana he told me how he ended up with the Sons of Shem:

'I am Gudea, of the land below the lands of the Sons of Shem. For many years the Sons of Shem grew rich as they learned the art of building ships and used them to raid the coastal settlements. But we soon moved our towns inland. The town where I live is called Sat-Am, on the shores of a salt lake.

'Other people used captured ships to learn the art themselves. My people – the Sin-Ad, soon became prosperous as we plundered the inland villages of neighbouring lands. Soon the Sons of Shem and the Sin-Ad were the bitterest of enemies. Me, I am not a warrior, as my fat belly must tell you,' Here he patted his many rolls of fat and burst into laughter.

'No, I am a trader – one who gathers furs from the forest in exchange for timber, or metal for cotton, or slaves for jewels. But I am an honest man. My fortune has been made by giving people what they want. My name is known – and respected – in all the lands of this enclosed salt sea. Except that of the Sons of Shem.

127

'One night they swooped down on us – just as they swooped on you. And in the same place. Those who are masters of the narrow waters are masters of the sea. In the night we had no chance. All my men were butchered and then the leader recognised me. He was the very one who received your answer to his challenge with a spear in his heart.' Again he roared with laughter and clutched my shoulders in a warm grasp.

'The leader kept me alive – not for love but for riches. We were waiting for another ship to take me back to their homeland – the very ship we are now sailing in. There I would be held for ransom. The ransom would be half the lands of Sin-Ad and the occupation of Sat-Am. I had them convinced that they would get their terms – just to spend a few more days alive. Thank you, Boaz, for saving me. I will do anything I can for you.'

'Except give me half of Sin-Ad – eh?' We both roared with laughter.

In the next few days we sailed, as in a dream. The wind caught hard in the fine-woven sail – which Gudea said was made from the cotton plant. He promised to give me seeds of this plant on our journey homeward.

It had taken much time, but I began to grow fond of Dana. I even told Pica I no longer wished to share her with him. He merely shrugged his shoulders and said, 'This ship is all the woman I'll ever need.'

I had watched Dana grow from a girl to a woman. In the few short weeks I had been with her, her breasts had budded and her skin was darkening daily in the burning sun. She was a good fighter and our natures fitted together like the wind into the sail. Together we watched the grand sights of the coastline: Ragged cliffs rolled down to smooth beaches; single rocks with waves pounding them from all sides. There were a few settlements by the coast. The people would scamper away as soon as they saw the outline of the ship. Other settlements were nothing but burned ruins.

The forests provided more meat than we needed. All the things that Viracocha poured out in his love were ours for the taking. I let my men dally and relax. My inner feelings told me that the time for the great battle would soon come.

We sailed past a long coast of beaches with an island at the bottom. A monster-mountain on the island spewed smoke towards the Sun. We sailed through the narrow band of water between it and the mainland. My men bowed in worship to the fire-mountain. This surely signalled that the gods were ready to lead the fight.

Once past the fire-mountain we spent days in the open sea. Gudea could not keep back the many questions he had about our coming. I told him the story, from the landing of the Moon-Mother up to the present. The fat man's face turned pale as the mist. He vowed again to help in every way he could.

One day Gudea pointed out islands in the distance which were inhabited by friends of his. As we neared the largest of the islands we were approached by a mass of small oar-driven boats. They were manned by dark-skinned warriors with red-metal helmets. Their blades of shiny black stone pointed towards the hated ship of the Sons of Shem.

Gudea quickly proved his worth. He climbed one of the two poles which held the sail and shouted in a strange language. I could only recognise his name. Instantly the blades were lowered and the small ships circled around us, waving and cheering. Though my men waved back, we were all too wary to let down our guard. It was not until the leader asked to come aboard that I relaxed.

He and Gudea embraced. Gudea told the story of the battle. The leader had curly black hair and was very tall. Yet he looked on me as one would look at a god. I did not understand this respect. If the Sons of Shem were such fierce fighters then we'd have no trouble conquering the whole world. Just me and my handful of men. The thought of it made me laugh. Gudea spoke:

'Joachim invites us to spend a while at his table. He knows much about the gods and peoples of these waters, Boaz. And his women are renowned on all shores of the sea.'

'I have little need for food or women, but tell him I will gladly put up at his harbour and learn of the coming of the Serpents. As long as you stay close by to preserve our safety.'

'Of course, my friend.'

'Pica,' I shouted, 'follow the boats into their harbour.' Joachim returned to his small boat and led us into a small, protected bay. Aroona was nervous but I calmed him down.

'If they were truly enemies,' I said, 'they could have wiped us out many times by now. Didn't you see the flame-tipped arrows they were about to shoot?'

'Yes, Boaz. It is not this that I worry about. Each day the Serpent grows bigger, stretching its jaws until they will swallow the world. We are just wasting time here.'

I pulled his hair playfully. 'Come, Aroona, we may learn much from these men – and their women.'

'We have suffered greatly together, Boaz. Our tribes have suffered worse. It is good that the Jaguar and the Condor hunt together, and good times should come. But the danger is too great for good times. Many more of us will die before we return to the Sacred Lake. Let us die sooner than later.'

'You are a good man, Aroona. We will only spend the night here and leave with the morning tide. I will learn all I can and keep away from women and Star-Juice.'

At this, Aroona's stern features broke against his will and he smiled.

'I have your permission to splash you with cold water if you don't wake up?'

'But of course, you do!' I said, imitating Gudea's broad gestures. Together, we watched, the rock-anchor splashing into shallow water.

I had never seen a settlement like it. Around the small bay stood a wall higher than the length of two men. The small boats were hoisted on the islanders' shoulders and carried through a gate. Behind the gate lay huts well-built with stone walls and plank roofs. They were set in straight lines halfway up a steep hill. Between them were straight paths where a tall and handsome people went about their business.

My men and I were taken above the lines of huts where the Chief's hut stood. It was no bigger than Nima's thatched hut. Inside we saw paintings in colours we had never seen before, painted onto shiny cotton sails and on smooth flat stones. They showed men wrestling with giant horned creatures and sea-scapes with boats and fish. Other pictures showed beautiful red-haired women looking proud and inviting.

A great feast was soon set before us. Fish cooked and raw, strange plants, birds and red meat were served with nuts and fruit. Joachim poured vessels full of sweet red Star-Juice and toasted the conquerers of the mighty Sea of the Sunset. As soon as our plates were empty they were replaced by full ones. I remembered my promise to Aroona

130

and used the Star-Juice only to wash the food down my throat.

After the feast I called for Gudea and Dana. The three of us walked outside with Joachim and sat under the sea of stars. I asked what Joachim knew of the Serpents who could swallow the world.

'There are many tribes who worship the serpent,' Joachim said scowling. 'But never have I heard of such a demon as the one you describe. There are only serpents who can swim in the sea and crawl ashore on short, mud-brown legs. They are worshipped as gods of darkness.'

'We have fought this demon and slain it,' I told him. 'Although it destroyed nearly half my men it was a creature of this world – or so it appeared. It had trouble swallowing even one of my men.'

'Sacred gods!' said Joachim. 'And you say you killed such a serpent?'

'We did – with the help of the gods. After all, you are not talking to a ghost, but a man who lived to tell the tale.'

'Mighty Boaz,' Joachim gasped. 'Your name will be long remembered.'

'Then let it be remembered for our final battle. Have you seen anything that flew without wings in the skies? Anything, be it serpent or comet or child of the Moon?'

Joachim furled his face, shaped by the wind and sea into deep lines and leathery skin. 'I myself have not. But I have heard stories of such things.'

'Tell me them,' I said, 'however odd they sound.'

'There was Chonos the fisherman. A full turning of the seasons it has been since he came to me with such a tale. He was blown off course by the wind and struggled to get back to our harbour. Suddenly he saw a cloud as bright as the sun but shapeless. It wobbled like a wounded bird high overhead and landed in the direction of the great river on the southern shores. It made the noise of many musical notes, or so he said.'

Now it was my turn to scowl. I could not place the description but somewhere in the back of my mind it made more sense than just a wild vision seen in a storm. 'Can you add anything else?' I asked. 'Or any other tales?'

'Well, yes.' Joachim looked uneasily towards Gudea. 'It was three moon-changes ago. Our allies on the mainland were engaged in a fierce battle with the Sons of Shem.

131

Suddenly the sound of thunder shook the clear sky. For a second the battle stopped as all eyes turned to the fire-god Etna. But there was no smoke nor fire in that direction. Then blades pointed upward as a – how do you call it – son of the Moon roared by so quickly that half the men could not even see it. The battle started again, to the Sons of Shems' advantage. Only a few men escaped to tell the story. Whether it is true I know not. But we ourselves heard a distant thunder.'

'In which direction did it go?' I asked, greatly excited by this description of Mahala's Moon-beast.

'In the direction of Sin-Ad,' he said. Gudea's face twitched in the moon-light.

'Do you know what this means?' Gudea asked me.

'For every answer I can think of, comes three questions to take its place. I must trust in the current of magic to take me where the Serpents dwell.'

Joachim closed his eyes, as if talking to the Spirit of his tribe. 'Your ship is only half full, Boaz. Let me fill it up with my strongest warriors. It would be a mighty honour.'

'I accept,' I told him gratefully, 'for the stories you tell give both hope and added danger.'

'Then come now,' said Joachim. 'We will stop our talk of battles and forget that they exist. Come inside and drink. There will be many days of sailing to clear your head.'

We walked into the Chief's hut and ate juicy green fruit still on the vine, both purple and green. I noticed that Aroona had forgotten his solemness as he stroked a woman with a deep-throated laugh. Her slim waist and full breasts danced under the Jaguar Chief's smoothing hands. Pica also had found more warmth in a red-haired woman than the creaking planks of the ship. My man-spear stayed sheathed in Dana throughout the night.

And in the morning it was Aroona who got the cold water awakening.

FOURTEEN

Two hands of tall warriors followed my men to the wooden craft. Joachim blessed them and us when we hoisted sail and rowed speedily away. The men were cheerful and relaxed as they tested each other in games of strength. The tall ones flexed their rippling muscles and rowed with more power, but my men rowed faster. Thus the strength was equal. In all other contests the same results were shown. I could not help but think that they would have slaughtered us in battle.

Smaller islands passed by. Rugged mountains gathered together along the mainland. Small figures dressed in furs saw us and scrambled into rocky crags and gulleys. Gradually, the magic river swung us out into the middle of the sea. A sudden squall tossed our craft like an old man mating with a strong woman. The planks shuddered and groaned in the short, fast rollers. Our reed boat would hardly have noticed the same waves that now made many men sick. Joachim's men were well used to it and laughed at our struggles. Lightning flashed amongst the darkening clouds.

Gudea grew more and more restless as we neared the shores of his homeland. The storm was not a good omen for him. He feared for his people. I told him that if the magic current stopped on his shores, then we would follow him ashore. If not, he would land alone and wait to hear from me.

As we pulled into a harbour of Sin-Ad I told him that our Moon-Gods might be somewhere in his land:

'Why they came here I don't know. But the current of magic pulls us southward – perhaps into the great southern river. Wherever it takes us we must follow.'

A narrow boat was coming for Gudea. The black-bearded oarsmen looked cautiously at the strange mixture of men in the enemy ship. Gudea took a necklace he was wearing and placed it around my neck. From it hung a cloudy blue jewel.

'Take this token of my devotion, Boaz the World Conquerer,' he said, his voice choked with feeling. 'It is not the prettiest of stones but the most useful. Even now, in the midst of a storm it will find the position of the sun.' He pointed it back and forth toward the grey sky until it caught fire and turned clear. 'There – it can save you when the magic current stops. No greater gift have the gods ever given to man. No humbler gift could I give you.' We hugged each other tight, his beard tickling my hairless face. He swung down a rope ladder saying, 'I'll wait for your word. Good health, my friend.'

'May you live as long as the sea.' I said.

The magic current pulled us away the moment the anchor left bottom. Blood-pumps of all my men beat faster as we sped fast as the wind. Waves died down but the clouds hung overhead. Ahead of us the land made a broad turn to the southerly shores. Now the sandy beaches seemed to flow forever back. There were fewer forests and signs of green. Only later did we see marshes and reeds – much like some parts of the Sacred Lake. Strong streams cut off slices of green from each other. The waves of the salt sea devoured the streams. No sign of man could be seen beyond the low, flowering banks and tall reeds. We were going so fast there was no need for the sail.

'Who knows this land?' I asked among the tall islanders. It was only then that I slapped my head in disgust. Gudea was the only one who knew their language. Dana asked the question in the language of the Sons of Shem. A broad-shouldered warrior stepped forward and spoke.

Dana listened and then repeated his words for us to understand: 'There are many branches of the great river, he says. They all lead to Giza, the largest settlement.'

'Can we turn into any of the small rivers?' I asked.

'No – not in this boat. He says he will show you where to turn – if the current of magic allows.'

The man shone his smile at me. Pica shouted from the steering oars:

'Boaz, there is a change. The current is loosening its grasp.'

We had been sailing alongside a wide bank of grassy land. As we rounded the bend the islander, whose name was Priam, raised his shiny-black blade with a massive arm and pointed. Into our view came a small body of water – only slightly larger than the others.

'Hoist the sail, Pica. Turn in here. Men, pray to the Moon-Gods – and to Viracocha. This is the greatest fight of all our lives . . .'

The oarsmen silently strained as Pica steered the timber ship through a narrow channel and into a fresh-water lake. The sail caught a strong wind and our eyes watched for the unknown enemy. Tall walls of reeds surrounded us as the ocean waves faded into the distance. The islander's blade pointed starboard where a white-frothed river churned into the lake.

Fast flying sea-birds cawed their warnings overhead. Carrion birds like Condors circled high above them. Could they

134

see Serpents creeping up to strike? Strong winds scattered the grey clouds as we entered the thickly flowing river. Even with all oars manned and the sail drawing full we moved very slowly. The magic current had vanished. The saviours of the world were on their own now in the land of the Serpents.

There were demons in our path: fierce scaly logs that broke oars with their savage teeth. They were the same as those in the River of Giants yet still more vicious. Mighty challenges roared from huge open mouths. Were these the Serpents or their creatures? Xinu's poison dart caught one in its maw. A few seconds later the beast was dead. No divine battle could be so easy.

We worked up our War-Glory by killing the sharp-toothed monsters, watching them twist and squirm on the ends of our spears. Their death-agonies made the river boil with blood and snapping jaws.

Soon we came to signs of man. . . . Nets left in haste, straw huts abandoned. If their owners saw us, we did not see them.

The reed island soon came to an end. We found ourselves in a river valley, green as the playlands of the gods. Plants sprang up alongside the banks. They grew too evenly for chance. Small white tufts rose from their tops. Perhaps these were the cotton plants of which we had heard.

Our boat hit a sandbank and lodged firm. The greatest muscles, the strongest curses could not set it free. On the land were a group of people coloured like the desert sands. They did not offer to help. Instead they ran off upstream. I ordered my men to destroy their camp. We trampled the fields of cotton and tore down their huts. There were many kinds of huts to tear down — rounded reed huts, the chief's hut built like a box, and a wooden altar hut enclosed by a fence. Inside, on the altar, above a basket of mud, was a series of golden circles that fitted into one another. Surrounding these circles were single lines curving inwards — the Serpent coiled and poised to strike.

We smashed the altar and waited to feel the Serpent's bite.

In the distance rose clouds of dust. It might have been a sandstorm but the sky was blue and the wind had dropped.

135

The clouds grew closer. Hands clutched weapons as my warriors and I ran up a rising slope of grassland. Only birds were flying in the deep blue sky. The Sun throbbed mightily overhead.

Then on the furthest edge of sight we saw things which could not be named: 'Monsters with moving wheels,' 'Land ships pulled by swift beasts,' 'The Serpents themselves,' were each whispered as the unknown visions thundered closer. A pack of them drew up in line a bow-shot away. Then three charged towards us. As the roar of the hurtling wheels and the beasts' hooves grew in our ears we started the War-Glory chant. At last – after losing so many of our friends and brothers! The Sun leapt on the metal of the strange thundering crafts. As they came closer we could see they were driven by men. Their faces were narrow and smooth, their hair dark and wavy. And they dared to smile!

It was the smiling which set off a moan of fright amongst my men. When the roaring beasts were almost on us, their leader extended an arm and raised it high. I knew not what weapon he was about to hurl. I ordered Pica to let loose a poisoned dart. The sand-skinned one let out a roar and fell backwards. His land-craft thundered into our midst.

A volley of arrows met the other two demons. One swung around and crouched low as he sheltered from flying death. The other, filled with arrows, lashed the beasts that carried his craft. It piled into our ranks, killing an Islander. The beasts kept running. They did not stop until they fell in the river and disappeared, a feast for the stomachs of the hungry river creatures.

We ran towards the two bodies. 'They have no weapons,' said Aroona.

'The Serpents sent them forward to test our power,' I said, unsure of my words.

'It looked to me as if their hands were raised in greeting,' said Dana.

I was angered by the possible truth in her words. I dismissed them from my mind;

'Look how the third demon races back to tell the enemy,' I said. 'I want guards watching in all directions. They could attack by river or over land.' Raising my voice I shouted: 'The first attack of the Serpents has been lost by them. It is as the gods will!' My men cheered at this. The Islanders, saddened by the loss of a man, buried him with a long ritual. Afterwards they kept silent and tense.

We tried again to move the ship from the sand bank. As we gave a mighty heave a loud crack was heard. The timber craft had not been made for the river and the bottom quickly filled with water. We unloaded our weapons and supplies. Nervously, I fingered the sun-stone Gudea had given me. Xinu and Pica tried to ease the tension by playing music together. I wished we had not destroyed the fishing village. Now there was no relief from the choking sun. And no relief from many unanswered questions. The islanders returned to the boat to try and repair the broken planks.

The line of land boats did not move. Nor did any more enemies appear to test our power. To show them our magic, we mounted the blackened, puffed-up corpse of Pica's victim onto his wheeled land-craft. Then I smacked the rump of its beast and it ran back across the grass lands between us and the enemy.

I called for Priam the Islander; 'What do you know about these people?' I asked him through Dana.

'They are fishers and planters,' he said. 'Not as advanced as the rest of the sea-peoples. Further up the river the tribes grow more savage. They make many raids into this land. For years the desert has been creeping closer to the river. Once there was no desert. The tribes are well used to fighting for the green land.'

'But how did simple people learn to make wheels and land-craft?' I asked.

Priam shrugged his shoulders, 'It can only be from the gods,' he said. 'Never have I seen such things before. But I have heard tell of them by one or two drunken seamen. They are called chariots, and are used mainly for war.'

For the first time since I had severed Nima's head, I began to feel uneasy as the Chief of chiefs. Here I was, surrounded by my loyal fighters in a strange land filled with deadly enemies. Perhaps those land-craft *had* come in welcome – but what could that mean? That the sandy-skinned ones had already defeated the Serpents? That they wanted us to join in the fight against them? We were a mere ship-load of men. Out there was a line of enemy that stretched halfway across our line of sight.

And if they weren't our enemies before – they surely were now.

We watched as a small number of land-craft crept

137

forward. They halted halfway between the two lines of warriors. My men were murmuring amongst themselves things I could not hear. The Sun began to set.

A thundering shook the air. Hands reached for their weapons.

But the enemy was not charging. Pica looked upward and screamed with joy—

'The Moon-Gods! They're back!'

It could have been the Moon itself. But it was brighter than the Moon. And the Moon does not swoop down and circle overhead. Nor does it put forth the sound of many thunderstorms. The gods had returned. The fiery Moon-beast settled down, flattening cotton plants.

The islanders had turned pale with fright. But when the metal tongue folded to the ground, their terror was complete. Some sank to their knees, some broke into a run. I yelled to Dana to tell them they were *our* gods. She had fainted.

The islanders stopped their trembling when they saw me calmly approach the Moon-beast. They watched dumbly as I stood before the metal steps, hesitated for a second, and then bound inside like a puma into a cave.

FIFTEEN

They were all there. All the ones I knew best. Askar was the only one who smiled, yet he said nothing. Mahala, the giant, loomed above me, arms crossed over his massive chest. His look was one of anger, of surprise, of menace. He too said nothing. Oraan was watching me carefully. Then his stone face shaped into a smile. He stepped forward and motioned to a sitting pad.

'Well done, Huanac,' he said as all sat except for Mahala. The giant turned his back to us and busied himself with the board of metal stones and sticks.

It was strange that Oraan had called me only Huanac. Was I no longer Chief to him, nor even the man called Boaz? I looked at him, meeting his cold smile with a few solemn words:

'We have done your bidding, great ones. Much blood has

138

been spilled. Many friends have we lost. But all is well, as Askar said it would be. I await your orders to attack.'

'All in good time,' said Oraan.

Askar interrupted the silence that followed: 'We've been watching your deeds with wonder, Boaz. The tribes of your homeland know of your bravery.'

'Have the Serpents attacked there since we've been gone?' I asked.

'No,' said Oraan. 'Nor will they ever again after this battle. As Askar said, your battles so far have been watched by us with surprise. We did not expect that you and your warriors would get this far.'

'That is what some of my men suspected. Why, then, did you send us on such a fatal journey?'

Oraan held up his pale white hand against my rising anger. 'All will be explained to you. But you *did* make it, and you now fit well into the Great Plan.'

Mahala turned and faced me, 'There will be a battle, the likes of which few worlds have ever seen. Sett has given the order. You will start the battle. We will finish it.'

'Let's take him up, Mahala,' spoke Oraan. The metal steps folded back into the wall of the shiny cave. The sound of muted thunder overcame all other noises. I was pressed into my seat as if a great hand was pushing me down.

I looked out through the clear ice, as I had long before. Instead of seeing the Sacred Lake and a frightened tribe I now saw my men waving, as small as ants below me. The great river valley stood out as a green ribbon in a golden desert of sand. The boat was like a rat drowning in a stream.

Then we flew high across the battlefield. The forward guard looked as a mouse looks to a hawk. But behind it many more mice were gathering. I saw a camp of many chariots, and armies of ants marching forward to join the camp.

'Tiki!' I said. 'How can even the Moon-Gods conquer such an army?'

Mahala laughed in a savage way.

'These are just the slaves of the Serpents,' said Oraan, 'We will show you where their masters dwell. Mahala, head for Geda.'

The mighty Moon-beast tilted and changed course. We followed the river, itself looking like a shiny winding serpent.

I likened myself to an old man who has seen all the

139

wonders and miracles that gods and man can make. This time when I had lifted off the ground in the Moon-beast, it was as a toughened warrior, not a wide-eyed savage.

Yet when I saw the dwelling place of the Serpents, I had to close my eyes and open them many times over. Each time my eyes showed me the same thing. Each time I became more and more amazed. Finally I could not pretend that I was in a dream. The smiles had disappeared from the Moon-Gods. Even Mahala now looked at the marvel with almost fearful eyes.

It was a mountain where there were no other mountains. Though its base was broad, its sides slanted inwards and upwards to form a sharp point high in the air. It was shaped like the fin of the grey sea-monsters. Or like an arrowhead carved of golden blocks of stone. It was the deadly fang of the Serpents, pointing up from the sands like a perfect volcano about to spew its deadly venom. Or had it already done so?

The ship began to shudder, like the wooden craft in a storm. Askar ran over to sit before an altar of shaking buttons and waving splinters. The steady thunder of the ship began to break up. The air itself suddenly grew hot. Since I was not in command, I allowed myself a frightened yell.

The Moon-beast swerved away until the temple was replaced by the sky. As we flew from the wondrous mountain the thunder became smooth, and so did the flight. Gradually the air grew cooler, along with my senses.

Askar spoke with hope in his voice; 'It's getting weaker. We were almost within range that time.'

'Their power is giving out,' said Oraan, watching the altar where flashing red brightness died and the splinters again pointed straight.

'So is the power of Brave Boaz,' said Mahala with a mocking voice.

'I am not afraid of what I know,' I said, 'only of what I don't know. Perhaps you could tell me more.'

'What do you want to know?' asked Oraan, also with a hint of mockery.

'How you are going to finish the battle.'

'With this,' said the god, his hand fondling a piece of the altar. He pushed his thumb in a groove and removed a piece of the altar. Beneath it was a button, no bigger or smaller than the others.

140

'Oraan,' I said, beginning to lose my patience, 'I did not ask my question in jest. 'You will finish the battle with that button?'

'Yes, Boaz, with this. And with this,' he said. As he replaced the cover he pressed another button. A part of the floor disappeared and the roar of thunder was deafening. He gestured towards a shiny metal box, pointed at one end and with small metal wings at the other. Below was the shiny river.

I looked at it carefully, but I could not catch its meaning. Such a small box against an army of as many men as stars in the sky?

Oraan pressed the button again and the floor slid back into place.

'Is it a weapon?' I asked.

'That is *the* weapon,' said Oraan. 'That is the God of All Power. With it we will melt the flesh of the Serpents. With it we shall make their mighty mountain into slingstones.'

'Then this is the God who devoured the Sacred Rock at the island temple,' I said, trying hard to figure it out.

'Yes,' said Askar, 'and without the help of your noble tribe and the tribes who followed you, this weapon could not have been made.'

'After the battle,' said Oraan, 'after the final battle, then earthmen will be set free. Many more of our ships will come from our part of the heavens.'

'What for – if earthmen shall be free?'

'Many will freely want to work with us – for we will bring gifts of such pleasures that men cannot imagine,' said Oraan. I noticed that we were flying over the battlefield without stopping to land. Within seconds we were over the white-peaked sea. 'We will take you back to our base,' Oraan continued. We have been waiting in the settlement of Sat-Am until the time was right to let loose the God of All Power. The great Mother-ship still rests by the shores of your sacred lake. For the God of All Power is used not only for war. On our victorious return, the Power will be used to repair and fuel the Mother-ship. Meanwhile we wait at Sat-Am for the power of the Serpent to die. This it is already doing. The magic of the Serpents gets weaker by the hour. Soon we will be able to fly over the Serpent's fang and drop the weapon on its very point. We will

141

destroy their mother-ship once and for all. It will melt the Serpents and their slaves to their bones.'

'What?' I said. 'The Serpents have a mother-ship like the Moon-Gods? Are they then man-shaped, like the Moon-Gods?'

Mahala burst out in a raging laughter. 'Poor savage,' he said to Oraan, 'you spoke too much and too fast for him. You've got him so confused he'll run in terror from an earthworm.'

'I do not run in terror from you, dead giant,' I said standing up and taking a step towards him. He lashed out to hit me but I caught his great wrist. We struggled for many blood-pumps until Askar stepped between us. Mahala pushed him aside and he fell against the altar.

'Both of you – stop!' Oraan was pointing the weapon of the red tongue at us. Mahala turned slowly and sat at the altar. I went to Askar and helped him up.

Oraan put aside his weapon. 'I think now we'll take you back to your warriors. Mahala, would you please?'

The ship turned sharply. I helped the wounded god to a seat. Askar smiled at me. He fumbled for an ointment which he asked me to apply to the wound. I did so silently. The nameless gods in the background looked on, stone-faced. Oraan sat turning white leaves and looking as if nothing had happened.

Soon came the mouth of the river and the green islands of marsh and reed. The ship landed in the same cotton field and the metal tongue swiftly unfolded. Oraan stood up.

'You will wait outside, Huanac,' he said. 'I will meet with you and Aroona shortly.'

As I walked to the steps I looked back. Oraan was standing by Mahala, who towered above him. The two were speaking fiercely in Moon-Tongue at each other. Mahala's face was red with rage. I saw Oraan strike the giant. Askar motioned me to quickly leave.

Once my feet set back on ground the stairs folded back. But the ship did not move. I put on a smile to greet the anxious looks of my men. My thoughts were in confusion. I called for Aroona.

'I know you, my friend,' he said as we walked toward the river, 'enough to see that your smile is false.'

'It is both real and false,' I said as we sat by a great rock and dangled our feet in the water. 'Look at the beasts on that rock,' I pointed to a number of carvings of strange animals. One had a neck that stretched three times higher than his body. 'Look. There are men trying to throw a rope around its neck. But we do not know if the animal escaped or was slaughtered.' Aroona spent more time studying my face than the carvings:

'Tell me, Boaz, what will happen to us? Will we escape or be slaughtered?'

'There are many, many warriors waiting for the next move,' I said, 'and the Serpents have built a mighty fortress where they hide their mother-craft.'

'Then the Moon-Gods have been playing with us – as I thought.'

'No, no, they have been helping us. I saw a weapon that looks like a great shiny box. They say it will finish the battle for ever.'

'Words like that should make me happy. But they do not.'

'We are like that long-necked animal,' I said. 'Strange creatures in a hostile land. The rope is ready to be thrown. But our very strangeness may help us to win.'

We heard steps crunching the powdery stone behind us. Oraan motioned for us to stay seated.

'Greetings, great Chiefs of the Sacred Lake,' he said with his voice now full of respect.

Aroona started to say something but my hand stilled him. The Chief of chiefs answered with dignity:

'Greetings, Moon-God. Have you had your meeting?'

'Yes, Boaz. In the times when the battle is over, you and Mahala will have much to laugh over. I told you before that the giant loses patience because we must wait to drop the weapon. He says . . . he is sorry for the ill-feeling between the two of you.'

'Then I, too, am sorry,' I said, watching Aroona's eyebrows raised at these untrue words. 'When will the weapon be dropped?' I asked.

'In a matter of days, Boaz. But the fighting will begin to-morrow, before dawn.'

'Eeee-eee! But how can we fight without the God of All Power?'

'How soon you forget the mighty battles you have fought and won without the final weapon,' said Oraan in rebuke. 'But we have helped you this far, and you can sleep tonight knowing the battle will be won tomorrow.'

'For every one of us there is a boatload of them,' snorted Aroona. 'How can we sleep well knowing that?'

'Under our protection, you need not worry. Have you both forgotten the red tongue of death?'

'Never!' sighed Aroona, for the first time relieved and eager to believe.

'Did you think you would be thrown into battle without the help of the gods? And have you forgotten your own sacred substance from the high plains?' Oraan tossed a pouch to the ground. It spilled open and coca leaves scattered amongst the rocks.

'Blessed be the gods,' said Aroona, stuffing the loose leaves back into the pouch. Oraan looked down on us, his smile feeding our sudden hope.

'You are the gods' children,' he said, 'and after the battle you may take your place amongst us. After the God of All Power smites the Serpents you will fly with us to the furthest reaches of the heavens. Whole worlds will be yours, new battles fought for pleasure. Women of every colour imaginable will be yours for the taking.'

'Get up, Children,' he said, 'and think – by tomorrow this river will flow red with the poisonous blood of the slaves. The more men you kill, the less the Serpents' magic powers will be. After the Power-God is dropped, you will fly with us to Sat-Am and have your pleasure with the women and boys. Then we will fly those who wish back to their families by the Sacred Lake. Any who wish to go elsewhere will be free to travel as gods amongst the savages of this planet.'

'Was it so with you, Oraan?' I asked.

'It was so with my distant ancestors,' he said. 'But go now and strengthen yourselves in the power of the leaves. I have also left jugs of Star-Juice with your warriors. Tomorrow we shall help you roast the flesh of our enemies.'

The Moon-God walked back to his ship as Aroona and I stuffed our mouths with the ancient power from the high-mountain leaves. Then we fell to laughing and wrestling as brothers by the shore of the river. The Moon-beast lifted off crackling thunder and spitting fire.

Aroona and I were soon surrounded by warriors. We passed out the leaves. Pica held out Star-Juice for us. We danced and laughed and playfully clashed blades with each other. The islanders and Xinu had never before chewed the

144

sacred leaves. Xinu suddenly thought himself the bravest of us all. To prove it he swam to the middle of the river with a blade between his teeth. There he struggled with a giant scaley beast. He was just able to drag the carcass ashore before the river was full of teeth snapping at his feet. The beast he killed was twice as big as the son of the jungle Chief. When he saw what he had truly done he praised us, the gods and the leaves, and fainted dead away.

We skinned the beast. Its meat provided many with full bellies. And Pica sang a song to the jungle man while Xinu awoke, reached for the Star-Juice and was hailed as a hero.

The women passed themselves around during the night, moving from warrior to warrior. The Islanders mostly kept their thoughts and the Star-Juice to themselves. The rest of us enjoyed the final night before battle, for we were at the end of our quest. Those who had stayed alive thus far were grateful to our totems, to the Moon-Gods, and to each other. If Xinu could survive in a river of thrashing death, the men of the Moon-Gods could conquer all the enemies of the world.

Only the Islanders slept at all. The rest of us had our cheeks puffed with coca for the first time since the River of Giants. So we felt the full effect of the sacred substance. The Lake tribes danced the ancient rites of War-Glory. As the fire cast strange shadows on our flexing bodies we fell into wild trances. In visions we saw the enemy crushed like ants beneath a stampede of llamas. There was much sacred power released in our shouts and invocations. Had the enemy heard us, the fear of our strength would have run shivers through their ranks.

I gathered my warriors together in the hours before dawn. The Moon was thin and gave no more light than the stars. Silent and confident, we armed ourselves and advanced. The women insisted on coming with us, rather than waiting helplessly behind. They trailed after us, their pale skin smeared with mud. They were armed with short bows and arrows, which Xinu had spent long hours teaching them to use.

The campfires of the forward post had burned into cinders. In their glow we saw the sleeping warriors of the enemy with only one guard half-awake. We crept forward on our bellies, as silently as the night changes into day.

I looked for the Moon-beast but it was not yet above us.

Had I not chewed on the coca all night I might have been more cautious and waited longer. But then I thought that the Moon-beast's thunder would quickly alert the enemy – so I knew once again that all was well. I motioned to Xinu, who dipped a dart in his black oil. He put his blow-pipe to his lips and his cheeks puffed out. The guard clutched at his throat and died before he could scream.

The beasts attached to the land-crafts grew nervous and started to beat their hoofs. Moon-beast or no Moon-beast, the time to attack could only be now.

At my signal we waded into the sleeping ranks of war-riors. In a fury of war screams our blades severed heads like oars cutting through water.

But there were more men on the forward post than I had expected. As we carved our way through the enemy more of them rose before us to take up the fight. The darkness was splintered by sparks from clashing blades. In the dis-tance, fires sprang to life – the alarm was given!

As the sky turned from black to grey the sound of many beasts rumbled towards us. But the coca and the promises of the gods fired our courage. The forward post was des-troyed, just as in our War-Glory visions of the night before.

I ordered my men to regroup and face the enemy falling upon us like an avalanche. We swung round the captured chariots of the forward post to face the attack and released the frenzied beasts which drew them.

The first line of enemy collided head-on with their own riderless chariots. We quickly slew the fallen men. Then we looked up to face an army of warriors charging us on foot.

Their faces were gentle but their weaponry was fierce. They slowed our advance and tried to circle around us. The women did well in checking this. Behind the foot-soldiers came another line of chariots. Arrows rained from both sides while sling-stones and blades split the enemy's skulls to their breast-bones.

Then the Serpents appeared.

They hovered above us, larger than our thoughts could grasp. Their black writhing filled the sky, blotting out the pure sun and turning day back into night.

These were the Sky-Devils we had journeyed so far to destroy, the monsters we had steeled our hearts to face. Yet still we froze with dread.

Their ghastly tongue-flickering faces leered down at us

146

from the thrashing sky, their hungry eyes red as setting suns. They were more terrifying than even our nightmares had imagined, more hideous than all the monsters of land and sea together.

The sight of them tore our breath moaning from our lips. Howls of fear rushed through our ranks like a fierce wind amongst winter peaks. The enemy echoed our fear, so dreadful were their Devil-gods to behold. Yet still they poured towards us, in numbers as many as leaves in a forest.

Only their faith in the gods held my warriors to the attack. They knew the gods were coming and with them the mighty God of All Power that was to destroy the Serpents. If it were not for this knowledge, they might have turned and fled screaming at first sight of the slimy nightmares that fouled the sky.

And I with them.

For only once before in my life had I ever felt such fear as that which gripped me now. Suddenly it was as if I was again a child, a small helpless boy trapped in the tightening coils of a monster python. Only this time there was no Snake-Killer to come and rescue me. I stood frozen, helpless as that child, my chest crushed by pounding fear.

So far the Serpents had not attacked. They hovered above the battlefield like gloating spectres laughing at the dead. I saw one of them, greater than all the rest, thrust down its head towards warriors clashing steel. Its fanged mouth seemed to clamp on dying men as if quenching its thirst on the blood of war. Venom dripped from its fangs. Those it touched screamed and fell blinded, clawing at the sand in agony as the poison ate into their brains.

All around me my warriors were fighting hard and brave. Wave after wave of the enemy threw itself upon us. The Warriors of the Sacred Lake and their friends of the Island held firm as a rock, and like a rock smashed every rushing wave. As great a battle as was fought around me, I fought inside myself. My mind waged war against the fear that held my body like strong ropes. I saw enemy warriors charging towards me and still I could not move. My war-club hung at my side, held by fingers numb with terror. I could not raise it even to save my life. Seeing me caught in some spell of the Serpents, Aroona leapt past me, placing himself between me and the attacking warriors. His

147

blade whistled a song of death and heads rolled in the reddening dust.

A cry of joy sang out from Pica's lips, a cry taken up by all my men when they too looked up into the sky. For the gods had kept their promise!

It was the Moon-beast bringing the God of All Power. The ship of the gods should have shone bright with victory. Yet never had it seemed so pale. Its light was as dim as a clouded moon as it struggled to break through the lashing coils of the giant Serpents. A few more moments and their tails would be lashing their death-agonies . . .

I wanted to add my cry of joy to those of my men. But even at the point of victory my tongue was as frozen as my limbs. I saw one of the sandy-skinned warriors moving straight towards me, grinning as he raised his spear to spill my blood upon the sand. Aroona was occupied with three other warriors and all my other men nearby had battles of their own. The warrior moved closer, confident of his kill. I could not raise my weapon. The power of the Serpent-fear still held me in its grip. I prayed silently to the gods to let me live long enough to see the Serpents slain.

Again I looked into the sky. I wanted to see the God of All Power scorch Serpent-flesh to ashes. Instead, the Moon-beast grew still more pale. It shivered as does a cloud-image upon a lake trembled by the wind. . . . Then it was gone. And with it our lives.

The cries of joy of my warriors became wails of despair.

Then the Serpents struck.

The greatest of them thrust downwards, tongue flicking over us. And its tongue was as deadly as the red tongue of the Moon-beast. The screams of the dying mingled with the sizzling of charred flesh. The tongue hissed through our ranks, men flaring into torches at its touch.

Anger swelled within me. Anger so great it snapped the bonds of fear that held my body trapped. I threw back my head and screamed my fury – my fury at the Serpents and at our traitor gods. Gods who had promised us heaven and left us to die in burning Hell.

A brightness flashed towards me. My war-club rose, smashing through the spear aimed at my heart. It rose and when it fell it smashed through the skull of the enemy who held the splintered spear. Behind him came more of his fellows, anxious to test the strength of my fury. A savage

148

cry bellowed from my throat I fell upon them with the rage of a maddened bear. My club snapped aside their weapons, hacked strong men to the ground. The last of them did not even dare fight back so fierce was my attack. They shrank to the ground, throwing up their arms for mercy. My club broke their arms and then their heads. Within ten breaths I was alone at the centre of a circle of broken bodies. Then I looked up to see with my eyes the horrors my ears already warned me of.

The Serpents' tongues had cut our army to burnt shreds of meat. Men ran past screaming, their hair and clothes aflame. Those of my men that still had legs to run wheeled and fled, their faces full of terror and despair. I looked quickly round for Aroona. Where I had last seen him there was nothing left but smoking death.

Then I saw the Serpents were not satisfied with our blood alone. We were but a small meal to them and they hungered for a feast. So great was their hunger that they fell upon their own slaves. The red tongue of death swept over the charging chariots of the enemy, turning beasts, craft and riders into one great mass of smoke and living flame. The Serpents were merciless. Nothing escaped their hunger. I saw hundreds of men devoured at a time. The enemy became a great pyre of flames, a burnt offering in honour of their terrible masters. Smoke rose in greasy clouds to further blacken the Serpent sky.

I had no sympathy for the enemy nor time to stand and watch them destroyed. I ran. And as I ran I saw the great Serpent with the tongue of fire streaking after me. I weaved amongst the smoking piles of dead to escape its fiery touch. I collided with another warrior running as fast as I, an enemy crazed with fear. My club released him from his fear. I wished he could have done the same for me for the Serpent was almost upon me, its hideous head filling the sky. Again I ran, blinded with pain and sweat from the heat. Too late I saw the burning chariot hurtling towards me, its galloping beasts wild with terror. I could not turn back – the Serpent's tongue was crackling nearer. I threw myself into the path of the chariot of fire and prayed that death be quick.

A roaring in my ears and I was seized in a burning fist of pain. Red scorching pain. I heard a scream that could have been my own. I smelt the burning flesh of men.

The fist clenched tighter, the pain burnt deeper. Too deep to bear.

Redness became blackness.

Then emptiness.

Again, I joined the Spirits of the dead.

SIXTEEN

Silence roared in the land of Spirits. The emptiness of death surrounded me. The last screams had long since died. The Chief of chiefs would wander until the last star faded, searching for his ancestors. Searching for the open arms of Snake-Killer. Searching out forgiveness from all the spirits he had misled.

This blackness – this blackness has a body. Inside the belly of the Serpent this blackness has thoughts.

But I had been here once before. In the blackness of death, yet somehow in the world of the living. Then my eyes had opened to a shiny cave and the metal spider webs piercing my body and brain.

But that time was long past.

Thoughts echoed through the black silence without beginning – without end. Aroona, Pica, Xina, Dana – forgive me, my friends, my fellow spirits. . . . Forgive me, ripe earth, for we have all been swallowed. The Moon is no more. We are empty spirits now, with no children to guide or bless. The Earth lies deep in the bowels of the Serpent. There is no one left to die.

The darkness opened to let in a shaft of hazy light. Not the shiny cave, but a room of sand-coloured stone – a burial chamber too small for eternity.

A low moan filled the empty room. A sharp throb of awaking pain. . . . Then as in a miracle – legs, arms, trunk and beating heart – all could be felt. All were mine.

Boaz lived.

To die another day.

My eyes slowly crept around the room. It was large and box-shaped. I lay upon a bed of skins.

Was I saved by the Moon-Gods and flown to Sat-Am? If so, the buildings of that town were built to last. There were

150

no windows, no other openings except a stairway in one corner leading upwards. Jewels on the walls shone with a dim green light. If this was Sat-Am then where were the women and boys? Where were the rest of my warriors?

I felt for my war-club but it was not there. I swung to my feet. The dizziness made me sick. I staggered around the room, looking for signs to tell me where I was. And how to get out.

I made a dash for the stairs, but the pounding in my head was too harsh. I rolled back down the stairs I had bounded. My neck was hot and sticky. Blood trickled from my wounds.

'Who keeps me here?' I called. 'If it's the Moon-Gods, tell my why you deserted us. . . . And if it's the Serpents – come finish me now!'

'Be still, Boaz,' The voice, low and soothing, came from everywhere at once. 'There are many strange things which must be told to you. Lie back and rest. Let your eyes answer many of your deepest questions.'

This was not the voice nor manner of the Moon-Gods. Then I knew without a doubt where I was – inside the man-mountain of the Serpents!

'Come, let the Serpents strike!' I challenged. 'I have been warned of your magic by the gods from the great Mother Moon.'

'Lie down, Boaz. There are riddles to be solved and mysteries to be explained. Only a calm mind can judge what is truth and what is false.'

My hands became fists as I struggled against the voice. But its magic was impossible to fight. There was no reason to obey the words, but obey them I did. I fell back on the skins. My terror and urge for the enemy's blood were somehow stilled for the moment. My body relaxed but my mind was racing. I judged the size of the stairway – too small to admit the Sky-Serpents that hovered above the battle-field. I grinned, knowing I would take down a hand of their wavy-haired slaves before they took my life.

When I awoke in the shiny cave of the Moon-Gods, the light had slowly faded. And so it did now. From a tiny hole behind me came a new beam of light. Suddenly the room filled with visions. As with the soothing voice, the visions were all around me. I was enclosed by them as dreams enclose a dreamer.

And, as in dreams, most of what I saw and heard was already known to me. Familiar yet strangely different.

First came the battle in the sky I had seen as Boaz the hunter. This time I did not feel the fear of that night. I was able to watch calmly. I saw two mother-craft in deadly battle. One of them was the great Moon-Child. The other was a brilliant white form throbbing with Sun-like rays.

'Is this not the sight you saw that night while hunting in the mountains?' the low voice asked, 'that night that the heavens raged above you. It was then that those you call the Moon-Gods attacked us as we studied your world for signs of life. The Moon-Gods are known to us as Sethians, and like us come from planets of distant stars. They are not gods, neither are we Serpents. Nor is it even the other way around. They are of the race of man, and their planet is in the constellation of Orion. We are of the same race as Earthmen and Sethians. Our homeland is a planet of the Dog-Star, Sirius. Think on these words, and watch.'

The two giant craft darted back and forth in this battle to the death. The familiar red-tongue from the Moon-Gods lashed out repeatedly towards the other craft, but was repelled by the great throbbing brightness. The Sun-like craft moved more swiftly, as if made of lightning, but the Moon-Ship chased after it like a hawk after a sparrow.

Then I saw a spinning cloud form itself from the white rays of the Serpent ship. Like a whirlpool it spun around the Moon-Craft. The white globe began to shake and grew fiery red. Then the Moon-craft shook loose from the whirling cloud and darted close to the other, Sun-like ship. Red shafts struck the Serpent ship, piercing through the rays. Fire began to drip from the Moon-ship and a loud explosion shook the heavens and Earth.

Both ships were damaged. They veered away from each other, the white cloud spinning back to its mother-ship. They fell away towards the earth below. The Moon-ship was spilling its fire as it plunged towards the Sacred Lake. The Sun-like form shot away over the mountains and oceans. I watched it land beside a great river. There was something familiar about the place where it settled down, rolling back clouds of swirling sand. Then I knew it was the same place where stood the great pointed man-mountain of the Serpents. How I knew this I knew not for there was no man-mountain in the vision. Nor were there fertile fields beside the river as I had seen from the Moon-beast. There were only sun-baked dunes sweeping into the distance, empty of life.

The vision faded and was gone.

'You see, Boaz,' said the Voice, 'we are not Serpents but men such as yourself and the Sethians . . . forced to land on your world when the Sethians crippled our mother-craft.'

'I see nothing!' I cried pointing to where the vision had been. 'It was all magic. Do you expect me to believe your lies when I saw your slimey shapes in the sky, saw them slaughtering my men all around me?'

'Did you, Boaz?' the Voice calmly asked. 'Now look again.'

I looked. Another vision took form. Anger swelled hot within me for the vision showed my men being burnt alive by the Serpent's flickering tongue. Yet there were no Serpents in the sky. Only Mahala's Moon-beast hovering above the battle, its tongue of flame bringing hideous death to warriors of both sides.

'What trickery is this?' I demanded.

'Sethian trickery,' the Voice firmly answered. 'A trick to make you see Serpents where there are none. And to turn aside blame from its rightful place . . . Did you not think it strange that only one Serpent had the tongue of death? Did you not see with your own eyes for a moment the Moon-beast as it hid behind the empty shadows of Serpents?'

The words struck me like Xinu's darts. It was true. I had seen the Moon-beast as it hung over the battle-field, its face pale and clouded.

'It cannot be!' I cried as the vision faded.

'It is the truth, Boaz,' said the Voice, now behind me, fearfully close.

I spun round prepared to fight, prepared to face any kind of demon. But I was not prepared for what I found – an old man, small and silver-haired. I could have broken him across my knee like a stick and yet I hesitated. It was his eyes that held my hand and pushed back my anger. They were not cruel like Mahala's. They were not cold like Oraan's nor full of doubts like those of Askar. Instead they were gentle as a mother's and full of sadness and wisdom. They spoke of a different world, of ways I did not know. Yet I know better than to trust what my eyes saw as true.

'This is another trick,' I growled.

The old Sky-devil smiled.

'Do you still think me a Serpent?'

He stretched his open hand towards me.

'Touch me,' he said. 'Do I have the coldness of a Serpent or the warmth of a man?'

I touched his hand and felt the heat of his blood. My hand sprang back as if from a serpent's bite.

'Who are you?' I said. I felt I should have been fighting this Devil-that-was-a-man, not talking.

'A man like yourself,' he said. 'But one who comes from another star. I am called Teramos. I am a stranger to you – but I know you very well.'

'I lose patience,' I snapped. 'Explain your words!'

'We have followed your journey with great interest, Boaz. And if you don't mind me saying so, I don't think you could have made it without our help. . . . For instance, when that unpleasant-looking monster attacked your boat – another Sethian trick but quite real this time – we persuaded the whales to rescue you. A lot of persuading it took too. . . . And when your rafts strayed hopelessly off course, we pointed you back in the right direction. And then . . .'

'Enough!' I yelled. 'Your lies hurt my head.'

'Then let me show rather than speak,' said the human Serpent in a gentler voice. As he spoke the darkness crept back and suddenly we were not alone. Conyori stood looking at me from the banks of a jungle river. She beckoned to me.

'Conyori!' I cried and stumbled across the room towards her. My arms closed on empty air and the vision disappeared in sudden brightness.

I turned angrily back to the old Devil.

'More of your magic?' I accused.

'Of course, the sudden appearance and disappearance of that delightful creature would seem like magic to you. But it is a trick made by machines – an amusement known on every advanced world. The only difference in the ways it may be used is this: the Sethians made you believe it was real and I am telling you it is an illusion. . . . Think, Boaz, did not your Moon-gods make the same magic before? When they showed you the Temple on the island before it was built? Even the appearance of Snake-Killer in the shiny cave was a trick.'

'You lie!'

'You must decide for yourself what is the truth,' said the old man. 'You have quite a good brain if only you knew how

154

to use it. . . . If you wish to return to the Sethians or go back to your homeland without helping either of us, we will not stop you.'

I sat down on the bed of skins and watched the old man suspiciously. I could not even be sure if he was an old man and not some monster human-shaped by magic. He seemed to mean me no harm. Yet I could believe nothing of what he said until I knew more.

'Think carefully on what you have seen and heard,' he said. 'You saw our two mother-ships battling for survival. We did not attack the Sethians when we saw them scouting the same planet as us. It was they that attacked us. We did not destroy them though we had the power then. We only crippled their ship to save ourselves from destruction – and even then we were careful not to harm or kill. . . . For the taking of any life, however evil, is against our belief.'

I laughed scornfully.

'Now I know your honeyed tongue hides a sting. I have seen the torn bodies of my people – killed by you when you destroyed the great Temple!'

He shook his head. If he had been a man I would have believed his sorrow to be real.

'We did not attack the place which you call a Temple. The mistakes of the Sethians themselves caused its destruction. They blamed us – or rather the Serpents – so you would not doubt they were gods. After all, gods don't make mistakes, do they?'

I ignored his smiling question.

'What of the mines?' I demanded.

His smile faded and he looked to the ground.

'If it is true the gods make no mistakes,' he said, his voice low, 'it is not true of men. We are men and we admit our mistakes. This was one of them.'

He raised his eyes to mine and held them steady.

'We thought that by overheating the mine we could stop the digging of the Sacred Rock. We did not foresee that the cruelty of the Sethians would force your people to stay in the mines and die. . . .'

I remembered what Olmec had told me. Of how Mahala had whipped the terrified miners back into the burning pit that became their grave.

'Why did you want to stop the digging in the mines?' I asked. 'Do you seek the Sacred Rock for yourselves?'

155

'No, Boaz. . . . Our only purpose in coming to your world was to observe the progress of your race. If we found that mankind had achieved its own conscience we were to serve as your teachers. The Sethians are here only to serve as your masters and to plunder your world. We have no desire to rob the human race of the minerals it will one day need.'

'If you are not Serpents and you are not gods, who do you worship? Are your gods more powerful than the God of All Power?'

'You have a questing mind, Boaz, which promises well for your future. But I fear my answers to such questions can only confuse you more.'

'Are you ashamed of your gods that you cannot speak of them?'

There was laughter in the womanish eyes of Teramos as he looked at me.

'For you, Boaz, I will try and explain the unexplainable. . . . We recognise only one god. Our god has no name for all names are his. Those who seek him cannot find him for he is everywhere. He has no face yet smiles behind every face. He is without shape yet manifests himself in every form. He is creation and destruction and all that passes in-between. We do not worship our god by kneeling before him as slaves before a tyrant. We worship him simply by being as we are. So it is that even those who do not believe in him worship him by their actions and by their every breath. For he is the Universal Energy that creates the need for everything to be as it is. . . .'

His words stretched my mind. Yet I found meaning in them. I said: 'What you speak of is close to Him I know as Viracocha, He who created all that there is – even the gods and totems that each tribe worships as its own.'

Teramos appeared delighted by what I had spoken.

'You speak wisely for one of your world,' he said. 'And you are closer to the truth than the Sethians. Those that seek God in Power find only the emptiness of self-destruction. And that which they call their God of All Power is to the Universal Energy as a humble servant to a great chief.'

'Then your god must be a terrible master to serve,' I said, for I knew too well the strength of the God of All Power.

'No, Boaz, He serves us as we serve him. For in the deepest centres of our minds, each man has his share of the Universal Energy to use as best he can. This power lies in

156

the minds of all men. In most of them it sleeps, waiting to be awakened. The Sethians have it but know it not. It is in your mind too, Boaz, like a seed ready to grow.'

His words excited me. It was as if he had revealed to me a secret I had always known but only as a feeling. Now the feeling had words to it and I could better understand. I hoped I would learn more of this secret.

'But don't let me preach to you, Boaz. You will learn all we have to teach in your own time,' said the old man who held the secrets of the gods. 'Now you must see what happened after you fell beneath the wheels of the chariot of fire . . .'

The room darkened. The battle raged all about me. Men died everywhere I looked. The red tongue of the Moon-beast slashed through the bodies of warriors of both sides. Then the vision let me come closer to the fighting so that I stood amongst the warriors as one of them. Yet they saw me not. Then I saw a strong-looking warrior of my people running through the smoke of death. He was neither handsome nor ugly but very much afraid. I wished he looked braver for the warrior was myself. I watched him scream when he saw the blazing chariot rushing towards him, the flames spread behind it like a brightly-coloured cloak. I shared his pain when he fell beneath the stamping hooves of the maddened beasts. . . .

The vision changed. Now I saw the Moon-beast prowling the field of dead as an owl hunts for mice. A white mist fell upon the Moon-beast with a noise as of many hornets. It was the same white cloud that had settled round our boat after the attack of the sea-monster. Then it had seemed friendly. Now it appeared full of hidden danger. White fire, brighter than lightning, flashed from its centre, striking the Moon-beast. The Moon-beast trembled. Then it sped quickly away towards the distant sea – fleeing as a jaguar with a belly full of cubs runs from a fight.

The great white light of the cloud flashed on the weapons of the warriors who still lived. I watched with grieving heart as the enemy surrounded my disheartened men and led them away prisoners. There were few of them and the faces of many friends were missing. Then I saw the bodies of my warriors scattered on the ground. Most of them were too horribly burnt to be recognised. Those I did recognise I wished I had not. No more would my lips smile at the songs of Pica. Nevermore would my tongue taste the sweetness of Dana..

I shook with grief and anger as the vision vanished and brightness splashed the room. I hurled my anger at the Sky-devil.

'If this is the truth you show me, why did you wait so long before driving away the Moon-gods? Why did you wait until my friends lay burnt and dead?'

Sorrow creased the ancient face of Teramos.

'Believe me, Boaz, if we could have avoided that terrible slaughter we would. To us the loss of one life is too many. But the attack of the Sethians destroyed that-which-focuses-Energy. Since then we have had almost none of the precious Universal Energy except that which comes from within us and nearly all of that has been needed to protect our base from attack. All of us are weary from the constant effort and we were barely able to summon enough Energy to drive away the Moon-beast. The strain was great and has used up more of our strength than we could afford. And if we are destroyed, who is to save your world from the Sethians?'

Bitter was my laughter that greeted these words.

'The Moon-gods say they want to save us from you and you say you want to save us from the Moon-gods. I say – who will save us from the both of you!'

'I understand your feelings,' said the old Devil-who-was-a-man. 'All I can say to comfort you is that many of your men are still alive.'

'Does Aroona live?' I anxiously asked.

'He lives. His wounds have already been treated.'

Great was my relief at hearing this. Yet my joy lasted but a brief moment before I remembered the loss of my well-loved Dana.

As if he knew of the feelings in my head, Teramos said: 'To show we intend you no harm, we are restoring the life of the girl called Dana. She was not so badly burned as many others.'

'You can bring Dana back from the dead!' Wonder swept sorrow away. I dared hardly believe the old man had spoken true. 'But will she not be a phantom like Conyori?'

'No, Boaz. She will be alive to see and warm to touch.'

'I must see her,' I said, climbing painfully to my feet. 'If this is some game to torture my hopes I will crush you with my bare hands, Serpent or not. Now take me to her.'

'Of course,' said Teramos. 'Your mind is full of wonder and confusion. The sight of your woman alive will help put your mind at peace. You will be better able to judge the truth of what you have seen and heard.'

'So far you have not tried to kill me,' I said. 'So I will not try to kill you. Beyond that I do not know.'

'Spoken like a true human being!' the old man laughed. 'Now shall I help you up the stairs?'

I pushed away his offered arm.

'Boaz has no need of help from man nor Devil!'

The face of Teramos grew again serious.

'Maybe not, Boaz. But many men need your help as you will learn.'

We slowly climbed a great stone staircase towards a distant square of light. As we trod the stone steps I thought of the greatness of the mountain whose belly we trod. I thought of its point that touched the stars and I felt as a man who drowns in stone.

'As you have guessed we are inside that which you call the pointed mountain and which we call a Generator,' said Teramos, his voice echoing hollowly. I thought his words strange for I had not spoken to him of the pointed mountain.

'It is a primitive device,' he continued, 'but useful for storing and generating the Universal Energy on which we depend. Our ancestors made many of them countless ages ago. Luckily we remembered the method since the Sethians destroyed all our Energising equipment in their attack and we could not have survived without it. . . . We hope also it will be seen by our ships beyond your world and serve as a signal to tell them we are here . . .'

'Did your slaves, the chariot people, build it for you?'

Teramos laughed.

'The river people that dwell here were kind enough to offer to help with the construction – but we found it faster to do most of the work ourselves at night whilst their workers slept . . . And we did not have to slay the last of an ancient race to build it as the Sethians ordered you to do. Nor were men killed and maimed in the building of it.'

We continued in silence. My tongue was silent but Thatwhich-makes-thoughts was not. It had split into two halves like a clam dropped on the rocks by a sea-bird. One side saw me walking alongside a treacherous Serpent, a leader of the Sky-demons who had twice attacked the Sacred Land

159

and waters of my people and made many widows amongst my tribe. The other side saw Teramos as the wisest of wise men. One who had known and spoken truths I should have known long before. I carried the war of the Moon-gods and the Sky-devils into my mind and That-which-makes-thoughts battled itself with great confusion. I could not yet tell who was winning.

But I knew that behind the two sides of the shell lay the meat: I, Boaz, Chief of the Huanacs, was pitting my life and the lives of many others on whatever I decided.

As we climbed closer towards the square of light awaiting us at the top of the great stairs, I felt as I did when Snake-Killer first took me to the hut of Initiation when I was a boy-to-become-a-man. The women were sent far away and strange howlings rose from the unknown spirits of the earth. Then too had I felt this same feeling of Joy mixed with Terror.

I felt like a baby first taken to its mother.

Or like a lamb to slaughter.

SEVENTEEN

Dana lay on a shining table, her pale skin covered with the frost of death. She was naked and I saw the Serpent's tongue of flame had eaten of her beauty. The marks of fire showed dark as smoke against her deathly paleness. They were marks such as appear on the hide of a deer when it is first hung over the cooking fires.

A young man with long sun-bleached hair and a face too womanish for a warrior sat beside her. He looked up as we approached.

'I can use you,' he said to us both. There was urgency in his voice.

'What is it, Criztau?' Teramos asked.

'I have need of your concentration. I am weak and the white light grows faint.'

Teramos looked deep into my eyes.

'There is little time to explain what we are doing. If you wish the girl to live again, do as I say. We need your help in raising the power that heals.'

'What can I do? I am a warrior not a Shaman.'

160

'Sit here, right here . . .' He guided me round the table and motioned that I should sit opposite the one called Criztau.

'And now you must close your eyes and pray to the Oneness you call Viracocha – in your own words and from your own heart. This will help. Believe me and it will.'

'I will do as you say.' I fought back my suspicions of the Serpent people. For Dana's sake.

I watched Teramos seat himself by Dana's head. He placed one hand on her forehead.

'Do not be frightened when the white light comes,' he said. 'You will know it well for it has already saved your life once before.'

I closed my eyes and tried to capture the feeling of Viracocha as I had felt it strongest. Back in the days before the Moon-gods had walked our shores and our ways were as they had always been. I thought of the Sun-rise touching the summit of the sacred mountains. I thought of His tears of sadness and happiness as they appeared in the falling rains, the frozen peaks and the distant jungle rivers. I thought of the hissing foam of the waves of the Great Salt Sea. I thought of the white light which had cast its cloak of brightness round our boat . . .

The White Light! I was flooded with it though my eyes were closed. It filled my mind with warmth, my ears with gentle music. I opened my eyes and beheld the light within the room. It came from Teramos. It came from Criztau. It came from me. It passed from one to the other of us, so fast it hardly seemed to move. Between us lay Dana. The White Light bathed her with its brilliance. She was like a virgin lying on a bed of whitest snow. Never had she seemed so beautiful as she now appeared.

Then, as I looked, the frost on her cheeks and lips melted, warmed away by a faint flush of blood. A vein began to throb in the paleness of her throat . . .

'You may watch,' said Criztau, 'but don't stop thinking of the blessings of your god.'

So we sat for a time that could have been long or short. Slowly the great White Light grew less bright. It did not die but was drawn like breath into Dana's body. I knew I was seeing the mighty Energy, the God of Teramos and his people.

The blackness of the Serpent's bite faded away before the healing light. Dana's colours of life returned. Her breasts

161

and ribs began to rise and fall. With Viracocha's name on my lips I reached out for her hand and grasped it tight. It thawed beneath my touch.

Dana slept a peaceful sleep. A sleep not of death but of life.

I rose to my feet. My head-throb was gone but I felt a great weariness. My eyes joined those of Teramos. He smiled at me, his face shining.

I had to remind myself he was not a god.

'Let us go now and rest,' he said. 'And then we have much to do, many more lives to save.'

I kissed Dana's lips. They burned with life. I followed Teramos from the room, leaving Criztau to watch over the girl who had died and now lived again.

As we walked back down the stairs, I voiced aloud my thought.

'Do you know that the Moon-gods – the Sethians as you call them – can also give life to the dead? Only they do not use the White Light but their sticks and boxes . . .'

'They cannot do as we do,' replied the old man with gentle firmness.

'But they can – they did it with me!' I had not forgotten Nima's blow that spilled my life. Nor my gratitude to the Moon-gods for robbing the jackals of a feast.

Teramos shook his head.

'They did not bring you back from the dead. They took you in while you were still alive and joined your arm to your body with great skill – if only they put all their skill to such good ends! But you were never dead, Boaz. Raising the dead is the one thing machines cannot do. How could they when they have never lived themselves?'

Now I knew that Teramos lied. For had not Olmec killed the giant Mahala? And did not Mahala still live to enjoy his cruel sport? I had given Teramos my trust so that Dana might live again. Now I withdrew my trust. I knew I had to be on my guard every beat of my heart. I chose my next question with care: 'Do the people of your world never die if they can be returned to life so easily?'

'Of course, we die,' Teramos answered. 'As must all living beings. When one of our race feels he has led as full a life as he could wish and learnt all the teachings that existence has to offer, he simply releases hold of his mortal shell. He becames again part of the vast sea of floating Energy. Until the next Awakening. For there are many levels to climb, many universes to enjoy . . .'

'You mean there are more worlds than this and yours and that of the Sethians?'

'As many as—' He made a despairing sweep of his arm through the air. 'As grains of sand upon the shores of this world . . . And behind each one lies always another.'

I felt my head beginning to throb again and I was glad when we reached the room where I had awakened with its bed of skins.

'Sleep now,' said Teramos, 'and when you have regained your strength I will take you to join Aroona and the rest of your men.'

Teramos left and I lay thankfully down upon the skins. The prayers to Viracocha had left me very weak. As I closed my eyes I wondered if Aroona and the others really lived or whether the old man's promise was some Serpent trick. I wondered if I would ever waken again or would they kill me as I slept? I wondered if I was already dead and whether all I had heard and seen was part of some dream of death. Then I slept and neither wondered nor cared.

I awoke with mind and muscles greatly refreshed. When I saw I was not alone I sprang up from the bed of skins.

Before me stood a girl. Her beauty was so great that the sight of it squeezed my body breathless. Her face shone like that of Teramos and she looked at me with eyes golden like the jaguar. Her hair was the colour of the Sun and stretched towards ripe pointed breasts. Only her breasts and the place of her woman-hood were covered and these sparkled with jewels. I felt my man-spear rising to the attack.

'Are you a Sky-devil?' I asked. 'If so I like this shape better than your Serpent-self.'

Her smile was golden as her eyes.

'I am Zalima,' she said, 'and I bring you food.'

With so much else about her to delight the eye, I had not noticed the platter which she held. It was heaped with fruit and there was a jar to quench my thirst. She laid the platter at my feet.

There was a great emptiness inside me which called to be filled. I fell lustily upon the platter and filled my mouth with figs. My hands tore at bright and unknown fruit.

'Is there no meat here to fill a warrior's hungry belly?'
I asked.

She shook her yellow hair.

'We do not eat dead flesh. Nor do we kill for food.'

I grunted and raised the jar to my lips. I hoped for the sting of Star-Juice but tasted instead the sweetness of liquid fruit. Its cooling taste washed away my thirst.

I ate my fill. As I ate I watched the golden one watching me. She made me think of other hungers to be fed.

'Have you never seen a man eating that you watch me so?'

'You are wrong, Boaz,' Zalima smiled. 'I have watched you eat many times. I have followed your journey here with much interest.'

'How is that possible?'

'In the same way as Teramos has shown.'

I nodded my understanding.

'Have you watched me fight?' I asked. 'Have you seen me crush skulls with my club of war?'

She looked past me as if seeing into a great distance.

'The sight gave me no pleasure. We are a peaceful race without interest in war or weapons.'

'And what of my man-spear?' I grinned'. 'Did that weapon not interest you when I thrust it into Dana and the others?'

Her eyes returned to mine.

'That pleased me more,' she smiled.

'I'm not surprised if all your men are as womanish as Teramos and the other one I saw.'

Her smile grew wider.

'I must go,' she said, moving away towards the stairs. 'I will see more of you, Boaz.'

'Much more, I hope, Devil-woman . . . Much more.'

My thoughts were pleasant as I finished eating the fruit. Since becoming Chief of the Huanacs I had enjoyed the women of many tribes and many colours. Then why not a woman from the stars?

If she was a woman . . . Again I remembered I was all alone in a Serpent Temple, a well-fed prisoner but still a prisoner. And I still knew not for sure who were my friends and who my enemies. My thoughts soon grew less pleasant.

Such was my thinking when Teramos appeared. The old one seemed more tired than when last I had seen him but his eyes still twinkled.

'I will take you to your men, Boaz, but first I want you to come to the council room to meet the rest of my crew.'

'Are you the chief of your people?' I asked as we again climbed the great stairs.

'None of us are chief – and yet all of us are . . .'

'Speak simpler thoughts,' I said. 'I do not want my head to throb again.'

'What I mean is that we join our thoughts together in a way not unlike the healing of your woman. By uniting our Energy into a single mind we are able to ponder our problems together and reach a decision as one.'

'You can do this and still you say you are not gods?'

'To the small child his mother and father are as gods . . . yet when he grows older in experience he sees they are not gods but people like himself save wiser in their years. And so the child becomes a man and takes his place amongst men. . . So it will be with you, Boaz. Because you are as a child you think us to be gods. Learn from us and you will take your place amongst us. You too will become a god amongst gods. And so may all men if they but watch and listen to our words and keep their hearts and minds pure and open.'

'No man calls Boaz a child,' I growled, 'yet I like this talk of becoming a god so I will let it pass . . . But tell me – does Dana still live?'

'She lives but sleeps. You may speak with her after the passing of another moon.'

'Speaking was not what I had in mind,' I laughed.

This time we did not climb all the steps but turned off into a passage. I followed Teramos into a large room shining with light. At its centre stood a great round table and around it sat more people of the race of Teramos. When the old one took his place there were two hands plus two of them and each looked at me as if they had never before seen a man. Amongst them I noticed Criztau who had helped heal Dana and also the female-devil called Zalima. There were other women too, each as beautiful as Zalima but in different ways. Many of the men had curling hair on their faces in the manner of Mahala. Their hair was the same golden yellow as the flowing hair of Zalima.

One of the men rose to greet me. His face was hairless and more serious than his youth should have allowed.

'I am Elanil,' he said, 'and I welcome you to our Council, Boaz, fighter of the tribes of Earth.' As he spoke he raised

165

his palm towards me. The others stood and did the same. I hesitated, then returned their salute.

'Greeting, Gods-who-are-not-gods,' I said.

They sat down, Elanil motioning for me to join them. I chose to stand.

'I speak for my fellows,' said Elanil. 'Teramos has shown you many visions. Criztau has shown that we wish to help the men and women of Earth by our powers. We know your mind has taken in much since you awakened within these stone walls. We hope by now that you will have realised that your world is in serious danger from the beings you call your gods. The Sethians are out of harmony with the universe. They care only for power. Yet their power is of a primitive kind. It comes from out of the ground and not out of the mind. We have watched them turn many worlds into lifeless balls of mud in their quest for greater power. Other worlds we have been able to save. We wish to save your green world but, as you know, our ship was stricken from the sky . . .'

'Is your ship still hurt?' I asked.

'Yes, and badly so. We are making repairs but it will take a long time without the proper tools. In the meantime our craft is concealed deep beneath the sand, deeper than enemy blasts can reach.'

'I should like to see this ship of yours and compare it with the might of the Moon-child.'

'If such is your wish, I will take you there later,' said Teramos.

'Because of the damage to our equipment,' Elanil continued, 'we have lost most of the precious Energy which is our strength. We are able to create a certain amount with our minds and with this primitive Generator. But it is not enough to withstand many more attacks. And if the Sethians drop upon us that which they call the God of All Power, we will be destroyed and the people of this river with us. Even now the Sethians based at Sat-Am prepare to attack us with this terrible weapon . . .'

'Sat-Am,' I repeated. I had heard that name before.

'Without Energy to defend ourselves, we are helpless. We can only wait to die, for it is against what we believe to fight or to kill . . . But it has been seen in a vision that a warrior of this world will defeat the Sethians in battle. Boaz, that warrior is you.'

166

'Tell me more of this,' I said.

'There is but this to say . . . In your young life you have seen your world change about you. We ask only that you think back over what has happened to you since you left on your great quest to destroy us. If you cannot see that the Sethians have used and betrayed you since the night they landed by your Sacred Lake, that they have enslaved your people and slain your friends, then we will let you go. As you are free to go even now. But if you believe the truth of our words and visions, we ask you to join us and make the prophecy come to be . . .'

Once more my mind split like a clam. There was much to say for either side. I could not be sure that the Moon-gods had betrayed us and the vision I had seen was not a Serpent trick. True, there was the cruelty of Mahala to be remembered. But also the friendship of Askara and the wisdom of Looth who had brought knowledge and healing to my tribe. Of Teramos and his people I knew only their magic was strong and that they had restored the life of Dana. But had they not also taken her life to begin with?

'I cannot decide,' I said. 'First I must see my men. You will know my decision by my actions.'

Disappointment showed on every face.

'Very well, Boaz,' said Elanil with regret, 'we can but hope you make your choice with care.'

'Of that you can be sure,' I said, speaking as a Chief.

Elanil turned to speak to his people.

'Is there anything further for the attention of the Council?' he asked.

One with much hair on his face rose to his feet and spoke: 'King Zulid has sent us a spy from Sat-Am whom his men have seized. He sends word that we may torture him as we wish.'

These words sent a ripple of laughter through the seated men-gods.

'Thank you, Kulkan,' said Elanil, smiling faintly. 'Have him enter so we may look upon this spy.'

The bearded one left the room and returned a moment later with two warriors of the Chariot People who held between them the spy from Sat-Am. The spy was fat and sweating – but less fat than when I had last seen him.

'Greetings, Gudea!' I called out. 'Have you come to spy on the food of the Serpents – or their women?'

The eyes of the fat merchant filled with relief when he saw me. He ran forward from his guards and threw himself shaking at my feet.

'Boaz!' he shrieked. 'In the name of friendship, don't let them torture me! Tell them who I am!'

'Don't worry,' I said, helping him to his feet and pushing back the guards. 'They will not harm a friend of him who is to save the world. . . .'

The Chariot Men raised their blades but hesitated to strike. They looked to the one called Kulkan for their command. He waved for them to leave.

'Is this man known to you?' Teramos asked.

'To me – and to many women of these lands!'

Gudea tried to laugh yet looked as if he might weep.

'Can you vouch for his trustworthiness?' questioned Elanil.

I glared at him. 'Boaz is not a friend to spies and traitors!'

'As you will,' said Teramos patiently. 'Now I will take you to join your men. Your friend may come with us.'

Gudea and I followed Teramos through passages and down cold stone steps. He could have been leading us to our deaths and I would not have cared, so pleased I was to see fat Gudea once again.

We walked along a flat-walled passageway and turned a corner. I cried out as the brightness of the Sun glaring from the sand hit me like a splash of water. Shielding my eyes from its blaze I stepped out and was greeted by the cheers of my warriors. Of my whole army only five hands of men now remained. I noticed no one guarded these men who had attacked as enemies not so long ago.

'Speak with your men,' said Teramos. 'I will come back later and take you to see our ship as I promised.' I watched the old man-god walk back into the great pointed mountain that hid one whole side of the sky. Then I was being fiercely embraced by Aroona, Xinu and many others. There was much heartiness and good cheer. And many sad silent moments when we spoke the names of those who were no more.

I learned from my men that they too had been shown visions that drew the blame for our misfortunes away from the Serpent-people and back onto the Moon-gods. And like me, none knew what to believe.

'But what are you doing here?' I asked of Gudea. 'And

168

why do you come not as a successful merchant but as an unsuccessful spy?'

Gudea's head hung wearily and tears dribbled from his eyes.

'When I returned home to Sat-Am, I found everything changed,' he said amid sobs. 'The men you call your gods had come and taken charge. At first they gave my people gifts and were kind. Then they made our men work in their temples and made them dig for the black liquid that bubbles from the ground. Many men suffered burns. They lost interest in their women and the dissatisfied women gave themselves to the Moon-gods. Now my people are but slaves and whores. My own daughters were . . . were stripped naked in the street and ravished by the cruel, drunken gods! I escaped and raced across the desert as quick as I could to ask for help – even from the Serpents!'

More sobs shook the fat body of Gudea.

I thought about his words. It seemed to me that the Sethians made better gods than the womanish race of Teramos: those who were afraid to fight or taste of bloodied meat. When the Sethians wanted something, they took it. That was the way of the gods. And of a warrior.

'The Serpent swallows its own tail,' said Aroona, repeating the words of Conyori to me. 'The blood of the Moon is our own.'

I too saw the words clearly now.

'Someone give me a sword,' I said, 'that I may feel again a man.' I took the sharp gray blade offered me by Priam and strapped it on.

'Think hard, Gudea,' I said, taking hold of him by the shoulders. 'Is there a giant amongst the Sethians?'

The fat merchant nodded tearfully.

'The giant who makes families' fight against each other – who casts away broken bodies like the bones of a devoured lamb . . . Yes, there is such a giant.'

'And where is their Moon-beast?'

'By the shores of the Salt Sea. It sometimes leaves but always it returns.'

'How long did it take for you to reach here?' I asked.

'Two crossings of the Sun and Moon.'

'Can you get beasts for Aroona and I to ride?'

Gudea nodded. There were no tears now as his hope grew with my own.

'Yes, my people need cotton and healing herbs. The goods are being loaded onto the river ferry at this moment . . .'

'We have no time to take your goods,' I said, 'for we leave within the hour. Go now, Gudea, to the ferry and prepare for our departure.'

I watched the fat merchant waddling away as fast as his legs could carry him. When I looked up, Teramos was approaching us with a strange smile on his face.

'I will take you now to see the ship,' he said. 'If you are ready?'

'I am ready,' I replied. And it was true for I had reached my decision. I had weighed the two sides against each other and made my choice.

Aroona and I followed the old Sky-devil across the burning sand towards a massive dune. At the foot of the wind-carved slope stood a stone marker. As we neared it, I could see a stone stairway leading down steeply into the depths of the earth.

Holding on to the marker for support, Teramos climbed down the first step. He looked up at me, smiling. It was the moment about which I'd been thinking. But the time for thought was over. It was time for action.

I swung my blade high in the air . . .

'No!' cried Aroona, seeing my intention.

My blade fell and sliced through the neck of Teramos with a hiss and a thud. The head fell onto the sand. The blood-spewing body tumbled down the steps and disappeared from sight.

I grabbed the head of Teramos by the silver hair and ran. Turning, I saw Aroona frozen to the spot.

'Are you a woman or a warrior?' I challenged. 'Follow me or stay and weep!'

Aroona snapped out of his shock and followed.

By the time we reached the ferry, both of us were breathless. Gudea stood anxiously awaiting us. He paled when he saw what I carried in my hand.

We jumped aboard the ferry and I ordered the boatman to push off. I pulled up the gangplank. The boatman just stood looking at the bloody head and shaking with fear. I slapped him hard and that persuaded him to seize his steering oar.

Gudea handed us some loose-fitting robes as worn by the people of the desert. We slipped them on whilst the ferry glided across the river. I looked back to the shore we had just left. There were not yet signs of pursuit.

'Strip the wares off the three fastest camels,' I told Gudea. 'And three more to ride when they get tired.'

When we bumped against the opposite shore, we mounted the llama-like beasts and rode quickly from the boat. As I tossed and rolled between the two humps of the galloping beast, I felt the same sickness as when bad weather rocked our boat of reeds.

We rode long and hard, over sand and barren rock. The desert was as silent as our mouths.

No one followed.

When the second set of camels could be whipped no further, we rested for a few hours. The vicious Sun seemed to set fire to the very air around us.

That night we crossed over a range of wind-smoothed mountains. The Sun's first rays brought us in sight of the distant peaks beyond which lay the Salt Sea and Sat-Am. We rode all through the day, though the heat choked our breath and blinded our sight. As the Sun set we reined in at the roots of the mountains. Before us a small stream trickled into a pool. After men and beasts had drunk of its welcome sweetness, we moved on through the night, guided by Gudea over a winding pass.

'Once this route was busy with the caravans of merchants,' he told us. 'Now no one dares to travel here.'

In the morning we saw Sat-Am in the hollow below us. By the glow of early sunrise, it seemed a noble and prosperous settlement. But as the sky changed colour its reed and stone buildings appeared cracked and lifeless like dwellings of the dead.

We rode towards the waiting buildings. The desert around us grew green with fields. But the crops were choked with weeds. Carcasses of animals floated on the scum of stagnant water-holes. In the distance trees-that-were-not-trees pierced the reddened sky.

'Those suck from the earth the black mud sacred to the Moon-gods,' said Gudea.

My blood-pump raced like the pounding hooves of the chariot-beasts as we rode into the town. But no guards appeared to challenge us. The huts we passed seemed empty but for the screams and laughs of madness that rose to greet us.

171

'It is just as I left it,' said Gudea. 'The town that I helped bring to life is dead.'

As he spoke a rabble of drunken boys poured out from the doorways of the huts. Their faces were painted like those of women and they chattered with the tongues of girls. They surrounded us. They reached out to touch our flesh, calling on us to favour them with our embrace.

Gudea kicked his camel into the shrill-voiced mob and, reaching down, seized the hair of a painted youth.

'Now my own son has joined them!' cried Gudea with disgust. The other youths closed about him, striking at him with puny fists.

I drew my blade and held it so its light struck their faces.

'Begone,' I warned, 'or suffer the wrath of the Warriors of the Gods!' The boys looked at my blade and that of Aroona, then slunk away with anger on their painted lips.

Gudea slapped the face of his struggling son. The boy stopped fighting and kicking and began to sob with shame. His father's face lost its fierceness and Gudea smoothed the boy's black locks into place.

'It's alright now, Ura,' he said in a gentle voice. 'We have friends now who have come to help us if they can.' His son raised his paint-streaked face to see the Chiefs of the Sacred Lake. Gradually his weeping stopped. Gudea pulled the boy up onto his camel and we continued through the town.

More people had awakened. They filled the streets to see Gudea leading two strange warriors past their huts, one holding a severed head in a strong grip.

Women and girls stood naked in the doorways. They thrust their breasts towards us with looks of lust. They rubbed their woman-lips and called to us as had the boys. Their words stroked at my man-spear.

I made as if I did not see nor hear.

'This must be the Heaven the gods promised us,' said Aroona swinging round his camel to stop before a sweet-faced girl.

'Later, Aroona,' I said and urged him on. He blew a kiss to the girl then put heels to his camel to catch me up.

'Later,' he snorted. 'I hope there is a later to enjoy. The Moon-gods may not share the joy of these girls at seeing us appear.'

'We shall soon know,' I replied. 'Gudea, where are all the men of your town?'

'Slaving for the Moon-gods – or drunk or dead!' He pointed towards the shores of the Salt Sea now sparkling before us, hate twisting his fat face.

'Beyond lies the ship of your false gods – it lies in a great pit beneath the sand as with the Serpent craft.' Sudden anger quivered his body and his fist shook towards the sky.

'I curse them both!' he cried. 'We do not need them in this land. We do not need to be children of the Sun, nor slaves of the Moon. Before they brought down their war from the heavens we lived simply but with happiness. Now we live like goats – like worms!'

Ura patted his father's shaking arm. 'We must hurry, father. We must not be seen with these strangers any longer . . .'

Gudea looked at his son with tenderness.

'Go then,' he said to Aroona and I. 'Go back to your Moon-gods. I wish you safety and all the blessings of this world.'

With these words, he swung away, kicking his camel towards a distant dwelling of stone.

Aroona sang an ancient Jaguar chant as we rode in the direction of the Moon-beast. I chewed the last of the coca leaves I had kept. There were only a few but enough to ease the ache of my thoughts and muscles after our long sleepless journey.

'You know I will never forgive you for stealing Olani,' said Aroona. 'But I have felt proud to fight at your side.'

'Sometimes I thought I would never forgive you for letting me steal her.' I laughed. 'Yet a warrior could not have a closer brother than you. But enough of this – we are both speaking as if over the other's grave. Only we have yet to die.'

Aroona looked about the sun-baked slopes of sand. 'I think you are right,' he said. 'The Sun shines too brightly for the land of the dead.'

Soon the Moon-beast was before us. It lay in a great pit dug by the hands of the people of Sat-Am. Stone steps led from the rim of the pit down to the metal tongue of the ship. The tongue was unfolded as if waiting to swallow us.

173

I hid the head of Teramos inside one loose flowing sleeve of my desert robe. Then I climbed up the familiar metal steps into the Moon-beast, Aroona agape with wonder at my heels.

Strong hands seized us as we entered the shiny cave. Two gods without name held us tight, pushing us before the gaze of Oraan and Mahala and another without name.

'Greetings, great Gods,' I smiled.

'Hail to the Moon-gods,' Aroona echoed at my side.

Oraan shook his head as one amused by the antics of a small child.

'You never fail to surprise and amaze us, Boaz,' said the chief of the Moon-beast. 'Can you tell us what you're doing here when you're supposed to be dead?'

'I have returned to serve your great will as I have done all along,' I said with pride.

'Our will . . . I wonder?' said Oraan. 'No doubt you have an interesting story to tell, of what happened to you since last we met?'

'My story is but what I have seen and felt and heard.' I spoke in an urgent whisper, my eyes wide: 'After the battle I awoke in the Serpents' pointed mountain. They told me lots of stupid lies, of how my eyes saw things that could not be. I pretended to believe their lies so I would live another day. I waited until I had their trust. Then I was able to escape with Aroona. And here we are, ready to help you kill the womanish Sky-devils and avenge all our warriors that they slew!'

Mahala had been silent all this time, his huge face dark with suspicion. Now he stepped forward, looking closely at Aroona and then at me.

'I don't believe any of it,' he growled. 'This is some trick dreamt up by those Siriun cowards!'

Oraan motioned to the nameless ones to release us. They stepped back but kept their hands near to their pain-sticks.

'Tell me, Boaz,' said Oraan, 'how could you possibly escape from the Serpents and their warrior-slaves?'

I shrugged modestly.

'I gained the trust of one of their leaders and made him take me to the place where their ship lies buried. And then I killed him.'

'You killed him!' Mahala scoffed. 'Just like that!'

'Just like . . . *this*!' I said, pulling the head from my robe and tossing it to him.

He caught it between two great hands. His face changed from horror to pleasure.

'*Teramos!*' he cried and joyfully held up the head for the other gods to see. They shared his pleasure at the sight.

'His preaching tongue will wag no more!' the giant laughed and spat in the dead face of Teramos. He flung the head against the wall. It fell and rolled across the room. Mahala grinned at me, friendlier than he had ever been.

'I misjudged you, Boaz,' he said. 'You have proved useful after all.'

Oraan looked with displeasure at the drops of blood on his shiny wall.

'That's enough, Mahala,' he snapped. 'You're not in your quarters now. . . . Why don't you go into the town and take your aggression out on the women and boys?'

Still grinning at me, the giant moved as if to leave. Then he paused, doubt clouding his face.

'Wait – how did you find us here? How did you get to Sat-Am?'

The Moon-gods looked at me and waited. I smiled at each in turn.

'I met the merchant Gudea in the land of the Serpents,' I explained. 'He was to return with a camel-train of goods. I persuaded him we were more valuable than his load of cotton.'

'I know this Gudea,' said Mahala, 'though I know his daughters better. I wonder if his words will agree with yours?'

'You have but to ask him.'

'Perhaps I will at that . . .'

Mahala left, taking his suspicions with him.

'He means you no rudeness, Boaz,' said Oraan in a soothing voice. 'It is his excitement knowing the Serpents will soon be but legends.'

'The thought of victory excites me too,' I said. 'Our victory and revenge.'

'Greetings, Boaz, brave chief of the Huanacs!' a voice behind me sang. 'And to Aroona, no-less brave Jaguar chief!'

We turned. It was Askar who greeted us. My heart filled with warmth at the sight of the young god who was not too proud to be a friend of men.

I looked at him closely as we greeted him in turn. For he looked older than before. Older and wiser in the ways of war.

175

Oraan dismissed the nameless ones who had been our guards. It was easier to speak without the thought of a pain-stick at our backs.

For Askar's ears I again told the tale of our capture and escape. He listened carefully and with wonder, making me repeat all that Teramos had said. When I pointed out the old one's head where it had fallen on the ground, he did not show the same pleasure as Mahala or Oraan.

Aroona told how the Serpents had tried to make him and the rest of the men believe the same lies as they had told to me. Oraan and the plump god called Obaal, the chief of the base at Sat-Am, asked many questions about the defences of the Siriuns and the damage to their ship. These I answered as best I could. I told of their precious Energy and the magic of the great white light. I told of how the Energy was nearly all gone and how easy it would be to kill the Serpents when they had none. All these things gave pleasure to the gods to hear.

'We owe you much, Boaz, and you too, Aroona,' said Oraan. 'Of all men of your world, you two have helped us most. You will not find us ungrateful. I promised you Heaven and you shall have it. You will sit with us as gods and live the life of the gods. And tomorrow you will join us to watch the Serpents die.'

'Today many tribes are coming to Sat-Am, bringing their virgins as offerings to the gods,' said Obaal in a leering way. 'Why don't you come and help us unwrap these pretty gifts?'

His words put me in mind of the virgins of the Huanacs, those whom the gods had put into their Moon-beasts and taken from us. I shook my head.

'We are honoured by your invitation, great ones, but we have travelled for three crossings of the Sun and Moon. without sleep. My eyes have trouble seeing, my legs cannot walk and my man-spear could but droop with slumber with the rest of me . . .'

Oraan added his laughter to that of Obaal.

'Very well, sleep then if you must,' said Obaal. 'Perhaps I shall send some virgins back for you so you awake in the arms of bliss . . . that is, if there are any virgins left!'

'Hail to the Moon-gods!' Aroona echoed my cry of thanks.

'Are you coming with us?' Oraan asked Askar as he rose from his table.

'If I must,' said the young god without enthusiasm. His

176

eyes were on mine and his look was strange. Then he turned away, following after Oraan.

'Sleep well—and wake as gods!' Obaal laughed, then he too was gone. Only the two nameless gods who had seized us remained. They busied themselves in god-like ways, scratching on white leaves with the burnt ends of pointed sticks.

Aroona and I lay down on the raised beds of the gods. The beds were soft as women and whispered to our weary bodies of sleep.

It was difficult not to sleep.

Eyes closed, I lay awake listening to the two gods complaining in their Moon-tongue. Soon there was silence but for the scratching of their sticks.

I touched Aroona with my feet.

At my signal Aroona slid from his bed and I followed. We crept across the Moon-beast, silent as hunters stalking deer. Except that we were not hunting deer but gods.

The two gods were bent over their scratchings at the table. One of them glanced up as we approached. He screamed a warning. Before they could touch their pain-sticks, our blades were in their throats. Olmec had not lied. The gods could die and their blood was red as that of men!

The head of Teramos lay where it had fallen. I sprang across the room and picked it up. The wise face stared emptily into mine. The head was bruised from its fall. I hoped Teramos would not mind a black eye when Criztau gave him back his life. But there was much to do before that time.

'What now?' Aroona asked.

'Now we feel the wrath of the God of All Power. . . .'

I laid the head gently down on the table. Then I moved quickly over to the altar of the Moon-beast. I removed a part of it as Oraan had done. Beneath it was the red button he had shown me.

'Watch, Aroona,' I said. 'When I squeeze his nipple, the God will roar . . .'

My hand moved to touch the button. Then stopped. I looked up at Aroona.

'His anger will be terrible,' I said. 'It may be the last thing we ever hear.'

Aroona said nothing, his eyes fixed on the button.

I raised my hand and smashed my fist down onto the button.

177

From the guts of the Moon-beast came a faint hissing and clicking. Then silence.

The Chief of the Jaguar People looked at the Chief of the Huanacs.

'If that is the roar of the God of All Power,' said Aroona, 'I don't thing much of his power.'

My thoughts ran faster than chariot-beasts.

'Destroy everything that looks important,' I said. 'It is all we can do to save the yellow-haired ones.'

Our blades rose and fell, above the altar, smashing discs of ice and blazing jewels.

Sparks and smoke rose in the air as the altar died beneath our anger. Then came a serpent-hiss. A red tongue of flame melted my blade. I threw it from my scorched hand, turning to face Mahala.

The giant stood in the doorway, a smoking pain-stick in his hand. Again the burning tongue flew across the room. Aroona dropped his weapon with a yell.

Mahala glared at the bodies of the dead gods, his face becoming as red as their torn throats.

'Your whole world will drown in blood for this,' he growled. 'Every savage that lives will curse your names for the suffering and pain they'll feel because of you. And here's a taste of what they'll feel . . .'

As he spoke, he fingered his pain-stick. The tongue of flame licked at Aroona's shoulder. Aroona screamed and fell, blood bubbling from his burning wound. The giant's laughter was loud as the screaming. I knew I would be next. The thought made me desperate. I sprang weaponless for his throat.

My fury knocked the pain-stick from his hand. We fell to the ground, struggling and rolling. My hands clawed his face, pounded his body. Thoughts of the giant's cruelty made me wild, gave strength to my tired muscles. Yet the giant's strength was greater. Each blow of his fists was like the striking of an axe. He seized my hair and beat my head against the floor. Pain filled my being. Through red waves I saw him reach across the floor for his fallen pain-stick. I tried to rise. His fist smashed me down again. His hand closed on the pain-stick. He raised it and pointed it in my face . . .

The tongue of fire darted through the air.

Hair ablaze, Mahala screamed and twisted round to look into the flaming end of the pain-stick held by Askar. His face grew red then black. His scream died with him. He fell back and as he fell the red tongue of his pain-stick sliced the air, slashing across the belly of Askar. The young god gasped and clutched the wound. He swayed but did not fall. I climbed to my feet and ran to him. His belly was a red swamp beneath his clawing hand. I eased him to a chair.

'I knew he would come back,' said Askar through his pain. 'They never meant you to live, not as gods and not as men. There was nothing more you could do for them . . .'

Aroona joined us, blood gushing from his own wound.

Askar looked from his face into mine.

'Boaz, I knew you had too much cleverness in you to believe the lies you told Oraan or that you could ever have trusted us after talking to the Siriuns. But Oraan and the others saw in you only a savage. That has always been their trouble. And so they believed you.' His face curled in pain and a moment passed before he spoke again: 'What I don't understand is . . . why you came back at all?'

'To destroy the God of All Power,' I said, 'and so to save the people of Teramos. And all the people of this world.'

'I do not blame you for hating my people,' Askar continued through gritted teeth, 'they have exploited many races, many worlds with their greed. They have enslaved your tribes and the people of Sat-Am . . . Already here they have tested a ray so there will be fewer births – just enough to grow into slaves . . . We teach farming and healing and we take away pride. It's a poor exchange.'

'I have pushed his button,' I said impatiently, 'but the God of All Power does not reply.'

Askar looked at the God's red nipple then back at me. He managed a smile despite his pain. 'It takes the special knowledge of the gods to play with fire . . .' he said. Pushing away my hands, Askar struggled to his feet. He clutched at the table for support.

'Go now,' he said. 'What you have started cannot be changed. Head for the mountains as fast as you can and you might have a chance . . .'

'Come with us, Askar!' I said. 'The man-gods you fight against will welcome you – you are more like them than one of Sett's tribe.'

'I know, Boaz . . . We are not all like Mahala. On my world there are many who think like me . . . But it's too late for me. Much too late.'

179

I looked at his wound and saw his words were true.

'Go quickly,' he urged. 'Don't worry about me . . . And whatever happens, don't look back!'

'He speaks wisely,' said Aroona. 'Come, let us go whilst we can.'

I grabbed the head of Teramos off the table and followed Aroona towards the doorway. I had to step over the body of the dead giant. As I did so I looked at his face. The face I knew as Mahala was black and crisp and burnt away. Beneth it lay another face, a face I did not know. Then I knew that Teramos had not lied: this was not Mahala I had fought and the Moon-gods could not raise the dead. The true Mahala had long ago made food for worms.

We turned in the doorway to look once more upon Askar.

'You alone are a god amongst those who would be gods,' praised Aroona.

'May your ancestors welcome you as a hero!' I shouted in parting.

Askar kneeled before the smashed altar, his hands moving over jewels lit with danger.

'I think they will understand,' he said.

Our camels awaited us still at the top of the pit. We whipped them towards the mountains which now looked so far away. We rode past the town. It seemed bursting with people. To our ears came the sounds of drunken songs. And screaming.

Along the track into the mountains we found a body. It was covered with burns but still we recognised it as Ura, son of Gudea. We did not stop but sped towards the mountains.

Gudea was waiting with more camels at the appointed place. With him were his wife and four daughters. The daughters were comforting their mother whose face was wet with tears. Gudea's own eyes were moist.

'We have done all we can,' I told him. 'Now we must escape.'

One of the daughters wrapped a bandage around Aroona's wound. Then we hurried on.

'I had to tell him,' Gudea wept as we rode. 'The giant tortured my son. He burned the flesh from his bones until I told the truth.'

'It is over now,' I said. 'Let us speak of it no more.'

Soon we reached the mountains. We started up the pass.

180

Not for a moment had the mother of Ura stopped her wailing. Gudea begged us to rest a while so that she could be comforted. No sooner had we reined our camels than Gudea's wife sprang down from her beast and ran back down the track, crying out to the spirit of her unburied son. She ran from the cover of the rocks throwing out her arms towards the distant walls of the town we had fled.

A fierce brightness blinded the sun. Thunder rocked the earth and drowned the running woman's scream. A demon wind seized her in its grip and flung her against the rocks. It slapped us to the ground. Gudea started to rise. I threw him down again. The ground shook like a wind-blown sail. The sky grew red with blood. The very mountains shook with fear and showered us with stones.

It seemed as if night and day were at war. I thought of the night when the Sun had battled the Moon. That was as nothing compared to this combat that shattered the earth and bled the sky. The spirits of the dead howled through the pass, screaming in our ears. There must have been great numbers of them for it was many moments before the screaming ceased. Aroona and I held the daughters down until the thunder faded and the Sun dared show its face once more.

At last we raised our heads. When we did the girls shrieked out with fear. For before us rose a great Tree of Death reaching towards heavens streaked with blood. Its roots were flames and from its branches which stretched across the sky hung the corpses of the dead, numerous as leaves. And as leaves are shaken by the wind, so every corpse upon the tree writhed in a dance of burning death.

Gudea ran forward searching for his wife. When he found her, he drew back, a wail of madness rushing from his lips. I moved to his side and looked. She lay upon the rocks, more a scorched shadow than a body. As moss becomes one with the rocks on which it grows, so had she. All that remained of Gudea's plump wife was a charred layer of bleeding skin clinging to the rock. Her very eyes had melted into stone.

Below us, the desert through which we had passed was black as ash. The silence of death reigned complete. I looked in vain for the Moon-beast or the town of Sat-Am. They had become one with the great Salt Sea. I felt no pity for

181

the people of the town. Their spirits had been dead long before their bodies died.

Gudea's face was empty like one stricken dumb. I pulled him back to Aroona and the howling girls.

I said: 'We have seen what the eyes of men were never meant to see. Let us be gone and hope one day to forget.'

We held each other close that night. We shared our life and strength as one and gave thanks to be alive. In the blind thrusts of passion we escaped our thoughts. But after came the dreams.

And those we could not escape.

NINETEEN

With the Moon-beast dead we had no reason now for haste and we made the journey back at an easy pace. By the time we reached the land of the pointed mountain, the head of Teramos was black and shrivelled and death or our victory had tugged its blackened smile into a grin. In the glow of our night-fires the eyes sparkled as they had in life. Whilst others slept I held the head before me and sought the wisdom hidden in its gaze.

'Why do you keep staring at that dreadful thing?' asked Gunrum, the prettiest of Gudea's daughters and she who now shared my camel and my skin. 'Do you expect its mouth to open and speak? And what could the dead tell that the living would care to know?'

I smiled knowingly at her ignorance, for I had secret knowledge she could not hope to share, knowledge of the great white light, the Energy that breathed life into death and other teachings of the gods.

'These dead lips have spoken much wisdom in their life,' I told her, 'and they will do so again. When we reach the Temple that touches the stars, they will tell of how we roasted the Moon-gods over their own fires.'

'How can that be,' she pouted, 'that such an old dead thing should speak?'

'You do not know the power of these man-gods from the Sun . . . Such is their magic that they can raise the dead from their tombs by the power of their minds alone.'

She shivered and moved her arm on mine.

'Have you seen such terrors?' she asked, wide-eyed.

182

I nodded sagely, as though I were one of the gods myself.

'There was a girl called Dana. She lay cold and dead, her beauty burned from her bones . . . With my help the gods made her live again. She awaits me now, beside herself with eagerness to thank me for the gift of life.'

Gunrum drew back her head, her face becoming sharp.

'Is this Dana pretty?' she asked, knowing it was so.

'As the blooms of an oasis against the desert sand . . .'

'Then I wish she was still dead.'

'You are only an ignorant savage,' I told her, 'and I, Boaz, champion of the Sun-gods, pity you for what you are. Even dead, Teramos here . . .' I thrust the blackened head close to hers, 'speaks more sense than you alive.'

Her lips parted in anger. And met with mine in lust.

The head of Teramos rolled to one side and turned its eyes away.

The plains on the other side of the river were thick with a forest of cheering warriors of the Chariot People, stretching all the way to the pointed mountains which chewed the sky like one of Viracocha's teeth. The sandy-skinned tribe we had so recently attacked now welcomed us with cries of joy.

Women and children ran forward to touch our strength and strew flowers in our path. Aroona and I raised our blades to the Sun in salute. Boaz, Chief of the Huanacs, was returning to the Sun-gods with the prize of victory clutched in my hand as firmly as the head of Teramos.

The cheers which greeted us should have made me feel the greatest warrior alive. Yet my head swarmed with doubts. As the mountain of secrets, the Temple of the Sun-gods, loomed before me, I felt like a man wading through a sea of mysteries, searching for answers as a fisherman seeks fish to spear. Some of the answers lay with the yellow-haired Sun-gods I felt sure. There was still much I had to learn about their ways. I hungered to know the secrets at which Teramos had but hinted. Secrets that raised men to the height of gods. I hoped he would teach me more. I hoped he had spoken true and that his words had not covered lies as a robe conceals a knife.

So far the Sun-gods had smiled on me as fathers on an eager son. But then so had the Moon-gods when they made me a chief of slaves. I hoped the smiles of the Siriuns hid nothing worse than their teeth.

Yet the faces of the river people cheering us on every side were not those of slaves. They were happy faces, falling easily into smiles. I wondered if there were still many such smiles amongst the tribe of the Huanacs.

The land of the Sacred Lake lay so far beyond the sky that my life there seemed as a dream or a life lived by another. Yet it was the land of my fathers and its people were my people. And over them stood the might of the Moon-gods – as a foot raised above a nest of ants. Perhaps the Moon-gods had told my people I was dead and all my warriors with me. Shomu would believe them and others like him. Spirit-Catcher would add the lies of his flapping tongue. But Olani would not believe. She would be waiting for my return. And Curu too. And all in whose hearts the spirit of the Huanacs still beat strong. They would be waiting for the day when the Moon-gods would be tossed into their flaming pits as they tossed in their lumps of sacred rock. The day when my people would be slaves no longer but free as the condor sweeping through the sky.

That day would never come unless I returned. But how could I return without boats and without warriors to fill the boats? These thoughts dragged my spirit low.

But before me waited the last of my men and behind them, the man-gods of the Sun. And perhaps some answers too.

Like a small wave the warriors of the Sacred Lake broke from the sea of Chariot people and threw themselves at us. Their greetings and victory cries chased the heaviness from my thoughts. I slipped down from my camel into welcoming arms. I touched heads with Xinu and Jambal and Bola and many others. When they had embraced me they embraced Aroona, then each of the four daughters in turn, forgetting Gudea entirely.

I pushed through them when I beheld Dana. She ran to me. My arms found her waist and my mouth her lips. My hands searched her unfrosted skin and found no chill.

Elanil awaited me at the opening of the Temple which rose before me like a cliff. Beside him stood a tall man so richly dressed I knew him immediately to be Zulid, Chief of the Chariot People.

'Tonight I will see if all of you is thawed – or only the outside,' I promised Dana. I left her with another kiss and moved to join Elanil.

Zulid was the first to greet me. The tall Chief looked him-

184

self a god. His face was painted gold and his robes blazed with colours brighter than a parrot's. A high head-dress rose from his noble brow and in one hand he carried a golden serpent staff. I had yet to see a real snake in this supposed land of Serpents.

Zulid took my arm in his.

'You have saved my kingdom, brave chief of distant lands,' he said. 'Receive my thanks and the thanks of my people – and even of the spirits of my warriors you have slain . . . for it is a better fate to be dead, slain by a great warrior, than to be alive and a slave to evil gods.'

'The spirits of your brave warriors will be avenged,' I promised him, 'for many of the Moon-gods still live to be killed another time. And when that time comes we will fight together, not as enemies but as comrades in battle.'

'It shall be so,' agreed the Chief of the Chariot People. 'And until that great day comes, you and your men shall not want for gifts or pleasure.'

Elanil next stepped forward and greeted me.

'We have no love of violence,' said the Sun-god, 'but that the Sethians should be destroyed by their own evil weapons is but the law of the Universe. You have saved our lives and given us hope of returning to our world once our ship is repaired. For this we are grateful and extend to you our sincere thanks. But more important than our lives, you have returned to your people what the Sethians tried to take from your own world – the hope of a future.'

'Whatever thanks are given are better offered to the memory of one called Askar,' I said, 'for without him our victory cries would be wails for the dead.'

'We knew of Askar,' Elanil smiled. 'His spirit has already touched us and we have felt its warmth . . . But, come, let us enter. The others await us in the council room.'

The Sun-god led me into his great Temple and I followed him up the stairs to the council room.

The Sun-gods were seated around their sun-shaped table. They stretched their palms to me as before and I returned their greeting. I looked for Teramos amongst them. I saw Criztau and the bearded god called Kulkan. I saw Zalima and felt the caress of her warm smile.

Teramos was not there.

Elanil took his place at the table. I remained standing.

'I do not see Teramos,' I said. 'Did you need his head

185

to return him to life? I did not think you would.'

I pulled the head from my robe and held it out to Elanil. Stiffly he took it, glancing but briefly at the blackened face, and placed it on the table.

He looked at me with gentle pity.

'Teramos is dead,' he said. 'As no one should know better than you.'

Elanil did not have the warmth of Teramos and his long face was not as easy to read. I felt a tightening of anger inside. Anger behind which hid fear.

'What mockery is this?' I seethed.

'No mockery, Boaz, you killed Teramos when you struck his head from his body.'

I turned from him to the others in the circle. I looked from face to face. Nothing there on which to seize.

'I have seen too much these recent days to laugh at feeble jests,' I warned.

'There is no jest, Boaz,' said Elanil. 'No one here laughs at you. Teramos died when you lopped off his head – as would any man.'

'And can you not raise the dead?' I raged. 'Or have I been fed on lies as a goat is fattened for slaughter?'

Suddenly, doomful thoughts were hammering in my skull. Had I helped destroy the true friends of man to deliver the world on a platter to treacherous gods of evil?

I glared at Criztau.

'Well, shaman, do you play the same tricks as the Moongods with Mahala? Was that Dana I just kissed or another with her face?'

'It was Dana and no other,' said Criztau. 'And as surely as she wanted to live, so Teramos was eager to die. He knew as well as you that the Sethians would not trust you without some sure gesture of faith. He was prepared to die to supply that gesture.'

I shook my head as if to shake some meaning from it. I looked to the head of Teramos. But it told me nothing. How could it? It was a dead man's rotting skull.

Elanil touched my shoulder as I had once comforted Gudea. That time seemed long past.

'Teramos was glad to die, Boaz,' he said. 'Can you imagine a nobler death than his – one that saved mankind from something worse than death?'

I threw off my anger but a greater weight pressed against

186

my soul: the loss of Teramos. The old god had wanted to show me ways that would make me more than a man. And I had repaid him with a bloody sword.

'Do not grieve or blame yourself, Boaz,' said Elanil. 'Teramos knew of your plan as soon as you yourself. We all did. Teramos saw it in your mind. Yet he made no attempt to stop you. He trusted you to give meaning to his death as he gave meaning to his life . . . Amongst our people there is no greater honour one man can pay another than that.'

'You could still have tried to bring him back to life!' I accused.

Elanil shook his head.

'We could have but he would not have wished it, truly he would not. He had lived a full life and drawn from this existence all the lessons it could teach. When you killed him all you did was release his spirit so it could continue on its great journey towards everlasting peace. You held the sword but he guided your hand.'

My mind fluttered round these words as a moth about a flame. It was not the first time I found myself struggling to understand the ways of these gods. I remembered Teramos telling me of the many levels he had still to climb, the universes to enjoy. Perhaps he had been trying to tell me of what was to come. Suddenly I felt what I was – a man amongst gods. I was a stranger to these shiny-faced beings who cared so little for their lives, who spoke of things that could not be seen. I looked into the faces of them whose friend I had killed. Hate I could understand but not those gentle smiles. I had hoped to be a friend to the Sun-gods and learn their ways and share their secrets. Now I felt closer to Mahala and his brothers. These Sun-haired gods did not know what it was like to hunt and kill. They did not have on them the stains of other men's blood.

'I must leave,' I said. 'There are many things I must think on and more I must forget. Aroona will come with me if he wishes and the rest of my men. Warriors can always find work for their weapons.'

'You must do as you think best, Boaz,' said Elanil. 'You are free, of course, to leave any time you wish. But first think on this . . . The death of Teramos has left an empty space at our council table. It was his wish that you take his place, if but once . . .'

He gestured with his head towards the gap in the circle.

'Please join us, Boaz. It will bring his spirit closer to ours. And it is fitting that a man of your world should share our council after we have shared a common victory.'

'As I told Teramos,' I said. 'I am not a shaman. It is not my talent to summon spirits but to fight.'

'We understand your doubts. Yet it requires no special talent to sit with us and become as one. The power is open to any man who can train his thoughts and guide his will. But especially to you, Boaz . . . When you took the life of Teramos his spirit passed through your blade. His spirit touched your spirit. It will help you now.'

'You say this was the wish of Teramos?'

'His last. He spoke it to us as he left here the final time.'

'Very well,' I said. 'I will do as he wished.'

The Sun-gods smiled in welcome and encouragement as I took my place with them. It was the wish of Teramos that I was there but I remembered it had also been my wish to sit amongst the gods.

'We are glad that you join us,' said Elanil, 'for the Energy we draw from inside ourselves grows weak. We could not defend ourselves if the Sethians attacked. You will make our circle strong again.'

'What must I do?'

'No more than when you helped Teramos return Dana from the region of the newly-dead. Think of the blessings of your god who is One . . . And it helps also to think upon the spirits of good men you have known. Think of what made them good and what they cherished from the gift of life. We too will be helping you with our own thoughts . . .'

'I am ready,' I said.

The gods linked hands and I linked hands with them.

Each of them had a face that could tell many stories. Yet now the same look grew on every face. They looked as if they were in a trance of War-Glory. But no – it was a trance of Peace.

I thought of Viracocha whose great spirit moves the clouds and the sweeping oceans. I thought of Teramos and Snake-Killer, or Askar and Olmec. I thought of Tamtanamka and Amrat and Pica. It was not hard to think like this. These brave men were often in my thoughts.

Their spirits answered. My body felt good as if it tasted the heat of the Sun. I felt my muscles growing loose, my doubts flowing away. I closed my eyes.

Yet I could still see. Bright visions filled the darkness of my skull. Every thought made a picture. I needed but to think of something and I saw it clearly. Then I saw myself. Seated at a table. From many directions at once. I opened my eyes and shivered when I saw the gods all watching me from around the table. I knew I had seen myself from the insides of their eyes.

I would have leapt from my seat as from a deadly spider. But the encouragement in the eyes of the gods was strong and firm. Like the hands gripping mine. I felt their smiles as a warm glow inside.

The gods began to chant. A single note gently but firmly repeated. It grew louder like the hum of approaching bees. I joined in. And felt a jolt as a tingling power ran through me from my fingers. Then I saw the white light. Faint at first, it grew slowly stronger. It flowed from our linked hands slowly up our arms like a huge bright glow-worm. As it grew so did the humming in my ears. The humming no longer seemed to come from our mouths. It was like a living thing. As if the very air about us was singing.

The white light flashed from each of us in turn. It began to move around the circle, faster and faster like the wheel of a chariot gathering speed. Its brightness met in the centre of the table and grew stronger still. Soon it filled the room, a blazing whirlpool of light.

I closed my eyes.

The white light was there too.

I was the white light.

I began to spin with it around the circle, my spirit moving from god to god. First I became Elanil. I felt as him. I saw as him. Then I was Zalima. I felt what it is to be a woman. And so with each of the gods in turn. I became them and they became me. Their strength flowed through me, mine through them. I had never known such strength. I felt I could leap from cliffs, swim great oceans, fly like a Moonbeast through the empty sky.

I felt their spirits all around me, pushing me, pulling me, drawing me towards the still heart of the whirlpool.

Then we were

One.

A twelve-legged spider within a flaming cobweb.

The Eye at the centre of the Temple.

From this centre I could see many things.

189

Every thing.

I saw the peaks of mountains and the bottom of the sea. I was a fish slicing through water, a condor climbing the clouds. I saw lakes and jungles and burning deserts. I saw many tribes in many lands. I watched their joys and their pains. I saw warriors dying, women giving birth. Then I saw a face I knew. *Teramos.*

I watched him walk across sand. Behind him walked Boaz. Boaz lifted his blade to strike off the god's head. As the blade fell, Teramos looked into my mind and made a secret sign. His head jumped from a neck erupting blood. It became the blood of the Huanacs. Streaming from the backs of my people as they slaved for the Moon-gods. I saw Shomu growing fat like a leech on the blood of his tribe. I saw Olani screaming and writhing beneath the thrusting weight of Vision-Catcher. The screams became those of a hungry child. A small new-born baby. The son I had never held.

The screaming grew shrill. Suddenly no longer a sound but a feeling. A warning that cut like a knife through the twelve who were One. Then the feeling became a vision – three angry Moon-beasts plunging through clouds, swooping like hawks on the hunt towards the pointed mountain of the Sun-gods. The Chariot People outside the Temple saw them too. They lost their happy smiles. They pointed and screamed. The crowds burst apart, dark ripples of screaming people spreading across the sand. The Moon-beast fell towards them, tongues of flame poised to strike.

I felt the terror of the running people as my own. In flashes like lightning I saw their faces. I saw those I knew helpless. I saw Aroona looking for an enemy he could fight. I saw Dana swept along by panic. I saw people falling beneath trampling feet.

The white light writhed like an angry beast. It tried to grow but something held it back. It thrashed around the room, a blind animal trapped in its cage.

A whispering in my head, a babble of many tongues: 'Not enough strength, not enough Energy . . .'

I thrust my spirit into the light. It felt as if tied with ropes. I broke the ropes. I pushed against a great rock blocking my path. It would not move.

'Too weak, too weak,' whispered the voices in my head. The hungry tongues of the Moon-beasts lanced through

190

the sky. Fire touched running bodies. Flesh became flame. Men fell scorched to the bone.

I hammered against the rock. I strained with all my being. My spirit screamed with effort. The rock would not budge. I called upon Teramos for help. And Askar and Snake-Killer. . . .

The Moon-beasts rose, turned, swooped again. Death ripped its claws through the screaming crowds.

Then the rock began to move. It moved faster and faster and rolled away. The white light drank of strength. It began to grow. It burst from the room, splashing down the great stone stairs. It filled the Temple of the Sun as water fills a jar. The mountain of stone became a mountain of light.

Still the brightness grew. It flooded across the sands. It swept over the running people. It drowned them in its blaze.

They stopped running, the woman and warriors and children. They stopped running and raised their eyes in wonder. For the light that covered them had shape. Its shape was as the Temple of the Sun. But many times larger.

The frightened people stood inside a brilliant peak of light, a shining cone ablaze with strength. The mountain of light towered above them. It dwarfed the Temple of the Gods. It spanned the desert and it speared the Sun. Its brilliance was as day to night. Its splendour filled the sky with gold.

At the centre of the mountain of light blazed a flaming Eye.

We looked out through the Eye—

Boaz and the gods of the Sun.

The three Moon-beasts dived out of the burning sky, their fiery tongues aimed for the crowds below. The tongues licked at the walls of the shining mountain. They licked furiously but the flames dripped from the walls as blood runs off a shield.

I felt the breath of the flames upon my skin. Its touch was cold. For the walls of the mountain were my skin.

Again and again the Moon-beasts swooped behind their tongues of red fire. But they could not pierce the mighty shield of light. Like molten lava pouring from a volcano, the crackling fire flowed down the sides of the Temple of Light. Its heat could not devour those it seeked.

Then the power of the gods thrust upwards to meet the attacking Moon-beasts. As a volcano erupts so the white light burst from the peak of the Temple. It rushed upwards, catching the Moon-beasts in its fierce blast. The Moon-beasts swayed and trembled. They danced like leaves in a gale.

Then they fled, shrieking towards the horizon. Within three beats of a heart they were gone.

Now the white light grew again weak. Its strength melted in the air. The huge Temple of Light shimmered and faded. The brilliance of a sun became the glow of embers. Then the darkness of my mind.

I opened my eyes.

Around the circle, all looked at each other.

All were weary. Hands were released and arms stretched. No one spoke. There was nothing to be said that had not been mightily felt.

Then, after a few moments, a voice at last spoke.

'*Boaz* . . .'

A croaking grinding voice, dry as ancient bones.

Through a mouth without lips, without tongue it spoke. Through death-grinning teeth.

It was the head of Teramos which spoke. The head but not the voice.

It spoke and when it had said its words it fell forever silent.

Skin peeled from bone and bone crumbled to dust.

Horror smothered the faces of the gods. There was a stunned silence around the sun-shaped table.

But not in my head.

The skull-spoken words rolled around my head with the roar and weight of boulders—

'*Boaz* . . . *Mighty is your quest and has only just begun. It will continue beyond this world and beyond this life. The first step is great and takes you far . . . Return to the land of the Sacred Lake and set your people free!*'